THE GAME CHANGER

CEDAR CREEK THUNDER

JULIA JARRETT

INTRODUCTION

Before you dive into this series, I need to make one thing clear.

The Cedar Creek Thunder are *not* a major league or professional baseball team. They are a part of a fictional independent league that I created. I have taken creative liberties with the rules and organization structure, and ask that you suspend reality just a teeny tiny bit.

If you're a die-hard sports fan, and can't handle things not being totally accurate, then this may not be the series for you. But if you love swoony men with great butts, and just the right amount of game play in between those spicy and romantic moments, then read on.

XOXO Julia

1

ISLA

"Thank you, parking gods." I breathe a sigh of relief as I pull into a spot right in front of a coffee shop my GPS says is close to my destination. As I climb out of my car, I take a few seconds to look around at downtown Cedar Creek. Despite only being a couple of hours farther north from Victoria, the city on Vancouver Island I've called home for the last eleven years, I've never been here.

From what little I've seen so far, it's cute. Somewhere between a small town and a bigger city. Vibrant and busy, yet not nearly as crowded and chaotic as Victoria can feel at times.

If things go well today, I could see a move to Cedar Creek being a good thing. Which means I need to impress the new owner of the Cedar Creek Thunder baseball team.

But first, caffeine.

The coffee shop I walk into is warm and inviting, with eclectic art on the walls and comfy-looking chairs. It's the sort of place I'd love to sit and read a good book someday. But not today, I've only got half an hour before my interview. So, with a cup of strong Earl Grey tea and a chocolate croissant in hand, I turn to head back to my car, only to run straight into someone.

"Oh! I'm so sorry," I cry out, realizing with dismay that I've managed to spill tea on not only my blouse, but also the man's shirt. "Crap, I hope that isn't burning you." I pluck the fabric away from my skin as I look up at the person I just bumped into.

Oh.

Oh my.

Tall, with dark hair that has silver threads shot throughout, and grey eyes that are piercing straight into me. A strong jaw, dusted with salt-and-pepper scruff, and thick, muscular shoulders covered in a perfectly form-fitted shirt. I'm fairly certain my heart skips a beat or two as my mouth goes dry. This man is beyond gorgeous and has all the long-forgotten parts of me sitting up and taking notice.

He's walking, talking sex on a stick, and I'm a single mom who has only had sex twice in her life, both times with a clueless, fumbling teenage boy. I've got a vagina that's so paranoid about how easy it was to make a baby, even with a condom, she's been hiding from the big, bad dick ever since. But for a man like this, I might be able to convince her to come out of hiding...

If I had time for dating, that is.

I'm so busy trying not to drool, I don't even realize he's talking until I blink back to reality and hear his deep, warm, rumbling voice.

"...my fault. Can I replace your drink?"

"No, no. It's fine," I blurt out, sidestepping the gorgeous man. "I've gotta go. Sorry again about your shirt."

I beat a hasty retreat to my car, not daring to look back. "Damn," I sigh as I let my head fall back against the headrest. It's not like I haven't been attracted to any men recently or enjoyed some self-made orgasms to fantasies of my celebrity crushes. But something about coffee shop guy hit differently. Deeper. Something tells me he'll be the star of those fantasies for a while now.

The cold dampness from my wet shirt has me grimacing and looking down at it. Light brown liquid has stained my pale green blouse, and it's not a good look.

But I'm a mom. Which means I'm always prepared for anything. A glance in my gym bag that's on the back seat proves this to be true, even if the Vancouver Tridents tank top that my kid got me for Christmas isn't the most appropriate business attire. Then again, I am interviewing for a position with a baseball team, so maybe it'll be okay.

It's going to have to be okay. Because a poop-brown tea stain in the middle of my chest is a lot worse than a tank top. Thank goodness for my blazer. And for my planning skills that allowed me to get here early enough that I won't be late for my interview, even with this wardrobe change.

A few minutes later, and I'm parked at the address I was given for the interview. I've got just long enough to devour the rich, flaky croissant and chug the last of my tea. One more glance in my rearview mirror to check my hair and my teeth for lip gloss before I pop a breath mint in my mouth.

"You can do this, Isla Forrester," I say to my reflection. "You are an amazing branding and marketing consultant. You are exactly what this organization is looking for and you're about to wow them with your ideas and expertise."

As far as pep talks go, it's not bad. Even if it does little to quell the nerves in my stomach. It's been a long three months on the unemployment list, and this job, while only temporary, could be my ticket out of Victoria and on to better things.

Besides, I love baseball, I know the game, and more importantly, I know how to create a killer marketing campaign.

I climb out of my car and give a tug on the bottom hem of my blazer as I look up at the low-rise building where the interview is to take place. I'd expected to meet at the stadium, or the team's head office, wherever that is. Instead, I'm at...a coworking space?

I quickly pull up the email inviting me to the interview and double-check I'm in the right place. Yep, this is it.

Opening the door, I step into a nondescript lobby area. Seated behind the one desk is an older man with a small sign in front of him that has "Cedar Creek Thunder" written on it. He gives me a smile.

"Are you here for the interview?"

I nod and smile back. "Yes. With Mr. Calloway?"

"Wonderful. I'm Gabe, his assistant. Let me take you back."

He leads me down a short hall and knocks on a door before pushing it slightly open. "Luca, your first interview is here."

I step up to take his place and put on a professional smile as the door opens more fully. "Mr. Calloway? I'm Isla Forrester."

My hand, which was outstretched to shake the one of my potential new boss, falls to my side as that smooth, warm voice from the coffee shop says just one word.

"You."

I can feel my eyes blinking rapidly, as if I'm trying to wake up from a dream. But this is no dream. No, the hot-as-sin man that I spilled tea on just half an hour ago is standing in front of me, a slight smile tugging at his lips.

"I see you were more fortunate than me and had some clothes to change into." He chuckles, reaching out a hand to me.

Almost mechanically, I lift mine to shake his, and the second we make contact, it's as if my entire body comes alive from a deep sleep.

"Y-yes. Sorry again about that. And about wearing this to an interview." I gesture to my shirt. "Hope it's not too much of a faux pas to wear another team's shirt."

He chuckles again, that rich sound vibrating through me. "Nah, I'll consider it a good omen that you're enough of a baseball fan to have had another team's merch in your car." He points to the chairs in front of his desk. "Shall we sit and get started?"

I inwardly heave a sigh of relief. *Thanks for the save, Charlie.*

I sit down, angling toward him, and lift my portfolio

out of my bag. "Thank you for extending the offer for an interview, Mr. Calloway."

He nods slowly, that slight smile still on his handsome cheeks. Up close, I can see the thin lines on either side of his eyes that tell me he either smiles a lot, spends time in the sun, or both. I hope it's both.

No. No, I don't. No inappropriate thoughts about the obviously older, very handsome man who is my potential future boss. *Bad Isla, bad.*

"Luca is fine. Let's get right into it. This is a nine-month contract position, with the possibility of turning into a permanent position. Your primary responsibility will be to head the relaunch of the Cedar Creek Thunder. What makes you think you'll be the right person to lead the marketing campaign?"

"Well, first of all, baseball is the best sport on earth, and anyone who tries to say otherwise is simply wrong. I don't care if that makes me a bad Canadian to not pick hockey or lacrosse, but I've been a baseball fan since I was six years old and my dad took me to my very first Vancouver Tridents game." I pause, wondering whether or not to share the next part. My being a former teen mom, now a single mom, doesn't affect my ability to do my job, but, it is part of why I *want* this job.

"I've got a twelve year old son."

His eyebrows raise. Yeah, I know I don't look old enough to have a kid who will be a teenager in a few months. That's what happens when you have a baby at seventeen. Thankfully, he doesn't say anything, and I continue.

"He's just as crazy about baseball as I am. In fact he's

who I have to thank for the wardrobe save," I gesture to my tank top. "Anyway. Me being a mother has nothing to do with my skills as a marketing consultant, but he is part of the reason I believe in what you're trying to achieve."

Luca nods. "And what is it you think I'm trying to achieve?"

I let a small smile break free. "It's not what I think, it's what I know. I'm friends with someone who knows one of your players. That's how I know that you want to make the Cedar Creek Thunder, and their stadium, a cornerstone in Cedar Creek. Which I think is a fantastic idea. Every town needs something that brings them together, and what better way than uniting them as a fan base for a local sports team. The opportunities to engage with the community throughout the process of rejuvenating the Thunder's brand are endless, and any project that brings business and community together is what I want to be working on. Because a strong community, a town full of connected residents, is the sort of place I want to raise my kid in."

Luca steeples his fingers together under his chin, looking at me with an expression I can't even begin to decipher. He's silent for a moment, and I force myself to keep my hands still and my gaze steady.

"Most marketing consultants would be focused on the team itself at first, not on the connection to community. You mentioned your son, so clearly family is important to you, but if I may ask, why else do you think the connection between the team and community is so crucial?"

"Because without the community behind you, the team doesn't have a chance to thrive and grow into a brand everyone can be proud of. The two are interconnected." My voice fills with passion as I continue. "Any successful business, big or small, needs to have the support of the people and infrastructure around it. Who else are you marketing to, and for, if not the community you serve?"

His face softens into a smile. "I can appreciate that."

Feeling bold, I decide it's my turn to ask a question. After all, this has been anything but a typical job interview so far. "Can I ask, why did you buy the team? Why does it matter so much to you?"

Leaning forward, he places his elbows on his knees, his gaze drifting down to the floor. "Excellent questions. I grew up in Cedar Creek. This town has been good to me, and I always wanted to find a way to give back. Now that I'm in a position to do so, it seemed logical to combine my love of baseball, with my fondness for the town." He straightens, and looks at me again. "Did you know that twenty years ago, every seat in the stadium was filled for every game? It was where everyone went on the weekends. There would be monthly fireworks shows after a game. The local little league teams would take turns walking out for the national anthems. Baseball was as much a part of this town as anything. But that started to fade, for some reason. I'm determined to rebuild the Cedar Creek Thunder to what it used to be. In every possible way." He quirks a grin. "There's a reason we're meeting here and not at the stadium, and that reason includes shag carpeting with mysterious stains."

We both laugh, and he continues. "The Thunder might only be an independent league team, far from the major leagues. But we can still be a team the town is proud of. A team that gives back, that supports and is supported by its town. And that's where you come in. I need someone equally determined to bring the town of Cedar Creek back to the baseball diamond as I am."

There's a second where something passes between us. Something that makes it clear there's more to Luca Calloway than what meets the eye.

I open my portfolio, and turn it to face him. "Then let me show you some examples of why I think I could be that someone."

———

Several hours later, back in the tiny kitchen of the rental apartment my son Charlie and I share in Victoria, I'm having to take my third deep breath in as many minutes.

"But Mom. Cedar Creek is so far away."

I swear his pitiful whine is equal parts aggravating and guilt-inducing.

"I know it seems that way," I say patiently. "But it's actually only about two hours. And Nana's new house is less than thirty minutes away. Now, are you going to come and eat dinner or not?"

Heaving a sigh, Charlie unfolds his gangly body from the couch and slowly shuffles over to the kitchen table, the grumpy orange cat Gus that we've had for four years draped over his shoulder.

When did he get so tall? How is he already twelve and a half? Am I completely screwing him up?

It's not the first time I've asked myself these questions and it certainly won't be the last. I set down our plates of food, and take a seat next to him.

"Aren't you excited by the idea of me working for a baseball team? We can probably get super cheap tickets," I say, continuing to try and get him on board. After meeting with Luca this morning, my hopes for getting the job are high. It might be temporary, but it could be the move we desperately need.

His shoulders lift in a shrug, as he shovels a bite of food into his mouth with his left arm. "Yeah, I guess."

I hold back my sigh. "C'mon, kid. Baseball is our thing. This could be super cool."

"It was our thing with Poppa."

A stab of hurt and grief slices through me. It's been three years since my dad died, and none of us are over it. He was the only father figure Charlie has ever had, and their bond was close.

"Don't you think he'd love the idea of us going to as many games as we could, stuffing our faces with hot dogs, and cheering for our local team?"

Another shrug. "Sure. Whatever."

Guess that's the best I'm going to get. "Okay. Anyway, rose and thorn time." I see his lips just barely quirk up at that. It's a game we've played every day at dinner for years as a way to catch up, sharing the best and worst part of our days.

"Rose, finally beating the boss level in my game.

Thorn," —his gaze drops down— "thinking about moving."

"Charlie," I murmur. But he shakes his head.

"What about you?"

I quietly exhale. "Rose, the sunrise on my drive to Cedar Creek. Thorn, spilling tea all over my shirt before the interview."

His eyes widen. "No way."

I nod with a smile. "Yes way. Thank goodness I had my gym bag with me, and that Tridents tank top you gave me for Christmas."

That gets me a small smile. *I'll take it.* The rest of dinner passes quickly, with a lot less tension. When Charlie's done, he pushes back from the table and finally lifts his gaze to mine. "Can I be excused?"

I nod. He stands and carries his plate in his hand to the sink.

My gaze follows him, watching him walk out of the kitchen, Gus following right after. His left hand reaches up to rub his right arm, just about where it stops at his elbow, where the rest of his forearm and hand never developed.

Even though hundreds of children are born with a congenital limb difference every year, and it was nothing that could have been prevented, there's no stopping the familiar wave of guilt that comes over me.

For years after he was born, I lived every day with a voice in the back of my head. Wondering if I did something wrong in the months before I realized that I wasn't just gaining weight, I was pregnant, to cause this. It took

a lot of therapy and a lot of educating myself about amniotic band syndrome to finally get that voice to mostly
stop. But that guilt never fully goes away. And every now
and then, it'll catch me off guard, like right now.

Charlie's a great kid. For the most part, a happy kid.
But last year, he hit middle school, and things changed.
He started coming home from school quiet and with-
drawn, only to tell me later during our quiet moments
together before bed that someone said something mean
about his missing hand, or he struggled with an activity
somehow.

All the therapy in the world can't stop words from
hurting. And unfortunately, the bullies can be relentless.
Right now he's not thrilled about the possibility of
moving. But I have to believe that a fresh start in a new
city could be good for him.

For both of us.

2

LUCA

THE SECOND THE door closes behind Isla Forrester's back, I exhale. *Holy fuck.* After giving myself a moment to gather my wits, I pick up my phone, and type out a quick message to my assistant. Although, calling Gabe that is really doing the man a disservice. He's been working for the Thunder for over a decade and knows the team—and the stadium—inside and out. He's been invaluable at helping me understand all the parts of the organization that were working, as well as the elements that were not.

> LUCA: Get me everything you can on Isla Forrester. She's an excellent candidate and I want to make her an offer she can't refuse.

I'm playing with fire. Hiring the first person I've interviewed is reckless. Even if it is based on her exemplary qualifications and expertise, and not the borderline uncontrollable pull I feel toward her.

You don't get to be a multimillionaire by the age of forty-two by being reckless.

So what the fuck am I doing?

Fine. Isla is an excellent candidate for the job. She knows her stuff when it comes to branding, and hearing her ideas and passion for baseball was sexy as fuck.

And that's the problem.

I can't be finding anything *sexy* about my potential future employee.

"What's got you glaring at that computer monitor so hard?"

I turn sharply at the sound of Dom's voice. My closest friend, part investor in the team, and new chief financial officer, is standing in the doorway to the conference room I've rented for interviews today, leaning against the frame with a smirk on his face.

"Don't tell me it's because of the bombshell that walked out of here wearing a blazer and skirt with a Vancouver Tridents shirt." He chuckles as he walks into the room and drops down into the chair Isla only recently vacated.

I turn my glare from my laptop to him. "Don't call our potential new marketing consultant a bombshell. It's not appropriate."

Yeah. Neither is lusting over her, dumbass.

Dom raises his eyebrows. "You offered her the job? I thought you had interviews all day."

"I haven't made an offer yet, but I plan to. Why waste time when she's the right person for the position." I can only hope my succinct response is enough. But I've known Dom almost my entire life, so I should know better.

"Luca. What the hell? We need someone experienced and competent who can get the job done in such a short time frame, and she looks like she got her degree last year."

Before I can fire back the reasons why Isla is the right hire, no matter how young she might be, my phone pings with a response from Gabe.

> Her resume and references all check out. Her former employer said she was the best consultant they had, and they felt awful for shutting down the business, which cost her the job.

I ignore Dom's pointed stare and type out a quick reply.

> Draft up an offer that includes a relocation allowance.

Hitting send, I look up at my best friend. "We're hiring her. She's passionate about engaging with the town, and she can see the vision I have for making the Thunder an integral part of the community again. She knows baseball, and her references check out. All I need from you is to give me the numbers on what we can offer as a starting salary and a relocation allowance."

Dom sits up straight, his mouth curving down. "Relocation allowance? We never discussed offering that. We agreed all new hires would be temporary contracts until we know if we can even make this endeavour profitable. Giving a relocation allowance to everyone is going to eat into any possible profits, Luca." He sounds exasperated, the way he has every time I've wanted to spend money on something he doesn't agree with.

Tightwad.

I wave him away with my hand. "I'll pay it myself if I have to. She's the right person for the contract. We need to lock it down, Dom."

Folding his arms across his chest, Dom's brows pull together in a frown. "What were you saying about being appropriate toward our employees, Luca? Seems like you might be the one needing to remember that."

I meet his gaze head-on. "Trust me. I'm aware. There's nothing behind my decision except confidence that she's the right person based on her qualifications."

Lies.

Dom pushes to stand, still staring down at me. "Fine. I'll send you those numbers. *Minus* the relocation allowance."

I've known Dom most of my life. I can tell when I'm fighting a losing battle with him. "Fine."

"Excellent. We still on for lunch?"

I nod. "Yeah. But I'm still going to get Gabe to cancel the other interviews. I'll let you know what Isla says to our offer."

"I hope you know what you're doing."

His parting shot stays with me long after he leaves my office.

Do I? It's not like me to be impulsive. But truth be told, from the second I stumbled into her at the coffee shop, my shitty balance working in my favour for once, I felt something.

Having her walk into the interview just a short time later felt like a sign. Her being absolutely perfect for the job, another.

I might be setting myself up for nonstop torture every workday, seeing her and not being able to do a damn thing about it, but she needs a job, and I need a marketing expert.

Most of all, I need to see Isla Forrester again.

———

Gabe raises his eyebrows when I give him the task of canceling the three other interviews we had scheduled for the afternoon, but he does it anyway. And as soon as Dom confirms the starting salary we can offer, I take the letter Gabe has drafted, edit it to add a few things, and send it off to Isla.

With all that done, I push away from my desk and move to stand. But just as I push onto my feet, my left thigh cramps up.

"Fuck." I grimace as I dig my thumbs into the muscle above my knee. I don't get hit with these kind of cramps often, thanks to the rigorous exercise regime and regular physical therapy protocol I still follow. But every now and then, my body rebels.

The cramp turns into nerve pain, jolting down my leg, and into the thin air where my calf and foot should be. I glare down at the pant leg covering my prosthetic. I've never had a fucking foot on my left side, so why the hell does my brain seem to think I did? Phantom nerve pain is common for amputees, but nobody cut off my leg.

I just never had one to begin with. My mom explained it to me when I was old enough to understand. That when she was pregnant with me, a band of tissue from the amniotic sac wrapped around my leg, just below my knee. The limb never even had a chance to fully form.

But the nerve centers in my brain sure as shit think it did, and every now and then, they like to send lightning bolts down my leg that hurt like a son of a bitch.

I breathe through the pain and continue to massage the muscles of my quad until it eases to a tolerable level. Testing my balance, I push up to stand again, putting more of my weight on my right leg this time. Once I'm confident I can walk, I close my laptop and put it in my bag before heading out of the shared office space I've taken over for the time being.

With my day clear now, I want to head to the stadium and check out the renovation work being done, as well as see if I can meet the new manager who will head up the coaching staff, who arrived last week with his family from Vancouver.

Half an hour later, I'm pulling my sports car into a parking spot outside the Cedar Creek Thunder's home stadium. The building is a mix of chipped-paint-covered bricks and aging, cracked concrete. Decades of exposure to the elements, combined with a lack of upkeep and maintenance, have this place looking more like a creepy horror movie set than a place for families to enjoy the day at a ball game. From my parking spot, I can see that the corrugated metal paneling covering the upper levels of seating is a patchwork of rust. Same with the tall light towers that frame the outfield.

And yet, despite its current run-down state, there's something about the stadium that calls to me. This place matters. To me, to the team, and to the town. It's my job to remind everyone of that.

Fixing up the building and the field is the easy part. With enough money and a good construction crew, this place will look incredible in no time. And already, I can hear the sounds of the team I've hired hard at work.

Rebuilding the team and getting the town on board is another story. And that's why hiring Isla was so important. She gets it—the importance of having Cedar Creek believe in the Thunder again.

Because she's a mother... It's crossed my mind more than once that there might be a Mr. Forrester, even though I didn't notice a ring. She's a mother, which means her kid has a father. Honestly, if she does have a partner, it would be a good thing. I need something to shut down the instant attraction I felt for her.

The fact that she has a kid doesn't affect my decision to hire her in the slightest. But I could see it on her face when she mentioned her son; she was preparing for me to use that information against her. Instead, she achieved what I think she wanted to. She proved she was quite possibly the only candidate to have the right motivation to see this project through.

Not that I would know, seeing as I didn't interview anyone else...

Pressing the button on my key fob to lock my car, I

head inside and make my way to the locker room, and more importantly, the coaching offices next to it. I offered to temporarily set up the coaching staff in the shared office space I've rented, but the response was clear: they wanted to stay where the players would be.

Shag carpet, chipped paint, and all.

Sure enough, I find the man I'm looking for in the office. Rafe Montego is the former starting pitcher for the Vancouver Tridents major league team. He retired several years ago, and three months ago, I convinced him to come out of retirement and join us as the head of the coaching staff. He and his wife moved over in July, their only kid being in university, I believe.

And he's not alone. With him is the batting coach, Levi Hutton, who's been with the team a couple of years, with a similar background to Rafe. He played a season in the major leagues before having to retire after suffering a devastating knee injury.

"Luca, good to see you." Rafe stands up and reaches out a hand. I shake it firmly, nodding at him.

"Likewise. I had some time free up in my schedule and thought I'd stop by and see how things are progressing." I turn to Levi. "Levi, hope all is well."

He nods, lifting a chipped Thunder mug, which has the most tacky cartoon storm cloud logo on it, to his lips. Taking a sip, he then grimaces. "Aside from the sludge we're calling coffee around here, everything's fine."

I give him a small grin. "Coaches' office needs a new coffee maker. Noted."

He tilts the mug in my direction. "Appreciated. And

maybe a better logo?" He glances down at the mug. "This looks like something a toddler drew."

I bark out a laugh. "Couldn't agree more."

We chat for a while, going over the new players they want to take a look at recruiting, as well as equipment that needs to be replaced.

When I leave the stadium later, I feel good. Confident that things are moving in the right direction for the Thunder. I've got a solid coaching staff in place, the stadium is getting some much-needed repairs, and soon, I hope to have a team in place to help overhaul our image and reignite the town's love for the team.

A team that needs to include Isla Forrester, for reasons I don't fully want to think about. Back in the safety of my car, I open up my email and try to ignore the thrill I feel at seeing a response from Isla waiting for me.

Luca,

Thank you for the opportunity to interview for the position today. I am pleased to accept your offer. I do require time to secure housing prior to starting work, but I will make that my top priority and am happy to continue compiling a list of ideas for the Thunder's rebrand in the meantime.

It was a pleasure meeting you today. I look forward to working together soon.

Sincerely,

Isla Forrester

As much as I believe Isla is the right person for the job, a wave of trepidation flashes over me at her acceptance letter. It's what I wanted, and yet, I know now that I have to tamp down any attraction I felt toward her.

She's my employee, and I need her to make this plan a success. Acknowledging that she's beautiful and captivating is a distraction I cannot afford.

3
ISLA

IT'S BEEN two weeks since the day everything changed. The day I interviewed for a job with a man who has starred in far too many late-night fantasies since then.

"Mom, where are my skate shoes?" Charlie yells from the front door.

"Breathe, darling," my mom murmurs to me, rubbing my shoulder as she walks past. She's been a godsend. Not just with helping me pack up our life again, finding a place to live in Cedar Creek, and navigating the million and one little tasks associated with relocating a preteen in the middle of the school year. She's also run interference between me and my boy more than once.

When Charlie was born, I was still in high school, and still living with my parents. We stayed with them for several years, even after I managed to graduate. That led to them having a really close relationship with my son. When my father died, it was hard on all of us. Most of all, Mom. So when she moved just over a year ago to Dogwood Cove, a small town close to Cedar Creek, we supported her the whole way. Now she's repaying the favour, helping me make the move.

I can't wait to be closer to her again. It certainly helps that housing prices are way cheaper outside of the larger cities, meaning Charlie and I won't be crammed into a tiny apartment any longer.

Still, I'm already riddled with uncertainty about this decision, and the off-and-on guilt trips Charlie is piling on aren't helping. Combined with his apparent lack of attention or memory to just about *anything* to do with the move—including the fact that he himself packed his skate shoes into a box yesterday—and I'm at my wit's end.

I realize I'm luckier than most single parents in that I've always had my own parents' help and support. Even so, this shit will break even the strongest. And I'm close to that point.

I take a few deep breaths before finding my son haphazardly rummaging through one of the boxes of his clothes I painstakingly packed for him last night.

"You put them in the box marked garage," I reply, proud of how calm I manage to keep my tone. "And that box is already on the truck."

"But I wanted to go skateboarding," he says, his voice bordering on petulant. The defiant stare he gives me isn't fooling anyone. He's anxious about the move, even if it is only a couple of hours farther up Vancouver Island. Upset at leaving the only home he's known outside of my parent's house. At the same time, I know he's also grappling with feeling a bit excited and relieved. At least, that's what I overheard him saying to my mom the other night. He might not admit it to me, but at least I know he's not as mad about this upheaval as he seems.

There's hope.

"Then you'll have to skateboard in your regular shoes."

That statement earns me a sigh of annoyance that only a twelve-year-old boy can produce. "Fine." He turns to go, skateboard and helmet in hand, and I call out a reminder.

"I'm leaving with the moving truck in half an hour. Nana will bring you up to Cedar Creek before dinner. Listen to her, please."

"'Kay."

At least he acknowledged me.

I turn and walk back to the kitchen where my mother is putting the last of our dishes into a box.

She walks over and folds me into a hug, the warm, comforting type that only a mother can provide. "It's going to be okay. You and Charlie will adjust, and if it all flops, you know my door is always open. And I'll be a lot closer now."

I squeeze her tighter. "I know."

———

A couple of hours later, I pull in behind the moving truck I'm definitely glad Mom insisted on paying for. I'm in the driveway of the cute little house I was actually able to afford a small down payment on. It's close to the stadium, so my commute is pretty decent. Best of all, the mortgage is the same as what I was paying to rent an apartment back in Victoria.

My best friend Juniper is waiting in her car in the driveway, and as soon as I climb out of mine, she races over and pulls me in for a hug. "Oh my God, I can't believe you're finally here! This is gonna be so great. You're going to love working for the team. And if you don't, I'll get Cal to beat up whoever gives you a hard time."

I laugh and shake my head at her. She's the reason I knew about the job opportunity with the Thunder in the first place, thanks to her friendship with Cal Prescott, a player on the team. "Trust me, that won't be necessary. I'm sure the job will be fine, and even if it's not perfect, it's only temporary, right?"

She pulls me in for another hug. "But your move isn't, right? You're here to stay?"

I nod into her shoulder. "That's the plan. As long as I can find a permanent job before the contract with the Thunder runs out next year or somehow do a good enough job to make them hire me permanently."

Except that would mean working for Luca permanently. And that temptation might be too much for me.

We break apart and walk into the house, stepping around the movers who have already begun bringing in boxes. Coming to a stop in my new, very empty living room, I let out a low whistle. "Okay. We need to turn this place into somewhere Charlie won't turn his nose up at when he gets here in a few hours."

We make quick work of unloading my car, and once the movers finish, we get to work on setting up the living room, kitchen, and Charlie's room. Those were the spaces I deemed a priority to hopefully make things easier for Charlie. I can handle sleeping on my mattress on the floor for a few nights until Juniper or my mom can come and help me set up my bed.

"I can't wait to hit the town with you," Juni says excitedly as she tosses a throw pillow on the couch we've just set down. "There are some awesome boutiques downtown, and my favourite diner, and we can take Charlie on a day trip to Dogwood Cove. It's a super cute town. Oh, and there's an amazing winery, too!"

I lift my hands up to slow her down with a smile on my face. "Juniper, can we please remember I'm a single mom of a grumpy preteen who's just moved to a new town and is about to start a new job? I'm not going to have a lot of spare time on my hands."

She scoffs and comes over to stand in front of me, placing her hands on my shoulders. "You've got me, Isla. You're gonna rock the new job, and Charlie is gonna fall in love with this place. Everything is going to work out. You'll see."

I let her gather me in for a brief hug. "I hope you're right."

"I am. Now, let's finish up here, then take a lunch break. When I was unpacking the cooler, I saw your mom put in a container full of her pasta salad, and I'm hungry."

Just as we finish unpacking the last of the dishes in the kitchen, Juni gets a call from the office manager at the Cedar Creek Wildlife Rescue that she runs.

"Crap, I gotta go. Someone's found an injured female

deer near the highway. We need to make sure there isn't a fawn nearby. Tell Charlie and your mom I'm sad I missed them and we'll do dinner soon."

"Go rescue Bambi. Love you and thank you for your help." We hug quickly before she dashes off to her car.

A couple of hours later, I walk in from the back deck where I've just set up the patio furniture, and see my mother in the kitchen, smiling fondly at Charlie, who's looking around with wide eyes. He turns to me, and my soul sags in relief when I see an excited—yet guarded—expression on his face.

"Hey bud," I say, pasting on a wide grin. "What do you think? Have you seen your room yet? Aunt Juni and I set it up for you."

"I guess it's okay," Charlie says, his shoulders slouched. It's then that I pull out my secret weapon.

"Did you drive past the skate park on your way here?"

His eyes widen, and behind him, I see my mom's grin as she flashes me a thumbs-up. I held onto this piece of information, knowing it could be the clincher in getting my boy on board with the move.

"No, where is it?"

"Close enough for you to go by yourself." I hold up my hand when he starts to visibly bounce with excitement. "As long as you have your phone with you and are back at whatever time we agree on."

"Deal. Can I go now?" he asks, then his face falls. "Oh wait. It's almost dark."

"The park is lit," I say gently, "but why don't we have some dinner with Nana, then you and I can go there together since it'll be your first time. I promise not to be too annoying."

I get the first genuine smile I've seen flashed my way in weeks. My boy, the light of my life, walks over and gives me his perfect one-armed hug. "Sounds good."

He scampers off after our all too brief embrace, calling over his shoulder, "I'm gonna check out my room."

After he bounds up the stairs, I drop down into the nearest chair. "Thank God he doesn't know how to hold a grudge."

Mom bustles into the kitchen, pulling together the dinner she insisted on preparing. "He's a good kid, and he loves you. He knows this move isn't meant to be a bad thing, just give him time to adjust."

And later that night, when I'm sitting on a cold concrete wall, watching my boy skateboard around the dips and ramps of the nearby skate park, I breathe a sigh of relief. Because now that we're here, I can feel myself finally starting to believe that Mom and Juni might be right.

Moving to Cedar Creek *will* be a good thing.

4
LUCA

It's absolutely ridiculous that I feel nervous right now, staring out the window that looks down onto the field where most of the players, the few temporary staff we've hired, and a smattering of family members are starting to mill about.

My goal today was to bring everyone together for the simple job of getting to know each other. It also gives me a chance to try and feel everyone out in terms of what they might want to see happen with the Thunder.

I should be down there with them all, but instead, I'm standing in my office, if you can call it that, at the stadium. This place is still a dump. I have no furniture, and there's stains on the walls and a broken light bulb in the retro track lighting above me.

I insisted that my office be one of the last spaces fixed up. I'm more than capable of working from home, or from anywhere until everything else is dealt with. After all, the owner of a team isn't as important as the players, the coaching staff, and everyone else who actually brings fans into the stadium.

But it's not my run-down office making me nervous. It's not the players that I haven't met yet, or the renovations that seem to be taking forever.

No, these nerves are one hundred percent caused by the stunning woman with wavy red hair pulled back in a high ponytail who just walked in. Against my better judgment, I don't stop my gaze from traveling down her curvy body, covered in figure-hugging denim and an off-the-shoulder sweater that's almost an exact match for the shade of blue on the Thunder's home uniform.

My jaw clenches. I can't be doing this. I can't be looking at Isla and seeing anything other than the competent marketing consultant I've hired to help me turn this team around over the next several months. Yet every damn time I've seen her since she started last week, I've fought a battle. A struggle between the devil on one shoulder, telling me no one has caught my interest like Isla does since my ex-girlfriend back in Toronto, and the angel on the other shoulder, reminding me just how much younger than me she is. To say nothing of her being my fucking employee. Everything about Isla is off-limits.

It doesn't help that I overheard a conversation between her and Gabe in which she admitted to being single. All that did was make the devil even louder.

But the devil doesn't care that me pursuing her could end in disaster. For me, if she is offended by my advances. For her, if anyone suspected she got the job based on my attraction and not based on her skills. And for the team, if I lose the perfect person to make Cedar Creek fall in love with their baseball team again.

"Son, you ready?"

I turn at my dad's voice. His back is stooped, his hair fully silver, but even at eighty years old, he's still the strong man who raised me to be who I am today. Focused, driven, yet compassionate and generous. Those qualities are what I pride myself on, and I can't allow one beautiful woman to throw me off course.

"You bet. Is Mom downstairs?"

He chuckles as I make my way over to him. "Of course she is. Probably convincing those players of yours to eat more vegetables."

We both laugh. My mother is a retired therapist, with an uncanny way of getting people to spill their life's story. She's also been a vegetarian since the seventies, and is constantly trying to get everyone around her, strangers and all, to see what she calls the "benefits of a rainbow diet." She's good-natured about it, and never forces or judges anyone, but it's become a running joke for Dad and me, trying to predict who her next target will be whenever we're out.

It could be the cashier at a store, or an usher at a theater. Heck, I've seen her try to peddle carrot soup as an alternative to lobster bisque at an upscale restaurant.

She's determined, that's for sure. Guess I come by my own tenacity honestly. And my propensity toward healthy eating.

Dad and I make our way downstairs and head down

the tunnel toward the field. The sound of voices gets louder as we grow closer. Dad pulls me to a stop just before we round the corner that will take us out onto the grass. Turning me to face him, he places his wrinkled hands on my shoulders and looks in my eyes. "Luca, I'm proud of you. I know you felt untethered for a while after selling off GaitSync. And I know coming back to Cedar Creek may not have been your first choice, but your mother and I really did appreciate the help after my fall."

"Dad, stop. Moving home was the right decision, and I don't regret it. "

Of course, that lack of regret was also the proof I needed that my last relationship was at its end. Because moving back to be closer to my parents was more important to me than staying in Toronto like my ex wanted. Truly, it was a timely wake-up call to the fact that we'd both been settling instead of chasing our happiness.

"Well, still, I hope you don't hold yourself back from finding someone again. Anyone would be damn lucky to have you. Look at you now, owner of the Cedar Creek Thunder, doing great things for the community. I just..." he trails off, a soft smile creasing his face. "I'm just so damn proud of you, son."

I pull him in for a gentle hug, feeling how frail he seems in my arms. It fucking sucks having aging parents, and when Dad fell from a ladder last winter, it really brought that hard truth home. I'd missed too many years, and who knew how many more I'd have left.

"Thanks, Dad. But remember, no one here knows I'm connected to GaitSync. I don't want any attention being on me, or my leg, or my money."

After graduating from the University of Toronto with both a Bachelor's of Electrical Engineering and a Master's degree in Biomedical Engineering, I spent over a decade living and working on the East Coast, developing GaitSync. A smart gait feedback module, it addressed the ongoing frustration of gait analysis wearing a prosthetic, and the constant adjustments needed to ensure no long-term joint damage was done.

When I eventually sold the technology to a Canadian company that specialized in advanced prosthetics in a private, anonymous sale that kept my name far away from it, I stayed back east, trying to think of my next step. My ex disagreed with me staying anonymous, and then the arguments over my lack of direction started up as well. I was so aimless, and she didn't understand that I hated it, too. I simply couldn't figure out what to do. GaitSync had been my whole life, my passion, for so long that when it was no longer mine, I felt lost.

I didn't want the fame or recognition in the tech world or the amputee world. I was plenty rich, but there was nothing in Ontario for me other than her. And soon, even that faded.

Moving here, my only thought was to be close to my parents as they got older. Buying the Thunder wasn't a part of any plan, but when the opportunity came up, I suddenly had a purpose. I had something that mattered to me, and I don't regret taking that leap.

"Thanks, Dad."

He slaps my back a couple times and we step back. "Let's go save your guys from your mother's nagging, shall we?"

We move into the late fall sunshine, which may be bright, but isn't exactly warm. Still, I squint and wish I had worn sunglasses. Moving through the crowd, I greet the players and staff I recognize, introduce myself to those I don't, and try not to be too obvious in looking to see where Isla is.

"Luca, good to see you."

I smile at Rafe and take his outstretched hand. "You too. Thanks for coming out today."

He places his free hand on the lower back of a smaller woman with a head of unruly red hair. "This is my wife, Imogen," he states proudly, and the love he feels for her is evident in that simple sentence.

"Great to meet you. Thanks for being willing to relocate so we could get your husband on board," I joke, shaking her hand, too. That earns me a peal of laughter.

"Are you kidding? I should be thanking you for getting him out on the diamond again. Seven years of retirement was enough for this guy, he was starting to drive me crazy."

Rafe leans over and kisses the side of her head. "Yeah right, as if you weren't enjoying having me around. And don't tell me you didn't love spending six months traveling Europe. That wouldn't have been possible if I hadn't retired, you know."

Imogen pats his chest as she rolls her eyes my way. "Yes, there are some perks. But you need to work, and you need to be on the field. Besides, I love it over here." She gives me an excited grin. "We found an adorable house in the next town over, Dogwood Cove. It's such a lovely town. And the commute isn't so bad for Rafe. I was able to get a job here in Cedar Creek as well, so it all just worked out perfectly."

"I'm glad to hear it. If you haven't already, visit The Nutty Muffin. It's got the best baked goods in town," I say, just as I spot Isla off to the side. It wouldn't be weird for me to say hi, would it? If anything, it would be weird if I didn't.

What's also weird is how this one woman has me feeling like a nervous teenager with his first crush.

"You eat pastries?" Rafe says teasingly. "I thought you were all about the organic healthy life. At least, that's what Dom said when I suggested bringing donuts to our last meeting."

I laugh. "He's not wrong. I'm not big on desserts. But I'm a sucker for Nutella, and they have a Nutella-filled puff pastry that is a once-in-a-while indulgence. And I've heard from others that their muffins are worth getting up early for, since they sell out fast."

It's a struggle not to be obvious in how I track Isla as she talks to one of the interns hired to help with the relaunch.

"It was great meeting you, Imogen. Make sure you get some food before the players demolish it all." I grin, gesturing to the long table filled with snacks that, sure enough, is surrounded by half the team.

I make my way over to Isla's side, politely ignoring anyone who tries to stop me. When I reach her, she's chatting with Dom, of all people. But his arms are folded across his chest, and his face doesn't exactly scream open and welcoming, making some rarely-used protective instinct inside of me fire. I know he doesn't fully trust that she's the right candidate for the job, but he trusts me. So he better not be giving her any shit.

"I see you've met the thorn in my side," I say, reaching the two of them. Isla startles, and Dom snorts. "I mean him, of course." I toss Isla a casual smile. "He's my best friend and holds the reins on what we can spend, so it's best to stay on his good side."

Isla purses her lips like she's trying not to smile back. "I'll keep that in mind when I start working up budget proposals."

"You make it sound like I'm a cheapskate, when all I'm trying to do is make sure we have enough money to pay the players when the season starts," Dom injects drily.

Isla's smile breaks free but only for a second and I clench my jaw, trying not to react, even if I am suddenly filled with a desire to see it again.

"Don't worry, Dom, I happen to be very good at finding cost-efficient ways to deliver high-impact results."

Fuck, hearing her talk about her work shouldn't turn me on.

"Good." Dom's gruff reply has me turning a frown on him, hoping Isla doesn't notice. But the asshole doesn't look at me, and continues, still staring at Isla. "We've got some pretty high expectations for what we want to achieve over the next nine months. Think you'll be able to give everything it'll take?"

"I think you'll find I'm more than capable. I've surpassed high expectations before, and I'll do it again," comes Isla's equally direct reply.

I clap my hands together, and plaster on a grin. "Listen, you two, we're gonna do whatever it takes to make Cedar Creek fall in love with the Thunder again."

"Go team," Isla says weakly, but she's smiling, and Dom seems to have softened, so I'll take it.

"That's right. Go team."

5

ISLA

"That was torture," I groan dramatically as Juniper and I walk out the door of the studio where she just made me sweat through an extremely intense yoga flow class.

"Agreed," Juni says, wiping her brow again with the small towel she brought. "Let's never do that again."

Giggling at our dramatics, we loop arms and walk down the sidewalk slowly. Charlie is visiting my mom this weekend, so when Juniper suggested a girls day, I eagerly agreed. We started the morning with some window-shopping along the "main drag" as Juni called it, a pedestrian-only street lined with adorable boutiques with colourful awnings. And then came the dreaded yoga class. Which we are both apparently grateful is now over.

"What are your thoughts on a chicken burger and fries?" Juni asks.

"My thoughts are good. Happy. Solid. Especially if those fries are sweet potato and come with a yummy dipping sauce," I reply, rubbing my stomach. Who knew yoga class would make me work up an appetite.

"Excellent, follow me."

I let my best friend tug me down the street, feeling incredibly happy and content in this moment. My job is going well, hot boss and all, my son seems to be settling in and has even made a couple of friends at his new school, and I have the entire day to spend with my best friend. Not to mention, tomorrow morning there won't be a hangry preteen to drag out of bed. No, I can sip hot tea on the back patio for as long as I want. I can blast my own music and linger in a bubble bath, all before lunchtime if I want.

Don't get me wrong. I love my son with my entire being. But being a single parent means time to myself is hard to find. So I cherish it when I get it.

Juniper comes to a stop out front of a building that definitely seems out of place in the city.

"Dot's Diner" blazes in neon bubble letters above a teal-coloured door with a round porthole window. Large windows let you see inside, where the place seems packed.

"Trust me, Dot makes the best food you've ever tasted."

We push open the door and are met with controlled chaos. That's the best way to describe the mix of kitsch and colour, with mismatched booths and chrome-legged tables standing on a classic black-and-white checkerboard floor.

"Woah, someone went all out with the decor," I murmur to Juni, taking in the sounds of patrons talking and staff shouting out orders to be picked up, all overlaid by music playing from an old jukebox in the corner.

"Oh, I know. Dot's obsessed with the fifties. I should warn you, she knows everything about everybody and will make it her mission to know everything about you." We make our way up to the counter just as an older woman with greying hair, up in a ridiculously high ponytail, bustles out from the kitchen. Best of all, she's wearing an honest-to-goodness poodle skirt.

"Juniper! Hey hon, gimme a sec, okay?" she calls out as she weaves between tables to deposit the food she's carrying. When she returns, she pulls Juniper in for a hug before turning and doing the same to me.

"Well, hi there. You have to be Juni's bestie Isla. We've heard so dang much about you, I'm just tickled pink to finally meet you."

I'm too shocked by her outburst of friendly affection to say anything at first, but I hug her back.

"Dottie, give her some space." Juniper laughs, tugging me free. "But yes, this is Isla. We just finished the hardest yoga class I've ever encountered and are in desperate need of a clucky burger and fries."

"No onions on mine, please," I pipe in.

Dottie smiles and taps the side of her head. "Got it. No onions for Isla. Troy's in the back. He'll have that ready in no time." Dot gestures to two stools lining the counter. "Tell me you'll sit there so we can chat?"

"Of course." Juni sits down and I follow suit as Dot hurries off to the window into the kitchen to put in our order.

"I see what you mean about her," I whisper with a smile, my brain finally catching up to the incredible energy of the place.

"Right? She's super cool, and her son Troy is the best diner cook out there. I don't know what he puts on the fries, he won't tell anyone, but damn, they're good. And she'll remember about you not liking onions every time you come in here. Trust me."

"Alright girls, lets get you hydrated," Dot says brightly, sliding two large glasses of water across the counter. "Now, Isla. How are you and your boy settling in?"

My eyes widen. Juni was right, Dot really does know everything.

"Good, so far. I'll have to bring him here sometime." I gesture to the glass case filled with pie. "He's obsessed with pecan pie."

"I'll send you home with a slice for him." Dot smiles, already pulling out a takeaway container.

I start to protest, but Juni nudges my leg with hers and says, "That's sweet of you, Dot. Thanks."

Just then, a deep voice from behind us bellows, "June bug!"

Juni spins around on her stool, flinging her arms out. I turn around as well, just in time to see a tall man swing her off her seat.

"You're back!"

When she's finally set back down, Juniper turns and grabs my hand. "Isla, this is Cal. Cal, meet my best friend Isla."

Cal's face falls into a sad puppy expression. "Damn, I thought I was your best friend."

Juniper's eyes roll as she shakes her head. "It's different, Cal. Boy best friend and girl best friend are two separate things. Deal with it."

His face lights up again in a grin as he sticks out his hand. "Cal Prescott. Nice to meet ya, girl best friend."

I take his enthusiastic shake, but mentally, I'm drawing connections. This is Cal? The guy Juni has a hundred stories about? I've seen his photo around the stadium, of course, and in pictures on Juniper's social media. But somehow, he's even better looking in person. Especially with that smile he's giving her, as if she's the only person he sees.

They've only known each other a few years, but she talks about him so much, I teased her once about their relationship being beyond friendship. She shot me down immediately.

"You play for the Thunder, right? I just started a couple weeks ago, running the marketing campaign for the relaunch. Were you at the barbecue on Wednesday?"

He shakes his head. "Nah, I was out of town helping my baby sister deal with some shit. But I heard the new boss hired a bunch of people to help turn things around. I'm excited to see what happens."

I give him a genuine smile back. "Me too."

Dot returns, sliding two big plates of food across the counter before turning to Cal. "What can I get you, big guy?"

He sneaks a fry off Juniper's plate. "This looks great, Dottie, can I have the same?"

"Of course, hon. How's your mom doing?"

Dot and Cal strike up a conversation and I spin Juni to face me, my eyebrows raised.

"What?" she mumbles around a mouthful of french fry.

I shake my head in amusement. Okay, she's oblivious. But before I can say anything more, a big arm is draped over her shoulder.

"So, Isla, what do you think the chances are of the team getting new uniforms?" Cal's hopeful puppy dog expression has me chuckling.

"Pretty good, actually."

"Thank God," he says before stealing another one of Juni's fries.

She slaps his hand away. "Wait for your own food!"

"But yours tastes better."

I hide my smirk as I watch them. Yep, oblivious. Both of them.

6

LUCA

WHO KNEW TRYING to revitalize a baseball team would involve so many goddamn meetings.

Yeah, the thought sounds ridiculously stupid as soon as I think it. But I'm used to a lot more hands-on *doing* to get shit done, and a lot less *talking* about it. That's part of why I sold GaitSync. Because I wasn't interested in the business side of distributing the technology, I just wanted to build it.

The payout from selling it didn't hurt, either. But how did I not realize buying a baseball team would mean endless conversations about budgets and plans.

Dom's waiting for me in his office space to discuss those very things. Budgets and plans.

Moving through the corridor on the bottom level of the stadium, away from the coaches offices where I've just finished reviewing our new player recruits with Rafe, I smile and nod at everyone I pass. It might be unconventional to be such a hands-on, present owner, but I don't care. This place is my legacy.

Normally I'd take the stairs, but my leg has been aching a lot lately, so instead, I head for the single elevator that provides access to all the levels of the building. I suppose I should be glad the previous team owners cared at least a little bit about accessibility. The elevator arrives, and I step in, thumbing through some unread emails on my phone. We've been waiting on someone to come and service the old elevator for a couple of weeks, nothing major, just routine maintenance. It starts to move upward, then comes to a stop just one level up. My gaze lifts as the doors open and meets a bright green one.

"Luca. Hi."

I smile. "Hey, wonder woman."

She blushes prettily. "Why would you call me that?" She moves to stand across from me, close, given the tight confines, but I wish she was closer. The elevator doors close and it slowly starts to move again. Pocketing my phone, I turn to her.

"Because I'm so impressed by everything you've managed to do in just a few weeks."

Her blush deepens. I'm toeing the line of inappropriate, and I know it. Thank fuck she doesn't seem upset.

What I hold back from admitting is the fact that ever since she started, Isla has had me tied up in fucking knots. Just looking at her makes me want to throw professionalism out the window and ask her if she'll let me take her to dinner.

It's ridiculous, seeing as I barely know her, but what I do know, I like.

Out of nowhere, the elevator shudders and comes to a complete stop, followed by an annoying alarm sound.

"Holy shit," Isla says, her hand coming up to cover her mouth. "What just happened?"

I turn to the panel and try to push the button to open the doors. "I don't know." Nothing works, so I press the call button next, hoping it's still connected to somewhere.

"Tyson Elevators, how may I assist you?" a tinny-sounding voice comes from the speaker. Thank fuck.

"Hi, this is Luca Calloway over at the Cedar Creek Thunder Stadium. Our main elevator just came to a stop between floors, and I'm stuck in here with one of my staff. Can you help?"

"I'm sorry to hear that Mr. Calloway, I can see there's been a small malfunction in your system. We'll dispatch emergency services right away to get you out of there and send a crew to repair the malfunction. Hang on, let me get you an ETA on your extraction."

I hear Isla stifle a giggle at the formal-sounding report, and turn away from the speaker to whisper, "Someone's been watching a few too many spy movies."

I can see her shoulders shake with silent laughter. At least she isn't freaking out.

"Alright, Cedar Creek Fire is on their way. They said it could be up to an hour, however. I will have an elevator technician on premises later this afternoon. Would you like me to stay on the line until rescue arrives?"

"No, we're fine. Thank you." The audible click of the call disconnecting echoes in the small space.

"Should we text anyone here to let them know?" Isla asks.

"Yeah. Good plan. Dom's probably wondering where

I am, actually, we were meant to be meeting right now. I'll let him and Gabe know what's happening." I quickly type out an explanation of our current predicament to the two of them, then pocket my phone. "So, I guess now we wait."

Isla's got her lower lip tugged between her teeth as she nods. "Guess so." She sits down, cross-legged, leaning against the wall and gestures to the wall behind me. "Might as well get comfy."

Shit. Sitting down on the floor isn't as simple for me as it is for her. I'm saved by her phone vibrating, and when she looks at it, I try to move as quickly as I can without it being obvious I've got a prosthetic leg. It means mine are outstretched, not folded like hers, and I make sure my pants are fully covering the bottom of my leg, even going so far as to cross my good one over top to cover any sign of my artificial limb.

It's silent for an awkward moment or two before I clear my throat. "How is your son liking Cedar Creek so far?"

That earns me a small smile. "I think he's doing okay. Back in Victoria, he was in a middle school, but here, he's already at the high school. Which could be a good thing, I guess. More options for classes and more kids." Her expression shutters. "He has a disability that he was getting bullied for at his old school. Time will tell if that's a problem here as well."

My blood boils at the thought of her son facing bullies. I had my share of tormentors in school. Not many, seeing as Cedar Creek was a smaller town back then, but enough.

"I hope not," I growl.

"Me too." She shifts in her seat, and I watch curiously as a visible change comes over her. As if she's putting on a coat of armour, masking her vulnerability. I wonder how often she has to do that. I wish she knew she didn't have to hide it with me. Because knowing her son has a disability and has been bullied for it only makes me want to protect them both.

"May I ask, is his disability serious? I know your temporary position doesn't cover extended medical benefits but if you need anything—"

"We're fine, but thank you," she interrupts stiffly. "He was born with a congenital limb difference. But after twelve and a half years, we know how to handle most things."

My heart pounds. Her son has the same disability as me? My thoughts spiral even faster, but I don't get another word out before she changes the subject.

"Want to play a game?" she asks, and my eyebrows raise.

"Okay, what kind of game?"

"Nothing too serious, just a twist on something Charlie and I do at dinner each night. It's called rose and thorn. The rose is the best part of something and the thorn is the worst. We use it as a way to catch up on our days."

I nod. "Sounds easy enough."

She smiles. "But the twist is, it doesn't have to be about our days. So what's your rose and thorn from, say, university?"

I consider my answer for a minute. There are things

I'm not ready to reveal. But I don't want to lie, so I get creative. "Rose would be my thesis project. Thorn would be the loan debt I had to pay off after graduating."

Isla laughs. "Tell me about it, I'm still trying to do that."

It's on the tip of my tongue to offer to pay it off for her as I'm hit with another spike of desire to protect her. Ridiculous, insane, and over-the-top as it might sound, I want to do that for her. But I'm smart enough not to say it. "Okay, your turn. Same question."

She lets her head fall back against the wall, her gaze going upward. "Rose, managing to graduate while raising a toddler. Thorn would be the statistics class I almost failed." She makes an adorable face. "I hate statistics."

I chuckle. "I don't blame you. There's a reason Dom is the numbers guy."

"You two are close."

"Very. We've been friends since we were kids. He and his wife are high school sweethearts, and probably the two people who know me the best, aside from my parents."

"Sounds like me and Juniper. She's my best friend."

We smile at each other, our gazes locked. The wall between us, that of boss and employee, feels like it's come down and we're just two people getting to know each other.

Which is dangerous and thrilling, all at the same time.

"My turn to pick a question," I say. I want to know

everything about this brilliant, beautiful woman. "Rose and thorn for luxury items."

"That's an intriguing question." Isla smiles. "Rose is definitely a high-quality Earl Grey tea with real bergamot. It's so much better than the stuff that uses artificial flavourings."

"Do you have a favourite brand?"

Her face falls slightly. "I've only had it a couple of times. The artificial flavouring is a lot more affordable." She laughs, but it sounds forced. I hate that and make a mental note to have Gabe research the best tea brands.

"Anyway, thorn would be private jets. I can't get past how bad it is for the environment. Carbon footprint and all."

"Agreed." I nod.

Her expression turns teasing. "You might be the only billionaire who doesn't have one."

"Millionaire." I correct with a shrug. "And first class can still be pretty damn luxurious." I wink and she giggles, shaking her head with a faint blush. God, she's pretty. I wonder how far down that blush goes. I don't realize we've both leaned in closer to each other until I register the dilation of her pupils and hear her intake of breath.

I shift back. Damn. I almost kissed her.

Isla's tongue darts out to lick her lower lip. My gaze zeros in on it.

Fuck.

Then she clears her throat. "My turn. Rose and thorn for food."

I welcome the distraction and try to convince my

dick to calm down. Nothing is going to happen right now. "Easy. Rose is the miso-glazed black cod with truffle-infused quinoa and roasted vegetables from The Lookout," I say, naming a high-end restaurant on the mainland. "Thorn would be pickles. Those things are nasty."

Isla's amused smirk makes her eyes sparkle. "That's one fancy-sounding dish. But I'm with you on the pickles. Totally gross."

"How about for yourself?"

She makes a humming sound. "Let's see, rose would be my dad's homemade pizza." Her face falls slightly. "Haven't had it in years, but it was the best. He'd make his own dough and sauce from scratch. Some of my favourite memories are of him and Charlie making pizza together."

There's something more to what she's saying, something that has made her sad. But it's not my place to ask what, and before I can say anything, she continues, blowing out a breath and shaking her head slightly.

"And um, my thorn would probably be cooked spinach. That texture is terrible."

I chuckle. "Don't ever let my mother hear that, she'll make it her mission in life to get you to like it."

"Not a chance," Isla says emphatically. She's not quite back to smiling, but she seems to be mostly over whatever it was that shifted her mood.

"She's a health nut," I say, hoping to distract her. "A lifelong vegetarian, which is how I was raised. Then, as an adult, I discovered the pure joy of a good steak with garlic mashed potatoes." I smile and rub my stomach.

"So good. Anyway, she's the kind of mom that refused to buy snacks from the grocery store and would make homemade granola bars and stuff. I hated it as a child, watching my friends get all kinds of treats while I had trail mix and dried fruit, but obviously, the habits stuck with me, since even now I tend to avoid sweets."

Isla shakes her head, her face a picture of mock horror. "You mean, no fruit snacks? No Dunkaroos? No Oreos? What a terrible childhood. I think Charlie would run away from home if I took away his Froot Loops. Do you eat *anything* sugary now?"

I grin. "Can I tell you a secret?"

She nods, leaning forward.

"I'm addicted to Nutella."

She bursts out laughing, and it lights up her entire face.

"Really. Chocolate and hazelnut. That's your vice?"

"Yep. I keep a jar in a mini fridge in my office for when I get a craving."

Just then, there's a loud banging above our heads. "Hello in the elevator, this is Captain Danson with the Cedar Creek Fire Department. Is everyone alright?"

"Yeah, we're fine," I call back, staring at Isla as she stands and smooths her hands over her hair.

"Good to hear it. We'll have you out in a minute, sir."

"Great. Thanks."

Then there's a screeching sound and the elevator door is forced open, revealing the smiling face of a firefighter.

"You two ready to get outta there?"

I nod and gesture to Isla. "Yeah, get her out first."

Thankfully, Isla's so focused on exiting the elevator that she doesn't look back. I awkwardly climb to my feet, realizing my legs are shaky. I'm literally weak in the knees for this woman. Which is a bigger problem than just hiding my leg.

I'm also hiding how I feel.

7

ISLA

I NORMALLY HATE conference rooms where every wall is glass. It feels like I'm in a fishbowl.

However, every time I've had to sit across from Luca in this space, I've found myself feeling quite grateful for the awareness that anyone and everyone can see us in here.

It's helping me keep my absolutely insane attraction to this man in check. An attraction that is even stronger after being stuck in an elevator with him for over an hour and getting to know him as a person, not just my employer.

Juniper thinks it's hilarious, the fact that my new boss has me thinking all kinds of things I have no right thinking. She immediately googled him the second I confessed to her how incredibly handsome I think he is, but he has a remarkably sparse online presence. Which I already knew from my own search before I agreed to take the job.

Juni asked if he was a *sexy silver fox* and while I agree

he's definitely sexy, and a fox, the silver is more salt-and-pepper.

Aaaand now I'm staring at his hair again.

"Which is why I was thinking of having Gabe handle the press that day." Luca leans back in his chair as I blink rapidly, trying to get my brain to catch up to whatever he was talking about while I was daydreaming.

"Right. Yes. I mean, that makes sense," I say, hoping fervently that whatever I'm agreeing to actually makes sense.

"That way, neither one of us are tied up showing them around," Luca continues.

Oh. That's what he's referring to, the stadium tour we're arranging for next week when the renovations are complete. Not tying me up. Or us being tied up together. In bed. Oh my God. Nope. Renovations, not bedroom kink.

I clear my throat. "And we're certain the crews are still on track to finish on time?" My gaze dips, skimming my list of notes in front of me, hoping it distracts my brain from other things. "Last time I was there, it looked like there was quite a bit left to do."

Luca's deep chuckle hits my ears. "Yes. I had to convince Dom to let me throw some more money at them, but they assure me next Thursday is their last day. The paint will be dry Friday morning, just in time for us to open the doors to the media. With no more elevator malfunctions."

I bite my cheek to stop from smiling. "Great." I glance up and see his storm-grey eyes focused on me. His stare is intense. He looks away the second our gaze meets, but

I flush, nonetheless. This isn't the first time I've caught him looking at me like that. It's never anything more than a look, nothing I would say is disrespectful at all. But every time I catch him, a wave of heat passes over me.

Mentally shaking my head, I reach for the carafe of hot water in the center of the table to refill my cup of tea. I've got one of my slightly more expensive tea bags in my mug, which means I can squeeze out a second cup.

Except, instead of the handle of the carafe, my hand brushes against warm, slightly rough skin.

"Oh. Sorry. You first," I say, snatching my hand away.

His lips quirk up slightly as he hands me the small package in his hand. "I just wanted to offer this instead of what you have there. Gotta keep you caffeinated," he continues in a teasing tone. "Last thing I want is a repeat of Monday."

I ignore his outstretched hand and give him a haughty look. "First of all, it was not because I hadn't drank my tea that I dropped that box of files."

"Oh, I remember, it was the smooth tile floor that tripped you," he says, openly laughing now. And I guess I can't blame him. It wasn't my best moment, tripping over absolutely nothing and spilling the box of trading card mock-ups I had made. Mock-ups he'll never see, since Dom insisted they were out of budget.

"Still, making sure my marketing expert has her tea isn't a bad idea." He grins, sitting back in his chair, looking every bit the sexy silver fox Juni named him.

"I'm glad you recognize that," I say with a smile of my own, settling back in my own chair. "Besides, if you remember our very first meeting, it was your fault I dumped tea all over you. You're the one who tripped over nothing that time."

I'm expecting him to laugh along with me, not clam up and drop his gaze to the table. An uneasy silence falls, and suddenly I panic that I've crossed the professional line and am getting way too comfortable around my boss. I clear my throat and try to redirect the conversation back to where it should be. On work.

"Anyway, let's circle back to the fundraiser gala."

"What about your tea?"

I look up to see him still holding out the paper-wrapped packet, an intense expression on his face. I take it, and when I bring it closer, the unmistakable aroma of bergamot fills my nostrils.

"Is this..." I trail off as I unwrap the paper. "Luca."

"It's a local tea company that uses all organic and sustainably sourced ingredients. I've got a bigger order on hold, if you like it, so there's enough at the office for you."

He remembered my rose. My luxury indulgence. More than that, he went to the effort of finding some and getting it for me?

I'm speechless. And confused. Is this a simple, kind gesture, or more? I mentally give my head a shake. This is not the time or place to swoon over tea.

"Thank you. That's very kind. I hope Dom didn't give you a hard time about the cost."

"It didn't come out of the budget."

Oh God. He paid for it himself. My cheeks start to heat. I don't know what to say.

Luca takes the package back from me and opens it. Inside are individual tea bags, and as soon as he takes one out, the bergamot aroma grows deeper. I watch as he places one in my cup and pours hot water over the top before sliding it back toward me.

"Let me know what you think."

I manage to lift my gaze to meet his and again say a simple yet heartfelt "thank you."

My head is still spinning as I try to compose myself, shuffling the papers in front of me. I scan my notes, not really reading them. "Did you give any more thought to the charity collaboration I suggested?"

"Yeah. I think working with the animal shelter is a great idea, especially with how close Dogwood Cove is to Cedar Creek. It extends our outreach beyond our town, which can only help in the long run."

Nodding in agreement, I go on to the next thing on our list. "Maybe we can ask Rafe to pick a few players to attend the gala. Then I'll get in contact with the director of the shelter and confirm our numbers and plans for the silent auction donations."

"And you'll be at the gala with me, right?"

I blink slowly. *With* him?

"Y-yes. I'll be there. To help make sure it all runs smoothly and generate more interest in the Thunder."

"Great. Let me know when and where to pick you up."

I manage to school my reaction enough to stop my jaw from dropping. But is he for real right now? "That's okay, you don't have to. I can just meet you there."

Luca fixes me with a look that leaves no room for arguing. "I'll pick you up, Forrester."

Okay, but why does his calling me by my last name send heat rushing through my body? And why am I now frantically thinking about what's in my closet, wondering if I have *anything* that can blend sexy with professional. Not that I need to be looking sexy. Oh my God, he's my boss.

Snap. Out. Of. It. Isla.

"F-fine," I stutter. He nods and checks his phone. "Next order of business, you wanted to show me some social media ideas?"

"Right. If you would open your preferred social media channel, I'll tell you what to search."

I pick up my mug and take a sip of the most decadent tea I've ever tasted, just barely stifling my moan of pleasure.

Over the rim of my cup, I watch Luca stand and move to walk around the table, stopping part way with a grimace he tries to hide, his hand coming to the side of his leg.

"Everything okay?" I ask, and he just nods.

"Yep. Just a cramp." He sits down beside me and gestures to my phone. "Okay, now you can just show me on your phone."

I look at him for a second, noting how his hand stays on his knee. Faint lines of pain are on his face, something I would have never noticed if he wasn't so close. Must be a bad cramp. But it's not my place to pry, so I turn my focus to my phone and open up the accounts I had saved to show him.

"Alright, so I think we need a multi-channel approach. Video and static posts, sharing stories from our players and team members, yourself included," I say, looking at him.

"Why me?"

"Because people are going to want to know why a former Cedar Creek resident came back and bought their baseball team. You're young, rich, and attractive. The trifecta for appealing to the masses on social media." I blurt it all out without thinking, then mentally slap myself. Seriously, Isla?

But Luca's enigmatic expression doesn't seem angry or insulted. If anything, he's amused. "I'd argue about the young part, but I'm more intrigued by the fact that you think I'm attractive enough for social media appeal." he teases.

I lift my hand and wave it weakly over him. "I mean. Yes." Turning back to my phone, I ignore my racing heart and continue. "We also need to go back in time. Look at what made the Thunder so popular with the town. Pull in the nostalgia angle. I'm thinking we can do that in both advertising campaigns and in our physical presence at the stadium. Vintage jerseys and caps, photos of past teams and players on the wall. Maybe the Cedar Creek News has some old photos of past news articles written about the team. We blend the old with the new, using modern approaches to remind everyone why they love this team."

Luca's studying me when I finish. "You're really fucking good at this, Isla." He glances down at the phone, where I've still got an account for a team in Washington open. "What about fan engagement? Loyalty programs? These guys do something cool with letting season ticket holders pick themes for fan nights."

I nod eagerly. "I love that. Yes. We can incorporate those as we go. Part of my approach is to be prepared for changing strategies on the fly. We always have a plan B in our back pocket, so that if one thing isn't working, we can pivot to something else. We've got the next few months to generate interest in the team, and then you'll have the season to make everyone fall in love with it."

The smile he gives me is proud and admiring, and I inwardly preen under the attention. I know I'm good at my job, but knowing I've impressed Luca Calloway? Even better.

Then he stands and stretches his arms overhead. "Alright. It's late, and I've kept you here far too long. Your kid must be wondering what's happened."

I stand as well and begin gathering everything up off the table. "It's okay, Charlie's a pretty self-sufficient kid."

Luca joins me in tidying up. "I'm guessing he gets that from you. Is his dad involved?" His hands freeze. "Shit. That's inappropriate, I have no business asking you that."

I place my hand on his, then snatch it away when he looks at me. "It's fine, Luca. Seriously, I'm not upset. And no, his biological father has never been in the picture." I shrug. "We were seventeen, he didn't want a kid to derail his plans. Last I heard, he went off to university on the East Coast. It's just me and Charlie. And my parents, they stepped up and were a huge help."

He nods, a soft smile creasing his face. "I'm glad you have them."

My responding smile is lined with grief. "Thanks. It's just my mom now, my father died a few years ago."

"Damn. I'm sorry."

I wave off his apology. "Please, don't apologize. Honestly, I shouldn't have said anything, you're my boss, not my friend. You don't need to know all my trauma."

"I don't want you to see me as just your boss, Isla. I hate the idea of being different, or somehow more important than anyone else here. Just because I pay the bills doesn't mean I don't care about everyone here. So if you want to talk about anything, I'm here. Okay?"

My tongue darts out to moisten my suddenly dry lips. And I nod. "Okay."

Luca exhales, his face relaxing from his intense expression. "And at the risk of being inappropriate again, I have to say one thing. You're an impressive woman. Certainly a talented marketer, and with the way you clearly care about your job and the team, I can only assume a great mom, also. Charlie is a lucky kid."

There's a heated moment of silence after his quiet compliment. It's not that I've never had someone praise me. But a man like Luca, who obviously has high standards and the drive to reach them, calling me talented and a good mother? It's hard to hold back from throwing my arms around his neck and hugging him in thanks.

Now *that* would be inappropriate.

Just then, my phone buzzes with an incoming call. We both glance down at the same time and see Charlie's name on the caller ID.

"I'll see you tomorrow, Isla, enjoy the tea," Luca says quietly before stepping out of the room.

I exhale.

He's my boss.

And the only man I have room for in my life is calling me.

"Hey kid, what's up?"

8

LUCA

"I swear to fucking God, your upper body is deceiving," Dom gripes as he swipes a towel over his face.

It's late, but we decided to stay after everyone else had gone home and take advantage of the newly finished fitness facilities at the stadium. Dom thought I was insane putting a state-of-the-art gym into a minor league baseball stadium, but now he's whistling a different tune.

"It's okay to just admit you're jealous," I tease, earning a shove that is not quite strong enough to make me trip. He's known me long enough to know the limits of my balance. And that upper body strength he's talking about? Comes from years of using crutches and years of needing that extra core and back strength just to walk around and perform normal activities. Things that others don't think twice about take me so much longer.

Yeah, I'm strong. Except for when I'm not.

We walk out onto the field, lit up by the also newly replaced stadium lights. Things are starting to come together after several months of hard work—and plenty of money.

"You think you can still hit off my curveball?" Dom shouts as he jogs out to the pitcher's mound.

I grin. "Depends on if you can still throw like you did when we were sixteen."

"If you mean deadly fast and accurate, then fuck yeah, I can." He rotates his shoulder while I get into position, making sure my prosthetic is firmly planted. It's been a long time since I swung a bat, but it feels good.

"If you hit this, I'll let you spend whatever you want on merch design."

My eyes widen and I nod enthusiastically. "You're on." The possibility of getting an unlimited budget to design new merchandise? Hell yeah, I'm gonna hit it.

He winds up, and my gaze zeros in on his arm. The ball leaves his glove, and thank fuck, he's just as rusty as I am because it moves slow enough for me to track the path it'll take and adjust.

I swing. And make contact. Not great, as the ball only goes a little past first, but there's contact.

"That was pathetic, Calloway," Dom jeers from the mound.

I scoff, taking a couple of practice swings. "Your pitch? Yeah, I know it was. Try harder."

He barks out a laugh and nods at me before taking his stance.

This time, my bat connects with a lot more force and the ball goes sailing into left field. "How 'bout that?" I crow, swinging my bat around.

"Yeah, yeah, fine. Bankrupt the organization with foam fingers and jerseys," Dom gripes, shaking his head.

"Forget fingers, I'm thinking giant foam lightning bolts."

"That would work if we were the Cedar Creek Lightning," he fires back, and I shrug with a smirk.

"Whatever. I get to do what I want. I hit the ball."

We go for a few more pitches before switching places. Except the slope to the pitching mound presents me with a challenge. After the first few shitty pitches, I throw my glove down in frustration.

"Fuck."

Dom jogs over. "Hey, everything okay?"

"Yeah. Fine," I bite out, bending down and massaging my quad. "Just can't get a good stance on the slope."

He frowns down at my leg. "Doesn't your fancy microchip thing help with that?"

I swear to God, this guy. He's known what GaitSync is for almost a decade and he still gets it wrong. "That's not what it—" I stop when I see him grinning. "Fuck you, Dom."

"Hey. It worked, didn't it? Got you to stop beating yourself up and get annoyed with me instead."

I shake my head as we move over to the dugout. I'm moving slower than normal, my leg starting to ache from the twisting motions that were unavoidable when I was batting. It's the same struggle I had when I was younger. I could play ball, but only for short stints. Thank fuck I had coaches willing to work with me, to adapt so I could play—even if it meant changing lineups on the fly when things would go wrong with my prosthetic.

GaitSync was meant to make all of that easier. To allow people like me to adjust their prosthesis in real time, without always having to go to their prosthetist for it. And most of the time, it works as intended. But I've been putting my leg through a lot lately, pushing myself in the gym and playing ball tonight. I could lie and say it's just to deal with the ongoing stress of the renovations and revitalization of the team, but it's not only that.

I sink down to the bench, and accept the water bottle Dom passes me, drinking from it deeply.

"So. Isla. How's *that* working out?"

I toss my now empty water bottle at him. "It's fine. She's doing good work."

Dom makes a sound, and my brows narrow into a hard stare. "What's your problem with her? Don't tell me you think she's not good at her job."

"I don't have a problem with her work. I have a problem with the way you look at her when you think no one's watching. She's your fucking employee, Luca, not some random woman you can pursue without thinking of the potential consequences."

My head falls back with a slight thud against the wall. "Trust me, I know. Nothing is gonna happen."

"Good." Dom slaps my shoulder. "Because we need her. A solid marketing plan is a huge element to our success. There's a hell of a lot at stake if you chase her off."

"Fuck off, Dom, I know." My voice is harsh. He's not saying anything I haven't already told myself. "But I can't just stop being attracted to her. I can't turn it off like a fucking light switch. She's beautiful, and funny, and smart. And so damn off-limits." I exhale slowly, letting my annoyance at my friend fade. "Besides, even if I wasn't her boss, there's no saying she'd be interested in a guy missing his fucking leg."

Dom snorts. "Are you serious? Look, I had my reservations when you hired her. I still do. After all, she was the only damn candidate you interviewed. But she's proving she can do the job. Even I can admit she's a good person. And while I definitely don't think you should be thinking about dating her, she doesn't strike me as the kinda woman who would care about shit like that."

I think back to what I've seen from Isla over the last few weeks. She's worked hard, every minute of every hour she's here. But she's also kind, and generous, and sweet. I've watched her take the time to learn almost everyone's name, from the players to the admin to the janitors. She brought in cookies the other day, including a special plate of nut-free ones for the outfielder who has a nut allergy. She always checks with everyone before going on a coffee or lunch run, and most often brings back an extra treat for whoever she's picking up a drink for. She's already made connections in the town, and they're all positive. Just last week, I received a call from the Cedar Creek Chamber of Commerce, complimenting me on my initiative to have our team sponsor a Little League team.

I didn't even know we were doing that. But it made my fucking heart swell to hear it.

Isla Forrester is a good person, through and through.

"It doesn't matter. At the end of the day, she's here to do a job for us. And I'm not gonna jeopardize that just because I'm attracted to her."

"I agree, Isla is off-limits. But what about dating someone else? I'm sure Coral could find someone to set you up with?" Dom asks before chugging the rest of his water.

"Your wife is a saint to put up with you, and a stellar woman. But I'm not letting her set me up," I scoff. "Besides, even if I was interested, I don't have time to date."

"Okay, what about just finding someone to have some fun with?"

"It's not that easy. Before my ex, the last two women I went out on a date with basically ran the other way when they found out I'm an amputee. Sex isn't as easy for me as it is for you. It takes effort and coordination and they don't want to deal with that. Fuck, the last girl flinched when she saw it. Flinched. That's great for a man's self-esteem." Dom is the only person I've ever allowed to see me this vulnerable.

"There are plenty of women out there who wouldn't give a damn about your leg. Don't let fear hold you back from finding someone, Luca. You're a good man, and you've worked too damn hard to get where you are to live only half a life."

He's right, I know this. But what am I meant to do when the only woman I want is the one woman I can't have?

More importantly, why do I feel like I'm fighting a

losing battle against the part of me that says it's wrong to want her...

9
ISLA

It's mid-October, six weeks into my contract with the Cedar Creek Thunder, and I feel like I'm hitting my stride. Plans are in place for a lot of town engagement events, and from what I see and hear, interest is starting to grow around the team.

Work couldn't be going better. Except when it comes to maintaining my boundaries around Luca. He's still my boss, and not someone I can ever be romantically involved with, but as I get to know him, I'm finding I also really like Luca the man. Except for when he's being a stubborn idiot, like he is right now. I try not to let my aggravation—or my amusement—show as I take a deep breath in and out. "Luca, I don't want to overstep, but I have to remind you that there's no reason for you to be opening your wallet every time we agree upon a marketing concept."

The arch of his brow tells me he's not buying it. So I pull up the list I've been compiling of all the things Dom tells him are out of budget and he goes ahead and pays for himself. At this rate, he'll lose his millionaire status in branded popcorn containers.

"I know the staff appreciate the special shirts you're providing for game days, and I agree that showing off team pride is important. However, I don't think everyone needed multiple colour options. And the booth for the Cedar Creek Fall Fair was over-the-top, even you admitted that. The signage for the exterior of the stadium was a good investment, I'll give you that, but we could have done something perfectly acceptable within budget. And this might not be marketing related, but if you think Dom didn't notice the *two* new espresso machines that showed up last week, you're wrong. I heard him grumbling even as he was sipping his cappuccino."

I fix him with what Charlie calls my *mom stare*. "You hired me to not only provide you with a marketing plan for the relaunch, but also a sustainable plan for going forward. So that the team has a positive presence that grows over time but is manageable at the same time and includes *community involvement*." I purposely emphasize those last two words before pushing over a piece of paper.

"I came up with a list of potential donors and sponsors last week and you still haven't told me which ones to approach. Locking down some solid sponsors for the big-ticket items, especially on the stadium itself, is key. Banners, spots in the fan store, collaboration on in-game events, these are the things we can offer. But we need to pick the right companies and individuals to approach.

So, please. Close your wallet and open your mind to choosing some sponsors!"

His lips quirk up into the sexiest smirk. "Yes, boss."

I feel my cheeks heat. But I hold his gaze. "Good. So you'll actually listen next time I suggest the better way to allocate funds, and you'll pick some sponsors?"

He leans forward, resting his muscular forearms on the table between us. We're still at the coworking space, as the offices at the stadium are not quite ready. "I listen to you. Every damn word you say, wonder woman."

My breath catches in my throat. Both at the undercurrent of his words, and at the nickname.

Juniper thinks I'm crazy for holding back. But that's easy for her to say. It isn't her entire life, and her son's life, that are at risk of imploding if I admit my attraction to him and it goes wrong. Just because I *think* he flirts with me doesn't mean he is. Besides, it's not like I'm all that experienced in this area. The last time someone showed interest in me, it was Charlie's bio dad, asking me to be his date to the senior dance. His idea of flirting was giving me his football jacket to wear.

And even if Luca is flirting, it certainly doesn't mean starting anything would be a good idea for anyone involved.

No, Luca Calloway the man will stay in my fantasies. And Luca Calloway my boss will stay as only that. Ethically and professionally, I have to keep the two separate. "Alright, if you've been listening, then tell me who, from this list, we should approach. Then we need to discuss your upcoming media interviews."

He takes the piece of paper and scans it quickly. I see

his brows draw together at one point but he quickly smooths them out.

"Let's reach out to Island Cidery, we can offer them a tap at the concession stands as well as banners. And I know the Devereaux Hotel chain would be a good one. Three Rivers Brewing is also an option. Same offer as the cidery. The property development company…" He pauses, and I can see his jaw clench. "Yeah. Whatever, we can reach out to them, too."

Briefly, I debate whether to push for an explanation of his reaction, but ultimately, it's none of my business. I'm just his temporary employee. "Okay, great. I'll reach out to those four to start with. Now, media. Have you ever done interviews with print or digital media?"

He looks away and shifts as if he's uncomfortable. "I can handle the media. What's next?"

"Well, the gala is coming up." I bite my lip. It's really not my business to ask my next question, his assistant can handle his RSVP. But I guess I'm a sucker for punishment. "Will you be bringing a plus-one? I only ask so I can give the shelter our final numbers and provide you with a plan for the evening in terms of what I'll need from you. I don't want you to feel like you're abandoning your date for me."

Luca's full lips quirk up in a grin. "Isla, you *are* my date. Remember?"

I squeeze my legs together. He has no right to sound so damn sexy with that low voice saying those words. It's not fair, even if I know he's just teasing.

"Hardly. I'm your colleague, helping you network and raise funds for the animal shelter and for the team."

He looks at me with an unreadable expression for several long minutes, to the point that I start to wonder what I said. Then he gives a brusque nod. "Right. Well, I'm not bringing anyone, and I was still planning to give you a lift there."

Pushing back from the table, Luca stands and picks up his phone. "I've gotta go. Feel free to get Gabe to set up any appointments with the sponsors, just make sure you can be there, too."

He leaves the conference room before I can reply, leaving me staring at the papers and my laptop in front of me. Why do I feel like even though we made forward progress on our work tasks, I just set myself back several steps when it comes to keeping the lines firmly drawn between me and Luca?

———

When I get home, Charlie and Juniper are sitting on the couch, looking at something on Juni's phone. Gus is curled up on Charlie's lap, purring, as Juni keeps a safe distance from his claws. He's been known to swipe a paw at someone even when he seems content with his kid.

"Hey," I say, kicking off my shoes. "Are we feeding you or did you bring dinner?"

"Aunt Juni brought stuff to make burritos!" Charlie says, barely glancing up from the phone.

"Awesome. I'll go shower, then we can eat." I wait for a second, but don't get a response from either of them. "Okay. What the heck are you looking at?"

The guilty looks they both give me as my best friend

flips her phone over have me placing my hands on my hips and dialing up the mom stare.

"It's nothing, Isla. Just a little research." Juni's lips are twitching like she wants to smile, and Charlie looks like he wants to burst out of his skin.

"Research for what?" I ask slowly.

"We'll tell you, but only if you promise to listen all the way before you say anything," Charlie says, hope and excitement bleeding from him.

I move to lean against the arm chair next to the couch, earning a glare from Gus, who seems offended I'm so close to the one human being he actually likes. "Okay, I promise."

"'Member I've told you about Miles, right?"

I nod. "Yeah, the kid from school you're hanging out with."

Charlie goes on. "Well, he plays baseball and asked if I wanted to come to his practice to hang out. I texted Aunt Juni and she said she'd meet me at the field."

I raise my eyebrows at my best friend who didn't tell me about this change in their after-school plan, but since Charlie did the right thing letting her know, I can't be too mad.

"Okay, so guess what? *Rhett Darlington* was there. He used to play for the Tridents, Mom! Anyway, while we were there, he came up and asked if I wanted to try throwing the ball. He didn't care about my arm, or that I couldn't catch. And it was so fun, Mom. I even got to try pitching! I wasn't very good, but I did it." Charlie bites his lip, and I do my best not to react to what I know is coming next.

"I think I wanna look at getting a prosthesis. So I can maybe play. Or at least do more stuff, y'know?"

My gaze flies over to Juni, and the reassuring nod she gives me helps me center my thoughts. We've tried prosthetic arms before, and Charlie hated them. Said he would rather have no arm than a robot arm—his words, not mine. But I've often wondered if he feels like he's missing out on things that require two arms. And if he'd ever want to try again. I'd never push him. Ever. It's his choice, and I'll support him the best I can.

Finding the money for specialized prosthesis right now, when we've recently moved and I've just started a new job, and a temporary one that doesn't have extended health benefits, is daunting. Without a doubt, the basic one that would be covered by our regular government benefits won't be good enough for Charlie to play baseball.

"You remember it's not a quick process, right?" I start gently. "We'll have lots of doctor's appointments, and fittings, and it'll be a while before you're used to a regular prosthetic arm before you can try the fancy ones for things like hitting a baseball."

He nods emphatically. "I know. But Coach Rhett said in the meantime I could come to practice and be a base runner and work on my throwing. There's stuff I can do, Mom. He'll help me. He's, like, the head of players or something."

"Head of player development," Juni supplies. "He was great with Charlie, and all the kids. It was pretty cool to watch this guy throw a ball around." She ruffles his hair and he ducks away, even though he's smiling. "We were just looking at different prosthetic attachments for baseball. There's some super cool stuff out there."

Yeah, I'm sure there is. I'm also sure they're super pricey. But that's my problem to worry about, not Charlie's.

"Alright. Well, let's talk more over dinner. And tomorrow I'll see if I can get an appointment with Doctor Kellan down in Victoria."

Charlie jumps off the couch, dislodging the cat, who lets out a grumpy *mrowp,* and throws his arms around me. "Thanks, Mom."

I hug him back tightly. It's been a rough few weeks for him, adjusting to the move. I'm thrilled he's finding his place in Cedar Creek and finding friends, even. "You can thank me by helping Aunt Juni with dinner while I shower. Deal?"

"Deal."

Several hours later, dinner and dishes are done, Charlie's homework is complete and in his backpack, and I've just finished tucking him into bed with Gus curled up at his feet. I sink down on the couch next to Juniper and lean over, resting my head on her shoulder. "How am I gonna do this, Juni? I want to give him everything he wants, everything he dreams about. But I don't know if I'll be able to."

What I don't have to say, because as my best friend, she already knows, is the harsh truth that being a single parent to a child with medical needs can mean having to decide between breaking my kid's heart or breaking the bank. If my parents hadn't stepped up and helped us over and over again, we never could have afforded the therapy he needed when he was younger to learn how to function with one arm.

Charlie deserves the world. He's a great kid. And what parent doesn't want to set their child up for success in any way possible? But doing that on my own is sometimes impossible.

Juni kisses the top of my head affectionately. "Babe, you're the best mom for that kid. I know you'll find a way to make it work, or you'll find an alternative that is just as good. And don't forget, I'm here to help if I can, and I know your mom is, too."

I sit up and face her, sitting cross-legged. "I know, but I just...I don't want to always need help from others, you know? I've accepted it when I've had no choice. When Charlie's well-being was on the line. But I hate it. I hate that I can't give him everything on my own."

"You can, and you do. Is it everything he has ever wanted? No, not always. But it's definitely everything he has ever needed. All the other stuff you've had help with, that's been extra. He benefited from it, sure. But I bet a billion dollars he would've been okay without it all, because he has you."

My eyes start to feel damp. "Thanks, Juni."

Everything will be okay, that much is true. Because Charlie deserves everything, and I'll do what it takes to give it to him.

10

LUCA

Sean Mulaney is the last person I want to meet with.

Fine, that's not entirely fair to the man, I've never even met him. His daughter Miranda? I've met her. Spent most of eleventh grade with a crush on her, and twelfth grade trying to avoid her and her clique after she turned down my invitation to go to a school dance. By laughing in my face, in front of everyone in the hallway at our high school.

"I'm not gonna dance with you, limpy. Eww."

Super original nickname, I know. I did limp back then. I would grow too fast for my prosthesis to keep up, and my parents couldn't always afford to upgrade when I needed it, so I'd often be stuck wearing something ill-fitting and uncomfortable.

The one downside to moving back to Cedar Creek is the risk of running into the people that made my high school years miserable. Even knowing I moved on and made more of myself and my life than they could ever hope to doesn't quite erase the damage that years of bullying can do.

But as I straighten my jacket outside the conference room at Peak Properties, Sean's property development firm that's responsible for most of the downtown core of Cedar Creek, I remind myself my meeting is with him, not his daughter. And Isla should be here soon, according to the text she sent saying she'd just dropped her son off after a doctor's appointment. I know she feels bad for being late to this sponsorship meeting, but really, I'm just glad she's coming. Lord knows it's not exactly her job, but we're a small organization and we all wear many hats. Besides, just the thought of seeing her, having her near me, soothes my soul in a way I don't want to look at too closely.

When I push open the frosted glass door, my stomach drops. Sean is standing to the side, looking at something on his phone. And there, seated across the table, directly in line with the door, is Miranda.

It's been over twenty years, but she still looks the same. I've got nothing against a woman doing whatever it takes to feel good about themselves. But to what lengths must someone go just to look exactly the same at forty-two as they did at seventeen?

Miranda's attention-grabbing appearance may have worked on me, as well as most of the guys in our class back in high school, but now, it does nothing to me.

Instead of letting it show that I could have happily gone another twenty years without seeing her, I let my gaze brush right over her, as if I not only don't recognize her, but don't notice her at all.

"Luca," Sean says in a booming voice. "Good to meet you. I'm excited to discuss how we can work together."

I shake his hand. "Nice to meet you as well. Thanks for your interest in partnering with the Thunder."

"This is my daughter Miranda, she's acting as my assistant for a few months before she jets off to Europe." He laughs, placing his hand on her back. "Actually, you two might know each other, you're around the same age, and didn't I read somewhere you grew up here?"

I put on a polite smile. "I can't say I recognize you, Miranda, but it's a pleasure to meet you."

"The pleasure's all mine, Luca," she purrs, and I fight to hide my grimace at the way she holds her hand out for me. I give it one firm handshake and then drop it immediately.

"We knew each other in high school, Daddy," she says with a tinkling laugh. "It would seem we've both grown up since then."

I don't know how her father is missing the heavily laced words she's saying. But somehow, I manage to ignore it, turning back to the man I'm here to meet with.

"My marketing consultant will be joining us shortly, she had to attend to an important matter first. But we can get started. Did you have some thoughts on what you'd like to see from our potential partnership?"

Sean launches into a speech about signage and branding opportunities, and I keep my attention firmly on him, doing my best to ignore the ridiculously obvious ways Miranda keeps trying to get my attention. She leans forward, making it impossible to avoid staring at her cleavage if I was looking directly at her, and barely five minutes later she's licking the end of her pen like it's a goddamn lollipop. She's shameless. And it's making me more and more uncomfortable by the minute. I don't know how I'll manage to work with Peak Properties if she's around for our meetings.

"Those all sound like potential plans, in-line with what my team is thinking," I say when Sean finishes.

"Excellent," Sean replies.

Just then, there's a knock on the conference room door. Any hope I have of it being Isla is dashed when a younger guy sticks his head in. "Sorry to interrupt, sir, but there's an urgent call for you on line two."

Sean looks to me. "Sorry, Luca. Do you mind?"

I wave my hand. "Go ahead. I'd rather wait for my staff to be here before we go too much further anyway."

I realize my mistake the second he exits the conference room. Miranda stands and sashays around the table, hitching her hip onto it right next to me.

"I find it hard to believe you don't remember me, Luca. High school wasn't that long ago," she says, giggling.

"Over twenty years is a long time," I reply drily. Her face barely moves, but I catch a slight narrowing of her eyes.

"You asked me to one of our school dances." She has the audacity to place a hand on my upper arm. "I always regretted turning you down, you know."

My eyebrows raise, but I say nothing.

"If you asked me out now, I'd have a different answer."

Holy hell, the guts on this woman. Does she truly not remember the bitch she was in high school?

I settle my expression into one of cool indifference and stare her straight in the eyes. "Too bad I never ask twice." I shake off her hand, push back from the table, and stand. "Excuse me, I'm going to check on where my employee is."

"Don't be shy, Luca, we're old friends." Miranda titters, standing as well and putting her fucking hand back on my arm, this time squeezing lightly.

I open my mouth, fed up with her antics and ready to burn this sponsorship to the ground if it gets me away from her, when a light knock precedes the opening of the conference room door. As soon as Isla breezes in, I feel my jaw unclench. I watch her take in the scene, Miranda leaning toward me, her hand on my bicep, my hands clenched tight at my side. *Fuck.* She better not think I want any of this. I give my head a subtle shake, keeping my eyes wide and lips in a thin line.

Mere seconds pass before she takes control in the most unexpected but not unwelcome way.

"Hey babe, sorry I'm late."

My eyebrows twitch upward at the casual endearment, but I immediately let them fall, only to have a different body part twitch when she struts up beside me, sliding her hand over mine and leaning in to press a kiss to my cheek.

"How have things gone so far?" She turns to Miranda and adopts a smile, one I can tell is obviously fake. "Oh, I'm so sorry, how unprofessional of me. I'm Isla. I'm heading up the marketing for the Cedar Creek Thunder relaunch. And you are?"

It's hard to tell underneath all the makeup, but I'm pretty sure Miranda turns bright red. For a brief moment, I worry she's going to reveal how we know each other. Which in turn could lead to Isla learning about my leg, something I'm not ready for yet. But to my immense surprise, Miranda backs down.

Well, sort of.

"Miranda Mulaney. My father owns this company." There's no mistaking the haughty tone to her words, but she doesn't make another move on me, thank fuck. "I'll leave you to your meeting." She turns her back partially on Isla and gives me what I would assume she intends to be a seductive gaze. "If things ever...change, you know how to find me."

Damn, that's bold.

Before I can say anything, Isla steps in again, sliding herself forward so she's partially between me and Miranda, and taking my hand, plants it firmly on her hip. My fingertips dig in of their own accord. This is so wrong. But damn, it feels so right, having her by my side like this, even if it is fake.

"Don't worry, he won't be needing to find you." She tips her head to the side and lifts her free hand in a small wave. "Bye now."

Neither one of us moves a muscle until Miranda has stormed out of the room, trying to slam the door behind her but since it's got soft-closing hinges, her dramatic exit loses a lot of its power.

"Holy shit, Forrester." I exhale, letting my forehead

fall to her shoulder. Then, I freeze. "Sorry." I drop my grip on her hip and lift my head quickly. "Thanks for the assist, you're a lifesaver."

Isla turns slowly to face me, a cautious expression on her face. "So, you're not mad I basically just pretended we were together in front of a sponsor's daughter? It wasn't exactly professional of me."

I let out a harsh laugh. "Definitely not mad. If anything, I should be apologizing for putting you in an uncomfortable situation." I run my fingers through my hair, aware Sean could be back any second. And I owe Isla at least a partial explanation. "Miranda and I went to high school together. She might not have been interested in me then, but apparently, she is now. Too bad the feeling isn't reciprocated."

Isla lets out an indelicate snort, then claps a hand over her mouth in embarrassment. I grin and pull it away.

"Anyway. I owe you big time."

"Great, you can buy lunch after we wrap this meeting."

"*Anything* you want."

I don't intend that to sound as laden in innuendo as it comes out, but with the way Isla's eyes darken, I don't regret it. Fuck, I want to feel my hands on her again. For real this time.

Just then the door opens, and Sean re-enters. "Sorry about that, everything is under control now, but my daughter said she was late for an appointment so it'll just be us," he says by way of greeting.

"No problem," I reply smoothly. "Sean, this is my

head of marketing, Isla Forrester. She's the brains behind everything." I gesture toward her with my hand. "Let's continue our meeting, shall we?"

For the next half hour, I sit back and watch in awe while Isla works. My gut hasn't steered me wrong before, and it didn't now. She's a fucking marvel to watch in action, and the way she understands my vision is incredible.

She's beautiful, competent, intelligent, and everything I could ever want in a woman.

The way she saved me from Miranda's borderline offensive approaches was entertaining...and confusing. I'm no idiot, I can tell we're both dancing around something when it comes to the attraction we have for each other. But I've somehow managed to keep a lid on it. To remember she's my employee and I owe her nothing but respect and professionalism.

Today she made it nearly impossible to remember that fact.

Today I felt her lips on my skin, albeit briefly.

Today I felt her hand on mine, not as an employee, but as a woman.

Today I realized I might not be able to contain this attraction for much longer.

And that could be a real fucking problem.

11

LUCA

It's been three days since our meeting with Peak Properties and the debacle with Miranda, and I'm not sure if it's intentional, but I feel like Isla's avoiding me.

Not that we've had a reason to meet, but on most days, I run into her at the administrative offices that are finally complete at the stadium at least once or twice. This week? Once. I've seen her once in three days, and all I got was a quick smile as she hurried in the opposite direction.

I'm a forty-two-year-old man. I don't obsess over things often. But the amount of mental energy I've expended thinking about Isla and wondering if she's avoiding me is ridiculous.

And exhausting.

"Don't take this the wrong way, boss, but are you sleeping okay? You look...tired," Rafe says as I walk into the coaches' office just next to the locker room.

I run my fingers through my already rumpled hair and let out a laugh. "Yeah, tired is one word."

Rafe just chuckles, pushing back from his desk. "For fun reasons, I hope."

I huff out a laugh of my own at the man who's becoming a good friend. Good enough that he feels comfortable teasing me like that, even if he has no clue how far off the mark he is. "Yeah, sure."

Not even slightly fun. More like pure torture, as sleep has eluded me every damn night this week. I toss and turn, thinking about Isla, worrying about how to handle my growing attraction to her, wondering whether she feels anything for me, and then wanting to kick my own ass for even thinking about that.

"Alright, well, the guys are ready for you. I told 'em to come up with questions or suggestions, but we'll see what they've got."

"Were you able to get everyone on the existing roster here?" I ask.

"Not quite, but most of them are here."

"Great. So, before we go in, have you and Levi thought some more on who you want to add to the roster?"

He nods. "Yes. The existing guys are good. Solid. You've got a strong starting lineup, although you need more pitchers. I read up on the league rules, and we don't have enough guys if we have a stretch of more than four games in a row. Remember the pitcher I told you about last week, Brady Dixon? My contact who told me about him tracked down his number, and I gave him a call yesterday. Turns out, he's very interested, and he's considering our offer. If we can lock him down, that would help."

"He's the one that was about to get called up to the big leagues, right?"

"That's him. No idea why he walked away, but it's good news for us."

"Definitely. Isla can market the hell out of that acquisition, if he's on board with some publicity. Can we find out why he walked away from the majors, just to make sure there's no skeletons in any closets that could come back to bite us in the ass?"

"Good plan. I'll ask some of my contacts in Vancouver if anyone has heard something. The head of media relations for the Tridents is the kind of woman who knows everything. I'll give Willow a call."

"Excellent," I say with a smile. "Let's make it happen."

Rafe nods again. "I've also been in touch with a couple of universities to let them know to pass on my name if they have any players who don't want to go to the majors but still want to play ball. They might be younger than some of our guys, but fresh skills never hurt."

"Sounds like a plan," I agree. "Let's go talk to the team."

We head into the locker room where twenty-odd players sit around chatting. The guys range in age from mid twenties to thirties. All of them have some experience playing at the college level or on major league farm teams. They share a passion for baseball, but for various reasons, it's not their primary career, making the independent league a perfect fit.

And best of all, I know from the brief conversations

I've had with many of them, they want to win. They want to be a team they can be proud of, a team the town is proud of.

I want to make damn sure that happens.

"Gentlemen, you all know Luca, which means you all know he pays your salaries. Which means you better shut up, listen up, and buckle up. He's got some things to share."

I chuckle at Rafe's introduction, but hell if it doesn't work. The guys all settle down and look at me.

"Thanks, Coach." I grin before turning back to the players. "Alright. First, thanks for coming in today. I know it's the offseason and you've probably got a lot of other things going on, but I wanted to make sure we had plenty of opportunities to sit down and chat about where things are headed for the Thunder. As you know, it's my goal to bring the Thunder back to its glory days, when everyone knew exactly how awesome the sport of baseball is and felt proud to call this team their home team. Now, I know, you all play your asses off out on the field. There's no doubt in my mind that the struggles the Thunder have been facing are not coming from in here. But change is needed. And in order to make that change for the better, I need your help. We're recruiting new players, we've renovated the stadium, we're working on a kick-ass marketing plan, but none of that will be possible without each and every one of you being on board as well."

I pause and look around the room. There's a mixture of reactions, from excitement, to pride, and more than a few looks of doubt. I don't blame them for wondering if I can deliver. They barely know me. I'll prove them wrong.

"You're all here because you love baseball and you love Cedar Creek. I know the last several seasons haven't been the greatest, and I hope to change that. My goal is to make this team a part of what makes Cedar Creek a great place to live. This might not be the big leagues, but I'm confident you can still play a fucking great game. We just have to get the town to see that. Which is why I'm hoping I can convince you to give me a little more of your time to do some publicity and be at some community events before spring training, so we can all work together to bring the Thunder out of the shadows and into the light again."

"Are we gonna be dancing and doing backflips like that team that's all over social media?" one of the players pipes up, tossing a ball into the air. "You know, the pineapples or whatever?"

The other guys all chuckle and talk amongst themselves. I grin and wait until they settle down. "Listen, if you want to bring some trick plays to the diamond, go for it. Just make sure you catch the damn ball. But dancing? Nah, not us. We want to entertain the fans, hell yeah, but with baseball first and foremost."

I get a few *hell yeah*'s and lots of murmurs of agreement to that.

"Alright, glad you're on board. Now, here's what I need from you today..."

———

Just under an hour later, I leave the locker room, satisfied I've got buy-in from the team. They're all talking animatedly about potential recruits, the new jerseys we handed out, and yes, trick play ideas.

I'm all for whatever gets everyone energized and excited once the season starts.

As I make my way back up to the executive offices, my mind turns from the meeting I just had to a different kind of meeting I *need* to have with a certain head of marketing. I'm still not entirely sure how to handle things with Isla, but the one thing I do know is that I want her. I don't have a fucking clue how to make that work, or if we even can, or hell—if she even wants me— but I'm pretty damn sure she does. Although, that could change when she finds out about my leg.

But none of that matters if I can't find the damn woman to have a conversation with her in the first place.

Apparently, luck is on my side. Because for once, Isla is in her office when I walk past. I knock on the door frame, and she looks up from her computer, her cheeks flushing as soon as she realizes it's me.

"Luca. Hi. How can I help you?"

I move into her office. "Just wanted to check-in, see how everything was going. And give you an update on the sponsorship situation."

"Oh, great. Please, take a seat."

I sit down in the chair opposite her desk and try to subtly move my prosthetic leg into a natural position. "We've got the gala tomorrow, and I convinced Dom we should donate a few sets of season tickets for the silent auction. The owner of Devereaux Hotels will also be there and agreed to partner up for a weekend getaway package with a hotel stay, restaurant voucher, and game tickets. And Peak Properties sent over their signed agreement yesterday."

"That's wonderful. I'll get to work on the signage designs immediately."

I nod slowly before leaning forward and resting my elbows on my knees. Her gaze drops to my forearms, and I mentally thank past me for rolling up my sleeves to my elbows. Good move, Calloway.

"There's one other thing we should discuss."

She tilts her head to the side, with an adorable small frown. "What's that?"

"You kissed me," I state with an amused smirk.

Her eyes grow wide as she flushes a deeper shade of pink. "On the cheek. It was a...a favour. You seemed uncomfortable with that woman, so I didn't think, I acted. I apologize if it was too much," she says, clearly sounding flustered by my direct approach. That's good, flustered I can handle. Avoidant, I can't.

"No apology needed." I lean in slightly. "I wanted to thank you for the *favour*, Isla. It was appreciated."

She nods, her green eyes flashing at me. Her tongue darts out to lick her lips and it's everything I can do not to close the distance and kiss her.

For real this time.

But kissing her at work? Bad fucking idea. So I force myself to back off.

"I'll be picking you up at six tomorrow evening for

the gala." I stand up straight and put my hands in my pockets. "Having you on my arm will definitely be a rose, not a thorn." I can't resist winking before I turn and walk away.

12

ISLA

A box is delivered to my house the following afternoon, shortly after Juniper arrives to help me get ready for the gala. With it came a handwritten note that instantly had my heart racing.

> Isla,
>
> I thought it would be fitting for my marketing expert to represent the team in Thunder blue.
>
> Luca

"Holy shit, Isla. This is a Da Silva original."

My jaw was already on the floor when I pulled out the gorgeous blue dress. But at Juniper's reverent whisper of the designer's name, it falls even farther.

"I can't wear this."

"You absolutely can and will."

I let Juniper take it from me, and she holds it up so we can see the whole thing.

The soft satin is floor-length, with a structured sweetheart neckline, and a slit up one leg. It's the kind of dress a woman dreams about wearing to a fancy event. And a dress that a single mom could never afford.

"It really is the perfect shade of blue," I murmur. "But I can't."

I've already turned to grab my phone, set on texting Luca and insisting this is too much.

"Isla, stop."

I lift my gaze at the command in her tone, blinking rapidly. "He sent me a dress, Juni."

She nods and sets the dress down before coming in front of me and picking up my hands. "He sent you a beautiful dress."

I exhale a shaky laugh. "Why would he do that?"

"Because he's a very rich, very smart man who recognizes that a woman like you deserves a dress like this. You're going to put it on, then I'm going to do your hair and makeup, and you're going to turn every head tonight with how stunning you are."

"I'm nervous, Juni."

I let her pull me in for a hug. "I know. Try to relax and just have a good time."

An hour later, Juniper has worked her magic. I'm just applying a little bit of hairspray when I see Charlie's reflection behind me in the bathroom mirror.

"You look really pretty, Mom."

"Thanks, kid," I say with a smile.

"So this guy picking you up. Your boss. Is he cool? Like, you're okay going with him?"

My heart melts as his voice cracks at the end. My tough guy, trying to protect his mama. That's the boy I know and love. I turn around and walk over to him.

"He's cool, I promise. And since he's my boss, you're gonna be respectful, right?" I narrow my gaze.

"Yeah, yeah," Charlie huffs, then turns on his feet to leave my room. "Aunt Juni and I are gonna order pizza now."

"No movie till you've emptied the dishwasher," I call after him before glancing back in the mirror to make sure my lipstick isn't on my teeth. Satisfied I look as good as I'm gonna get, I make my way to the living room where Juniper and Charlie are fiercely debating pizza toppings.

"Just get half and half," I say, right as there's a knock at the door. Like gophers popping out of their holes, my son's and my best friend's heads both pop up and swivel to look at the door. "Be. Cool," I hiss at both of them. Juniper smirks, and Charlie rolls his eyes. These two will be the death of me.

I smooth my hands down my sides and take a deep breath before opening the front door.

"Wow."

Luca's voice rumbles that one word, and I struggle not to melt into a puddle at the obvious admiration. To say nothing of how freaking gorgeous he looks.

"I knew that dress would be stunning on you."

I blush furiously. "Thank you again for it. Please, come in. I just need to grab my purse." I step back and gesture him inside, hoping my reaction to him isn't too obvious. "This is my son Charlie, and my best friend Juniper."

Luca gives them both a warm smile. "Nice to meet you both. Juniper, have we met?" His brow creases slightly. "You're quite familiar."

"I'm good friends with Cal Prescott," she explains, and he nods in understanding before turning to Charlie.

"How are you liking Cedar Creek?" he asks, perfectly polite, and I pray my son responds in-kind. Being protective of me is one thing, but being a jerk to my boss is another, and these days, preteen hormones are making Charlie anything but predictable.

Thankfully, he just shrugs. "It's cool, I guess." He stands up and looks my way. "Mom, can I have a pop before dinner?"

I nod, and he walks into the kitchen. I know what he's doing. He's purposefully walking past Luca in a way that his right arm is on full display and there's no chance of Luca not seeing it. He wants to see how my boss responds to his limb difference and to be honest, so do I.

Luca's eyes widen, which, fine, I can understand. It's not every day you see a kid missing part of his arm. But it's the way his one hand goes to the front of his left thigh that surprises me. He grips it tightly, for a second or two, before pulling his hand away and clenching it into a fist.

I can't wonder what that's all about right now, though, so I guess I'll just be thankful he's not horrified or asking stupid questions.

"Right, well, we should go." I give Juni's shoulder a squeeze as I walk by and call into the kitchen where

Charlie's rummaging in the fridge. "Good night, kid. Be good, love you."

"Night Mom, love you," is the muffled reply I get in return as I shrug into my wool coat and grab my purse.

"Have fun," Juni says with an enigmatic smirk. "Don't worry about rushing home, I'll stay as late as needed."

God, could she be more obvious? My cheeks flame, and I pointedly don't look in Luca's direction.

We're both quiet as we walk out the door to a waiting limo with a driver standing by the back door.

"I thought you were driving?" I say, coming to a stop.

His hand lands on my back. "This way, I can give you my full attention all evening."

My heart races even faster. He's treating this as more of a date and less of a business outing between two coworkers. Which is both thrilling and slightly terrifying.

I smile at the driver who's holding the door open, then carefully slide inside the dark interior. My gaze drinks in Luca greedily as he says something to the driver, then carefully steps in himself, sliding into the seat next to me.

He's 007 perfection in a crisp black suit and tie. His hair is artfully styled in that sort of messy way that looks completely intentional, and he's trimmed his scruff neatly. The threads of silver at his temples make him look dignified and far too sexy. Forget James Bond, he looks like a younger Patrick Dempsey, only somehow hotter.

It's funny, I'm normally drawn to a more rugged look. Jeans, T-shirts, plaid, that sort of thing. But being around Luca at work has me appreciating slacks and collared shirts in a new way. And this? Luca in a suit?

Hot enough to cause spontaneous combustion. Which makes me wonder if I should have slid an extra pair of panties in my tiny clutch somehow, because the ones I'm wearing feel damp already.

The way I react to this man should be illegal.

The limo pulls away slowly, and I look out the window for a minute before Luca speaks, drawing my attention his way.

"I take it your son loves baseball as much as you do? We need to get him hooked up with some of the new Thunder merch."

I can't hold back my laugh at that as I realize Charlie was wearing a Vancouver Tridents hoodie when I introduced him. "I'm sure he'd love that."

"Does he play?"

I bite my lip, struggling to decide how to respond. "He hasn't before, because of his arm. He was born that way and struggled to find a prosthetic that would work for him. But he wants to try one now. I guess the Little League here in town offered to help adapt things for him. Do you know much about the league?"

Luca offers me a small smile. "Yeah, I played with them when I was a kid. And the current head of player development is a former player for the Tridents. We've chatted several times about collaboration opportunities. He's a good guy, I'm sure he'll do what he can to help Charlie."

The drive to the gala only takes about twenty minutes, and the conversation between us flows the entire time. I try not to let it show how giddy I am to be in a limo, my first time ever. But when we pull up at the hotel, a part of me wishes the drive was a lot longer. Partly because of the limo, and partly so I could have more time with just Luca.

He exits the limo first, and I take his hand to get out. Even through my warm coat, I shiver when he slides it to the small of my back as he escorts me inside the Devereaux Hotel, where tonight's event is being held.

"Rafe said we have three of the players here tonight. They're on strict orders to smile and talk up the team alongside the animal shelter," Luca whispers to me.

I nod, even though he's not saying anything I didn't already know. My mind is still struggling to catch up to the look of him, the feel of his hand in mine earlier, and the close proximity of him to me.

He takes my coat and hands it to the staff manning the coat check, then offers me his arm with a crooked smile. "Shall we?"

Part of me feels like I've been transported to another world. A world where Luca Calloway is flirtatious and charming, and I'm free to respond in-kind.

"We shall." I slide my arm through his. To hell with professional boundaries. Just for tonight, I want to feel like Isla Forrester, a woman who is more than a mom, or an employee, or a marketing expert. I want to feel like someone who is beautiful and deserving of his flirting and charm. It's not as if anything bad will come of a few smiles and my arm looped with his. And if it does, I'll face the consequences of giving in to tempta-tion later.

Luca collects a glass of champagne for me and a soda water for himself at the bar.

"Don't you want a drink?" I ask after thanking him for my glass.

"I don't like alcohol, never have," he replies with an easy smile. "I see Rafe and the guys, shall we go and say hi?"

I file away his admission as we make our way over to the head coach, or rather the manager as Charlie corrected me. I've only spoken to him once or twice but he seems quite nice. He's standing with three men who are clearly the players, seeing as I recognize one of them.

"Luca, Isla, good to see you," he says warmly. "Isla, have you met these three?" He gestures to the other men. "Griff, Foxxy, and Cal have all been playing for the Thunder for several years."

"Hey Cal," I say, smiling at Juniper's friend. "Good to see you again."

Luca interjects with a chuckle. "Is Cal how you knew so much about my plans at the interview? Insider information?"

I lift my shoulders. "Maybe." He shakes his head with a soft smile as I turn and take the hand of the first player, who gives me a charming smirk.

"Griffin Voss. You're the marketing boss, right? Didn't realize you knew Pretty Boy." He tilts his head at Cal and I smother my laugh.

"Pretty Boy?" I look at Cal, who rolls his eyes.

"Don't tell Juniper."

I smirk. "We'll see." Then, looking back to Griffin, I nod. "To answer your question, yes, I'm the marketing consultant. Thanks for coming tonight. It helps to have you three here, putting a face to the team."

"Happy to oblige." The other player I don't know steps forward with a grin. "I'm Denver Foxx, but everyone calls me Foxxy." He jerks his thumb at Griffin. "I pitch, and Griff tries to catch my strikes when he can."

"Whatever," Griffin scoffs, but my smile grows warmer at their easy friendship.

We chat with the guys for a few more minutes before sending them off into the crowd to mingle. Luca stays by my side, escorting me around the room as we meet a few more people, including the mayor of Dogwood Cove, a man named Ethan, who's surprisingly young for someone to have been mayor for as long as he has. His wife, Summer, a stunning blonde, tells me she runs a beachfront resort. A romantic weekend getaway for two is up for auction, and she looks between Luca and me with a knowing smile.

"I think you'd really enjoy it."

Before I can correct her on our relationship, Luca cuts in smoothly. "We'll check it out, thank you."

We move on, meeting more Cedar Creek locals. I'm pleasantly surprised by how many people seem excited to hear of Luca's plans for the Thunder.

"Isla, Luca, I want you to meet someone."

We both turn at Griff's voice. He's walking up with an older gentleman at his side.

"This is Harold Moore. He lives in the same building as me and Foxxy and has a lot of stories about what the team used to be like." He turns to the older man. "This is

Luca, the new owner, and Isla is the head of marketing. They need to hear your stories."

He shoots us a wink, then steps back as Luca shakes hands with Harold.

As they talk, Griff piping in here and there, I take mental notes of the elements that make both of them chuckle with nostalgic memories. In-game events, fan interaction, and theme nights.

"You know, Harold," I interject with a smile, "we could use someone like you to head our voluntary advisory committee."

We don't have an advisory committee and judging by Luca's raised eyebrows, he's wondering what the hell I'm up to. But I forge on. "Luca's goal is to energize both the team and the community. What better way to do that than have a group of community members who still hold fond feelings and memories for the Cedar Creek Thunder to work as an advisory committee for our upcoming season? All it would take from you is a few meetings to discuss ideas on what to bring back to the ballpark, what changes to make, and you'd have a say in bringing the Thunder back to the team you remember, only better. There's a pair of season tickets in it for you, if you're willing?"

Luca turns his winning smile on the older man. "Isla's right. We need the right person to head up this project. I don't suppose you know of anyone else around town that might be like you, a baseball fan who wants to watch the game in his hometown and know he's going to have an excellent experience."

Harold puffs up with obvious pride. "Well now, I'd be

honoured. I think it's great what you're trying to do, and I'd be happy to talk to some buddies down at the Legion. There's a few of us that used to play ball when we were your age, you know. And I coached the Little League for a few seasons when my kids were younger."

I slip out my business card from my clutch and hand it to him. "Please give me a call next week and we'll set a time to chat. I'll take you and your friends to lunch, on the team, of course." I give him a wink, and next to me, Luca chuckles. Harold walks away with Griff after agreeing to call me.

Luca takes my elbow, turning me to face him, an amused smirk on his face. "So quick to give away my tickets and my money, wonder woman?"

I lift my shoulders and wink. "Whatever works. You've got a fan for life now."

He studies me, his smirk softening into something deeper, warmer. "Dance with me, Isla."

Without another word, he leads me out onto the dance floor where a few other couples are. I go into his arms without protest.

Only for tonight.

His large hand splayed on my back radiates heat through my body. I let him pull me in closer, my fingers brushing the back of his neck. God, he's all thick, corded muscle. We settle into a simple swaying movement, our feet stepping in a small circle. His gaze travels over my face, and I can't drag mine away from his.

The song ends far too soon, and the emcee asks everyone to take their seats for dinner.

For the rest of the evening, there's a charged tension

between us. An energy, thrumming, waiting to be set free. It's there in every touch of his hand against my back or my shoulder. It's there when he dips his head down close to me when he helps me into my coat at the end of the event. It's there when he takes my hand and walks me to my door.

And it's there when he doesn't let go.

Neither one of us speaks as we walk hand in hand up the path to my front door.

"Thank you for everything. The dress, the limo, it was a wonderful night," I say quietly, the words feeling flat and nowhere near encompassing how I feel. Something about spending this evening with him, both of us letting down our guard and allowing our attraction to peek through, was enchanting.

He was enchanting.

Luca turns to face me, his free hand coming up to cup my cheek. "Don't thank me, I'm the one who had the honour of having you on my arm tonight. You are incredible," he murmurs. "I'm in absolute awe of you, Isla. You're so stunning, you make it hard to focus on what I need to do most days. You're fucking brilliant at your job, kind, intelligent, just...you're amazing." The reverence in his voice has me swooning.

My lips curve up as I lean into his touch. My pulse is racing, my head is spinning, and not from the two glasses of champagne.

"What's your rose and thorn from tonight?" I whisper, staring up at him.

He smiles, his thumb stroking my cheek softly.

"That's easy. Rose is dancing with you. Thorn is the fact that the night is over. You?"

I don't think about it. I just speak the truth. "My rose was also dancing. But my thorn is the fact that you haven't kissed me yet."

I've barely whispered the last word before his lips land on mine. Softly at first, but quickly he pushes in firmer. His hand on my cheek holds me in place, as his lips explore, igniting every nerve in my body. My arms thread around his neck as I give in to what could be the greatest mistake of my life.

Or the greatest kiss of my life.

Or both.

When our lips finally part, we're both breathing heavily.

"I'm changing my answer for my rose," Luca whispers before kissing me again, softly and quickly this time. "Kissing you is definitely my rose."

13
LUCA

"One of these days, you'll let me pay for dinner," my dad grumbles as we meander slowly along one of the streets of downtown Cedar Creek. It's a quiet Saturday night, cold, seeing as it's the first week of November, but not so cold that it's uncomfortable to walk outside. The street lamps cast pools of warm light on the sidewalk. I'd say it's a romantic setting, if I wasn't with my parents.

Now, if it were Isla on my arm...

"One day," I reply with a smirk. "But not today."

Mom slips her arm through my elbow, hugging my side. "Thank you for dinner, honey, it was lovely to be able to spend some time with you. I feel like you're so busy these days."

"Turns out, owning a baseball team is a lot of work."

"Just don't forget there's more to life than work. You're building something incredible there, but what happens when it's done and the team is a success? You should have someone to share that with. Unless there already is someone and you're just not telling me," she says, clearly fishing for information.

I want to shrug off her hold. I love my mother to the very depths of my soul but sometimes she can be a little too pushy with her nosiness into my life. Especially now, after what happened with Isla last night, it's uncomfortable how close my mom is to the secret desire I have for my marketing consultant.

"Like you said, I'm really busy right now. I'll figure out dating when things slow down."

Just then, we pass a young couple walking hand in hand, smiling up at each other, and my dad says, "Remember when we were like that, Marjorie? Young and carefree, two kids in love."

Mom drops my arm and turns on her feet to place her hands on his shoulders. "Watch yourself Lou, I'm still carefree and in love."

Dad leans down and pecks a sweet kiss to her lips. "Just not so young anymore."

As a kid, I would get grossed out by how affectionate my parents could be sometimes. As an adult, it just makes me long for something I don't have.

"Well, Luca won't be so young, either, if he doesn't get a move on and find a partner to live life with," Mom presses on, but thankfully, Dad steals her focus with another kiss.

"Leave him alone, Marge."

Mom huffs but turns to me and smiles fondly. "Is it so bad for me to want my incredibly handsome and wonderful son to find someone to fall in love with? I just don't want you to wake up one day and realize you've gone through most of your life alone."

"You make it sound like I've never been in a relationship," I point out, stuffing my hands in my pockets as we come to a stop at the railing and look out at the water. Not that there's much to see with how black the night sky is this time of year.

"I do think you've never let yourself *fully* be with someone. You've always held yourself back, Luca. What I don't understand is why."

I scoff and start to speak, but this time, it's my father who pipes up. Apparently, they're double-teaming me tonight.

"Son, if you mention one thing about your leg, I'm gonna smack you silly, grown man or not. Missing part of your leg does not make you any less worthy of finding love."

"Nicely said, honey." Mom pats his chest lovingly before turning back to me. "You've been through a lot in life. More than any child should have to endure. It made you strong, but it also hurt you. Don't think we don't know that. Being alone won't make that hurt go away. If anything, it will make it fester. We'll stop nagging you as long as you promise to at least think about what we're saying. You deserve to be happy. Completely, fully happy."

"And I can't be happy alone?" I fire back, my voice full of more annoyance than they deserve. I can't help it, they've hit a nerve. One I don't want to look at too closely right now, when I just want to hold onto the memory of kissing Isla, and not get lost in the what-ifs and maybes of the future.

I know my parents mean well, but they don't realize that what they have, this perfect, unconditional love, isn't the norm. Not everyone gets to have that.

I've always believed I don't get to have that, and it would take a lot more than one perfect kiss to convince me otherwise.

"No, Luca, you can't. Some people, yes, absolutely, they can be fulfilled and perfectly happy living their life alone. But you have so much good, so much love in your heart, I know you'll never be fully content without someone to share that love."

———

My mom gets her wish, and I don't stop thinking about what she and Dad said all evening. I drop them at home, then return to my penthouse apartment. And I find myself noticing how stark and empty it is, in a way I haven't before.

It's big. Too big for one person. I bought it after my mom fell in love with the rooftop patio. A patio that has a hot tub and seating area I've used maybe half a dozen times in the months I've lived here.

The main living area is a blank canvas. Hell, it might as well be a hotel room. All there is in the way of decorations are a few photos on the mantel of me and my parents. Everything is off-white or grey, with the exception of my dark blue couch. I know without looking that there's only four sets of dishes and cutlery in the kitchen.

I never have people over other than my parents, or Dom and Coral, so why do I need more? Besides, when I left Ontario, and the apartment I shared with my ex, I let her keep just about everything.

But I've been in Cedar Creek for almost a year now. And what do I have to show for it, other than a baseball team I'm trying to rebuild? Since I moved back, I've been focused on my parents, and the team, and nothing else.

Depressed by my own damn thoughts, I move into the large open kitchen, open a cupboard, and reach into the back for the jar of Nutella I keep hidden away. Jar in hand, I fish around in the cutlery drawer for the special spoon my mom got me as a gag gift one Christmas, back when I was in university. It has "My Nutella Spoon" engraved on it, and I only ever use it at times like this, when I need the dopamine rush of a scoop of Nutella.

I take my treat over to the couch and sink down on one end. The same end I always sit in. On the only cushion that's even a little bit worn or sagging, seeing as it's rare for someone to be sitting in the other spots.

Fuck, that's pathetic.

Maybe Mom and Dad were right, and I won't ever be fully happy alone, but I can be content, right? And isn't that better than being in a relationship that will never measure up to the impossibly high standards they set with their marriage?

I probably shouldn't hold every relationship up to theirs, I'm sure there are plenty of other happy couples out there. But when you grow up witnessing firsthand what true, unconditional love and acceptance and support looks like, it's hard to accept anything less.

And no one has ever made me feel like unconditional love is possible for me. No one has ever sparked that deep of a connection.

No one until a particular redhead knocked my entire world off its axis with one kiss... I shut that train of thought down quickly.

I can't go there. Not yet. Not after only one damn kiss.

———

Sleep doesn't come easy, and when I wake up the next morning, I'm glad it's only Sunday. I drag myself out of bed, get ready, and head over to Dom and Coral's for brunch, a monthly tradition we've had since I moved back.

Coral opens the door, her tightly-cropped black curls covered in a colourful scarf. "Ooh, you brought the good croissants." She grabs the container out of my hands before stepping forward and kissing my cheek. "Morning, Luca."

"Morning," I reply, stepping inside their house. It's everything my apartment is not. Warm, cozy, full of colour, life, and love.

My best friend comes out from the kitchen wearing an apron that says "Kiss the Cook." All I do is look at him, and he lifts the pair of kitchen tongs he's holding and shakes them at me.

"Not one word, or I'm not cooking the rubbery shit you call bacon."

"There's nothing wrong with tempeh bacon," I say as we all move back into the kitchen.

Dom shudders as he returns to the stove where he's finishing up the food for brunch. "There's so much wrong with it, I don't know where to start."

Conversation is easy as we all work together to get food on the table. It's always like that with the three of us, which makes sense, considering we've been friends for over twenty-five years.

After we eat and clean up, we head into their living room and sit. None of us is in any hurry to get on with the day, but especially not me, since all I have to look forward to is going back to my empty apartment and overthinking everything some more.

"I need more coffee. I'm gonna go start a fresh pot," Dom announces during a break in conversation. He goes into the kitchen, and the sounds of him getting out the beans he likes to grind fresh filters back into the living room where Coral is now staring at me.

"Alright. Spill."

Damn it. "You're way too observant sometimes," I gripe, leaning forward and placing my elbows on my knees.

"Don't have to be that observant to realize you're caught up in your head about something, or my husband would've realized it."

I laugh. "Trust me, he knows, he just doesn't want to talk about it."

"Well, I do." Coral moves to the spot on the couch next to me, and leans her elbow against the back of it, tucking her leg under her body and giving me a soft smile. "What's going on, Luca?"

I lean back, letting my head fall against the back of the couch so I'm staring up at the ceiling. "Do you remember how I used to complain about my parents, how affectionate they can be with each other and how they finish each other's sentences and shit?"

Coral sighs. "Of course, I do. You and Dom thought it was corny and gross, and I thought it was romantic."

"Dom only thought it was corny and gross until he realized he was in love with you, and then he started doing the same damn shit."

Coral laughs, and her hand lightly slaps the back of my head. "Don't make fun of my man."

"It's kind of my job as his best friend."

"Whatever. So why are you bringing this up?"

I take a deep breath in and out. "I don't think I've ever believed a love like that was possible for me."

"Why the hell not?"

"I guess it just always seemed so perfect. *Too* perfect, you know? Out of reach for most, attainable by just a few. But I never believed I would be one of the lucky ones. I don't know who does get to have it, or why not me, I just know it's not me."

When I finish my confession, I feel raw. Exposed. Then Coral bursts into laughter.

"Luca Calloway, for a very smart man, you are being a big idiot right now. What the hell do you mean, true love isn't for you? There's not some finite limit on love, you dummy. If someone doesn't have it, that does not mean it doesn't exist." She heaves a loud sigh. "Look.

You're a great guy. Easy on the eyes, rich, smart, funny, and kind. You're a catch. But if you ever tell Dom I said that, I'll murder you. My point is, any woman would be lucky to be with you. But what matters is how you feel. Nothing is going to change unless you pull your head out of your ass and realize that maybe no one else will have a love exactly like your parents. But that's because no two people are exactly like them, either. Love isn't a one-size-fits-all thing. So shut your mouth and open your heart. And if there's a particular woman that's causing this very depressing self spiral of yours, smarten up and don't let her get away."

"Damn, Coral, tell me how you really feel." I try to sound light, but the truth is, she hit the bullseye.

"I am, Luca. You're too good of a guy to be alone forever. Don't deny the women of Cedar Creek a chance to be with you. And don't deny yourself the chance of finding someone who's really right for you."

Our conversation ends when Dom walks back in with fresh mugs of coffee for all of us, but I don't miss the meaningful look Coral gives me. The one telling me to shut up and listen to her.

The thing is, even if she's right, it might not matter. Because the one woman who I'm starting to feel could be the one for me is right in front of me. And I might have no choice but to let her get away...for now.

14
ISLA

When I pull up to the warehouse that holds the indoor sports facilities the Little League uses for some of their winter training sessions, Charlie's quiet. "You don't have to do this," I say. The last thing I want to do is give him excuses or make him feel like he can avoid hard things, but at the same time...my mama-bear instincts are clamouring to protect my boy from any embarrassment.

"I know, but Coach Rhett invited me and Miles said it's fun." He squares his shoulders, his one hand tightening around the glove he's spent the past week breaking in. "I wanna try." Turning to me, his lips quirk up in a wry grin. "You sure *you* wanna be here? I've got a good reason to suck, what's your excuse?"

I lightly punch his shoulder as he chuckles. "Watch it, kid, maybe I'm a baseball prodigy just waiting to be discovered."

Charlie gives me an epic preteen eye roll. "Sure Mom, sure. Watching the game and playing the game are two different things, y'know."

With that, we get out of the car and hurry into the building to get out of the freezing November rain. Charlie heads over to the group of kids and adults standing around a small set of bleachers behind floor-to-ceiling netting. There's a lot of energetic talking and laughing, but that's not what draws my attention.

No, it's the fact that the adults sitting on the bleachers are predominantly female, while the group holding gloves or carrying equipment are male. I've never been a fan of gender stereotypes, but they're every-where in sports. Apparently, even here, to my annoyance. Is there really not one female parent willing to throw a ball around with their kid? That's disappointing.

Most of the time, I don't begrudge Charlie's dad a thing. In fact, I'm grateful he walked away completely, avoiding any messy custody issues. We were kids ourselves, and he wasn't ready to raise one. Even with Charlie being born different, I rarely found myself wishing he'd stuck around.

But there are times, in moments like this, when I hate him for denying Charlie a father in his life. He could've at least agreed to stay in touch, to be available if or when Charlie ever wants to reach out. At least then, there could have been a way for my son to not be the odd one out, with his mother as his partner for this skills day, or whatever it is. Charlie came home one day, so excited about it. And when he said the parents were to partici-pate, I went out and bought myself a baseball glove.

It's got purple stitching. And I kind of love it.

I just didn't expect to be the only woman holding one today.

I also don't love the anxious nerves I feel inside, worrying I might do something to majorly embarrass my kid. Charlie's right, my love of watching baseball doesn't necessarily mean I'll be any good at playing.

"Alright everyone, c'mon over, let's get started." The ridiculously handsome guy I immediately recognize as Rhett Darlington speaks with a loud southern drawl.

So that's the former pro ballplayer who's got my kid finally wanting a prosthetic arm. I watch him interact with the kids, his smile genuine and wide for each of them. He gives Charlie a fist bump, and I guess Charlie must point me out because then I'm treated to a grin of my own as he makes his way over.

"Nice to meet ya, Isla. I've heard a lot about you from your boy. He's got a good arm for a rookie, I'm glad he's givin' it a try."

Dang, that southern accent is swoony. "Thanks, he's enjoying practice. We'll see if I can keep up." I smile as Rhett chuckles.

"Don't worry about it, darlin'. We've got plenty of other adults showin' up today to help out if needed. But you already know that, I'm guessing."

My brow furrows. "Know what?"

"Hey Rhett, I didn't have a chance to fill Isla in on our plan."

I spin around at Luca's voice and see him walking up to us with an easy smile. He's wearing black joggers and one of the new Cedar Creek Thunder hoodies. Behind him come the two players I recognize from the gala, Griff and Foxxy, if I remember their nicknames correctly. They're each carrying a large bag full of what looks suspiciously like our new merchandise. They veer off, over to a group of kids, obviously following instructions, and start pulling out Thunder-branded balls and caps, handing them out to all the kids present.

"Luca. What...what's going on?" I ask quietly, doing my best to not think about how good he looks, or how amazing our kiss was the night of the gala, and focus instead on how he pulled this off without me knowing.

"I completely forgot to mention it the other night, I was so...distracted by other things." He flashes me a wink that thankfully, no one else notices. "But when Rhett called me up earlier in the week to ask if we could join forces, he mentioned today and I figured it was the perfect opportunity." He leans in close enough for our shoulders to brush, his gaze going between Rhett and I. "Community engagement, right?"

"That's right. Now, we better get things started." Rhett claps his hands and moves back to stand in front of the larger group. "A'right. Here's how today is gonna go."

I tune him out almost immediately, too overcome with the close proximity of the man who rocked my world with a single kiss a few nights ago. Oddly enough our paths haven't crossed at the office, not even once, since the gala. Which means somehow, I've got to hold it together, maintain composure, and not let anyone see how affected I am by his presence.

The kids all stream out onto the turf area. I hang back, feeling even more uncertain about my involvement. It's one thing to make a fool of myself in front of my son and his friends, it's another thing entirely to make a fool of myself in front of my boss.

Who happens to own a baseball team.

"You joining them, Forrester?" Luca's low voice is full of amusement.

"Mm-hmm," I say, staring straight ahead.

"Mom? Let's go." Charlie hangs back, looking from me to Luca. "Hey, boss man. What are you doing here?"

Luca cracks a grin. "Making my players do some community service. Actually, it wasn't hard to convince them. They love any chance to play ball. That hat looks good on you."

Charlie lifts his hand up to touch the brim. "Thanks. Do you play?"

Luca nods. "I'm alright. Not the fastest runner, but I can hit."

Charlie's head tilts to the side, his eyes narrowing slightly. What's he up to? I know my kid, and that's the expression he gets when he's plotting something.

"Is it just your players that are participating or are you here to play, too?"

Luca's deep chuckle makes me feel warm. "I'm here to do whatever I need to do."

Charlie nods once, as if he's reached a decision. "Cool. Wanna be my partner? I'm guessing you'll be better than my mom." He turns and gives me a shoulder shrug. "No offense."

"None taken," I say, fighting my own grin, and let's be honest, a sigh of relief.

I'd much rather watch baseball than try to play it. Hand-eye coordination is not my strength.

I drop down onto the closest bleacher seat without looking around me. My gaze is fixed on the group setting up for a throwing and catching drill. I start to stand up, suddenly realizing there's no way for Charlie to do this with one hand, but freeze when I see Foxxy jog over to his side. He leans down and says something to Charlie, then calls over to Luca. The three of them laugh, and then to my amazement, Foxxy throws the ball for Luca before stepping back and letting Charlie field the catch.

"Your son is going to be the envy of the entire league," a kind voice from beside me says.

I look over at a young Asian woman wearing a sparkling diamond ring on her finger and a wide smile.

"Trust me, none of this was planned. I work for the team, but I had no idea this was going to happen."

She laughs and puts her hand on my leg. "Oh, I know. I'm engaged to Rhett. I heard him and Luca talking the other day, and I saw how surprised you were when he showed up. It's sweet, though. He obviously cares about you and your son."

I must look uncomfortable, because she leans in closer and drops her voice quieter. "Don't worry, I know all about unconventional relationships. Rhett is my older brother's best friend and we started out as roommates. Now look at us." She straightens and lifts her hand to shake mine. "I'm Evie Yamaki."

"Isla Forrester," I say weakly, trying to catch up. "Nice to meet you, but me and Luca, we aren't... There's nothing going on. He's my boss."

Evie just gives me a knowing look. "If you say so...but from where I'm sitting, that" —she nods her head to the field, and I look up in time to see Luca walk over to give Charlie a high-five— "is not nothing."

Someone draws Evie's attention away, but I continue staring at the two men on the field. My boss and my son.

They barely know each other, and yet, there they are, laughing and interacting as if they're old friends. My heart twists. I know Charlie misses my dad. If he were still alive, he'd be here throwing the ball back and forth. Instead, Luca's stepped up. And he probably has no clue how big of a deal that is.

I watch Luca give Charlie a tip on how to hold his glove, even going so far as to catch a ball with one of his arms behind his back to show him how it would work. Charlie seems to be soaking it up like a sponge. Even from here, I can see the focus and enthusiasm on his face, and it makes my heart ache for him all over again. Yes, partly for the things he's missed out on and the struggles he's faced, but also with pride at how hard he works to overcome every obstacle and go for whatever it is he wants in life.

And when my eyes are drawn to Luca, that ache in my heart turns to something different. Something soft, and warm, and fuzzy.

Something I have no business feeling but can't stop.

Correction, something I'm not so sure I *want* to stop feeling any longer.

15
ISLA

"Okay, love you kid. Make sure you finish your homework before you start video games." I end the call with Charlie and place my phone back down on my desk before letting out a weary sigh.

"That sound makes me think I'm working you too hard."

My head shoots up at Luca's voice, seeing him in the doorway to my finally furnished office, leaning against the frame with his arms folded across his chest. My palms grow sweaty just looking at him, corded muscular forearms on display, smirk on his face, and salt-and-pepper stubble lining his jaw.

"What would you do if I agreed?" I fire back, far more flirtatiously than I intended. Leaning back in my seat, I cross my legs, not missing the way his gaze drops to where they are, visible through my glass desk.

Slowly, he prowls into the room, coming to a stop across from me, placing his hands on the glass and leaning forward. "As your boss, I'd commend your work ethic but remind you about work-life balance. As..." he trails off, and in that pause, I know he's trying to label the other side of our dynamic. The as-yet-undefined part. "As just me, I'd get Gabe to schedule you a spa day and talk to Dom about increasing your salary."

That makes me choke. "Trust me, you're paying me plenty, and I don't have time for a spa day," I say, spreading my arms out wide. "If I did, do you think I'd be here at eight o'clock on a Thursday night?"

Luca chuckles, low and deep. "Fair point. Why are you here so late, anyway?" He settles into the chair across from me.

I heave another long sigh. "The college grad you hired to run the social media accounts got an offer to work in England for some up-and-coming fashion designer. Apparently it's their dream job, so they quit."

His eyebrows lift up. "Well, good for them, I guess, but where does that leave us?"

I gesture to my computer. "Now we only have a halfway set up online presence, a handful of collaborations discussed, and nothing more. They were going to start content creation this week, which is why I'm here now. Scouring other teams' platforms to see what's trending."

Without another word, Luca picks up his phone, tapping something out on it for a couple of minutes before looking back up at me. "Okay. How can I help? Put me in, coach," he says, smiling.

I stare at him. "Excuse me?"

He leans forward again, reaching his hand out to

cover mine. "What can I do to take some of the load off you?"

My head is already moving back and forth. "No, I'm sure you have better things to do with your evening. It's fine, I wasn't going to stay that much longer."

"Well. When you are ready to leave, then I'll walk you to your car. For now, let's get going."

He's serious. I can't deny the relief in my bones at the offer of help. "Alright, well, if you want to start looking at some of the major league teams' online presence, and then writing down any ideas for posts, that would be good. Static and video."

Luca gives me a mock salute. "On it, boss."

We work in silence for a while, only talking when bouncing an idea past each other. It's easy, fun, comfortable, and to my pleased surprise, Luca's got a great eye for trends. Some of his concepts are things I never would have considered.

It's been an hour or so when Luca stands. "I'll be right back." He starts to turn and stumbles, grabbing the back of his chair with a curse.

"Are you okay?" I push back from my desk and quickly start to move to his side, but he holds up his hand.

His reply is sharp. "I'm fine." He takes a step forward, and then another, not looking back at me. I watch as he moves to the door, his gait stiff, but seeming stable.

He's gone without another word, and I stare at the empty doorway, baffled by his behaviour. But I don't have long before he's back, carrying two paper bags that instantly make my stomach rumble with hunger.

I clutch my stomach. "Oh my God, that's embarrassing."

Luca sets the bags down on the desk and smirks. "Nah, I'm surprised you haven't heard mine all this time." He starts unpacking containers of food. "I wasn't sure what you liked, but tonight seemed like a good night for sushi, so I got a variety of rolls." He opens up all of the containers, and I try not to drool. Nodding at me, he says, "Ladies first."

I fill my plate, then sit down in the chair next to his. I can't help but check out the view of Luca standing in front of me as he selects his own food. His clothes are perfectly fitted to his body, the muscles of his back prominent when his shirt stretches as he reaches forward. My gaze travels down, and since he can't see me staring, I drink in the goodness that is Luca Calloway's ass. Damn.

My ogling comes to an end when he sits down in the chair next to me and I realize just how close he is. Our knees touch when he shifts in his seat to face me, lifting his chopsticks in a pseudo cheers. "To late nights at the office. May we not have many of them."

A chuckle escapes me as I lift my chopsticks to meet his. "You strike me as someone accustomed to late nights at the office."

He shrugs and gives me a wry grin. "You're not wrong. But that doesn't change the fact that there are plenty of other places I'd rather be late at night with a beautiful woman."

My breath catches. "Luca," I murmur, looking down at my plate of sushi. "We should talk about that kiss."

I hear him set down his food, and then I see his

hands cover mine as he takes my unfinished meal and sets it down on the desk as well.

"You're right, we should talk. I'm hoping you don't regret it, because I don't." I let him take my hands in his, only lifting my gaze to his when he squeezes them gently.

"You're an incredible woman, Isla Forrester." He smiles softly. "Stunning, intelligent, kind, talented, and *irresistible.*"

I hadn't realized my body had been shifting toward him until I feel the warmth of his breath on my cheek. It takes nothing at all to turn my head slightly, and then his lips are grazing over mine, pulling a whimper out of me.

He groans in return, pressing in deeper. My lips part for him, and I clutch at his shirt, dinner and any conversation we planned on having completely forgotten. Luca Calloway overtakes all reason, all of my senses, everything. With nothing but the press of his lips against mine.

A noise from down the hall has me pushing him away. We aren't alone. There's the nighttime cleaning staff, any one of whom could have seen us just now.

And that's enough to cut through the fog of lust that seems to surround me whenever I touch Luca.

"I can't do this now," I say, but the breathy way my voice sounds undermines how serious I am. I clear my throat, and try again, while Luca rakes his fingers through his hair, his other hand clenched around the arm of his chair.

"I...we..." I try again, scooting my chair back and standing up. I need to not be sitting next to him. "You hired me to do a job, and that's what I need to focus on. I've got Charlie to consider, and I can't do anything that will put his well-being at risk. Kissing my boss" —I let out a harsh laugh— "at the office, no less, is the definition of risky." I don't put voice to my real fear—that part of Luca's reason for choosing me for the contract was because of his potential attraction to me.

As if he can read my mind, Luca says, "I'm sorry. You're right, this is the wrong time and place to have this conversation. But Isla, I hope you know, I would never let anything that has happened between us affect the way I treat you in the office. I respect you and your work far too much to do that. And I also hope you trust me when I say this was not something I planned on happening when I hired you. I found you beautiful." He gives me a wry smile. "I'd have to be blind not to. But believe me when I say, I hired you because you're the right person for the job." His tone is gentle but firm as he puts that unspoken fear to rest. Yet, there's a tinge of regret in his voice that lets me know I'm not alone in wishing things were somehow different.

"You're right that this is messy." He sighs, and his body slumps ever so slightly. "I won't say it'll be easy to resist you, but I'll back off if that's what you need me to do."

My arms are wrapped around my stomach, but I manage to nod ever so slightly. Half of me is screaming no, I don't want him to do that, the other half is relieved that he understands where I'm coming from. "At least for now. While I work here, it wouldn't look good if anyone found out," I manage to whisper. "Yeah. So, we won't let this happen again. No more...kissing."

Luca nods, again with that mixture of resignation and regret clear on his face.

"Thank you," I say, my voice slightly stronger. "And I'm sorry, too. I shouldn't have let it happen in the first place."

Luca stands up slowly and moves toward me, stopping at an appropriate distance. He stuffs his hands in his pockets and gives me a rueful grin. "Forrester, you have nothing to apologize for. I'm your boss. I'm the one who was in the position of power, and I'm the one who should've known better. Please, if nothing else comes of this, know that you are not the one who screwed up here. I am." He pulls one hand free and holds it out to me for a handshake. "From now on, we are friendly coworkers, that's all."

I take his hand and shake it, pasting on a small smile of my own. "Friendly coworkers."

He tightens his grip and leans in slightly. "For a few more months, at least. But if you're still single when your contract is up, I hope you'll consider letting me take you out. I'm not ready to give you up entirely. Not yet."

I'm speechless at the hunger in his voice. His hand drops, and he turns, gathering up his unfinished dinner before walking to the door. There, he pauses and looks back at me. "Don't stay too late. And if you want someone to walk you to your car, text me, okay?"

Somehow, I find my voice. "You're not leaving?"

He shakes his head. "Not till you do. A friendly

coworker can still be concerned about your safety, right?"

Without waiting for me to respond, he walks out of my office, turning down the hall toward his own. My entire body sags in disappointment once he's gone.

I know pressing pause was the right thing to do. Then why do I regret it so much?

And why do I suddenly wish the next six months would go by a hell of a lot faster?

16

LUCA

WHY IS it that as soon as you can't have something, you become obsessed with it? At least, that's how it feels for me right now. In the days since Isla and I agreed not to act on our mutual attraction anymore, it seems I can't escape her.

I walk into a room, and the scent of her favourite Earl Grey tea lingers on the air even if she's nowhere to be seen.

I hear her voice walking down the hall of the office and find myself hoping she's coming to see me to talk about Charlie's baseball practices, disappointed when she isn't.

I can't stop staring at her during meetings and noticing things I really shouldn't. Like today, when I slip into the strategy meeting she's leading with her small team. If her blouse appears slightly sheer under these lights to me, showing the outline of a pale bra cupping breasts I fucking long to get my hands on, then that means it also might to others. Including the young intern she recently hired to take over the vacant social media role. It takes monumental effort not to glare at him, or worse, fire him on the spot for indecent workplace behaviour.

If anyone is having indecent thoughts, it's me. And I'm the goddamn boss.

I'm a fucking mess.

And the worst part is, Isla seems completely unaffected. As if putting a stop to the risky flirtation we were dancing around was no big deal. Like I'm the only one unable to sleep at night, wishing things were different.

The only thing keeping me going is the possibility that it's not a stop, it's a pause. And in just a few months I might have a chance with her again. Although, that would mean I don't get to see her around the office every day and that...is almost as depressing as seeing her and not being near her.

"Okay, any questions?" Her voice penetrates my thoughts, and I straighten in my chair, realizing I've been tuned out this entire meeting.

Not a good look, Calloway.

I plaster on what I can only hope is a professional, courteous expression that conveys the lie of totally knowing exactly what Isla was talking about. My employees filter out of the room while I stay seated. Some of them nod and say hi, and I nod back, not looking to the front of the room where she's unplugging her computer.

Even when the room is empty, I don't move. I don't trust myself not to walk over to her and just kiss her the way I want to. To beg her to change her mind and give us a chance to see what this could be, all the reasons not to do so be damned.

"I didn't realize you were planning on sitting in for this meeting."

She sounds worried, in a way. And that's enough to push me into action. Standing up, I move next to her and lean against the table. "I should've emailed you. Sorry if it made you uncomfortable."

The expression on her face when she turns and looks at me is a mixture of incredulity and longing. "You don't make me uncomfortable, Luca. Please don't think that."

Before I can stop myself, I'm leaning in closer so my hand brushes against hers. My other lifts up to tuck a piece of hair behind her ear, but then I freeze. My hand falls and bunches into a fist.

Her eyes flutter closed, and I see her take in a breath before she shifts away.

"Sorry," I mutter. What the hell is wrong with me that I can't respect her wishes and stay away?

"No, don't apologize." Her eyes open and she looks at me again. "This is hard for me, too. As much as I know I shouldn't, I wish things could be different. You make me feel..." she trails off, and I open my mouth to beg her to tell me what she feels, when there's a voice from the doorway.

"Hey Isla. Oh. Sorry. Didn't know you were still meeting with Mr. C."

It's the fucking intern.

I turn to him, a brittle smile on my face. "Not a problem, Nick. We're done here."

I glance back at Isla, noting the flush of pink on her cheeks.

Fuck, I wish we weren't done.

––––––

The next afternoon, I stare out my office window at the cold November rain pelting down onto the field. There's puddles of water everywhere, the skies are dark grey, and it matches my mood perfectly.

This is so much harder than I thought it would be. I've never wanted someone the way I want Isla, even with barely a chance to have her. A couple of kisses shouldn't wind me up in knots like this, but it does. *She* does.

I turn away from the stormy weather outside and gather up my computer and some files to take home. I'm not getting any damn work done here today, might as well go home and not get any work done there. At least at home I can wear sweatpants and take my leg off.

The elevator opens on the main floor, just in time for me to see Isla struggling with an umbrella outside the front door. I pick up my pace as lightning flashes across the parking lot.

"Shit," I mutter as I hurry to her side. "Here, use mine." I open my umbrella and hold it over her already wet hair. "Why didn't you go back inside to open it?" I ask, gesturing to her broken umbrella.

She blinks up at me, water droplets on her skin and eyelashes. "It's bad luck to open an umbrella inside." Her small smile has me chuckling, but my laughter dies when

I see her shiver. I hand the umbrella to her and shrug out of my jacket, draping it over her shoulders. Do my hands linger on her arms? Maybe. Do I say anything? Fuck no.

"Thanks," she murmurs, passing the umbrella back to me and tugging the edges of my coat together. We make our way into the parking lot and over to her car. I stand like a silent sentinel as she unlocks the vehicle and opens the door before pulling off my coat and offering it back to me.

"You gonna be okay driving home in this?" I ask in a gruff voice, gripping my coat tightly to stop myself from reaching out to her.

"Yeah, I'll be fine." She pauses, her eyes moving back and forth over my face. Her tongue darts out to lick a raindrop from her lips. I stay frozen in place when she lifts one hand up, her fingers lightly brushing over my cheek.

"Isla," I rumble.

"I'm sorry. We can't. I know we can't." Her face falls as she pulls her hand away and steps back. "I'll see you tomorrow." She slips into her car, and I move a few steps back, out of the way as she turns it on and slowly drives away from me.

I can't have her. But I want to. Fucking hell, I want to.

My drive home is slow, the rain pouring steadily down on my windshield. Once I'm in my austere apartment, the silence feeling oppressive, I move on autopilot. I change into workout clothes before going to the room I've set up as a personal gym. The all-white walls seem even more barren tonight. But maybe it's not the walls, but me who feels empty, lost, and alone.

The punching bag in the corner by one of the large floor-to-ceiling windows is my destination, and for a while, I simply let it all out. All the frustration, all the tension, all the fucking *longing* for the one woman I want, the one woman I can't have, is poured into the bag.

I think about her deep red hair when I deliver an uppercut. I think about her smile when I execute a right hook. I picture her and Charlie, and a life I can all too easily see myself sliding into. But it's a life I can't have as long as she works for me, or more importantly, as long as I'm keeping such a huge part of myself from her. She doesn't know about my missing limb. About the fact that I understand what her son lives with better than anyone.

I pull my last punch and let the bag swing as I breathe heavily, staring at myself in the mirror positioned in front of the weight bench. Who the fuck do I think I am, pining over a woman when I can't find the courage to tell her I have the exact same condition as her son?

I move over to the bench and sink down on it, draping a towel around my neck. My leg starts to cramp, and I bend down and detach my prosthesis. As I peel away the compression sleeve and sock that covers my residual limb, I grimace.

Yeah, lusting after Isla when I still haven't told her about my leg? Quite possibly the worst thing about this entire situation. Even if we never have a chance to be together, I owe it to her to come clean and tell her I have the same condition as Charlie. I just hope that when I do tell her, she doesn't hate me for keeping it from her.

Pushing myself up with my hands, I grab the pair of

crutches I keep in the gym room and make my way into the living room. Sitting on the couch, I grab my phone from the small side table where it sits, and unlock it, tapping into my messages. One hand massages the end of my leg while the other holds my phone, and I stare down at the message thread I have with Isla. The last thing we exchanged was a discussion about banner sizes. I hesitate for a second, maybe longer, then type out a message.

LUCA: I wish things were different.

Fuck. I can't say that. I delete it, and then, before I can think better of it, I type again.

LUCA: How is it possible that I miss you when I haven't ever had you.

Shit. Nope. Can't say that, either, even if it is the goddamn truth. I quickly hit the delete button, watching my message disappear. It doesn't matter what I wish I could say, or how I wish things were different and I was free to pursue her. I'm not. She made that clear the other night, and I have to respect it.

I drop my phone back down and push up to stand, grabbing the damn crutches again and move into my kitchen, filling a glass with some water and chugging it down. The cool liquid quenches my throat but does nothing for the other heat building inside of me. A drop spills onto my lip, and I lift my thumb to swipe it away, the movement reminding me of Isla's hand grazing my wet cheek earlier in the rain.

I pivot and head for the master bedroom, pausing to strip my sweaty shirt off and drop it in the laundry basket as I go. In the bathroom, I turn on the shower before setting the crutches aside and sitting down on the chair next to my shower.

Most of the time, I'm accepting of my disability. Hell, sometimes I forget about it entirely. But ever since meeting Isla, I've found myself resenting it more than normal. I hate being different. Feeling incomplete. Like she could look at me and find me lacking. I hate that I need crutches, and fucking chairs or benches to shower. I hate that I'll never be a regular guy, free to pursue a woman without worrying she'll be turned off when she sees the stump I have instead of a leg.

I shove my shorts down and transfer into the shower onto the custom bench designed to make everything easy for me. All the fucking money in the world might buy me accessibility and fancy gadgets, but it can't buy me a fully-formed leg.

I shower quickly, then dry off and pull on a clean pair of shorts before crutching back into the kitchen and throwing some leftovers in the microwave. I ditch one crutch and precariously—even though I've done it plenty of times—carry my food in one hand and crutch-hop over to the couch.

From my pocket, my phone starts to vibrate, and I'll be damned if I don't wonder if it's Isla.

It's not. It's my mom.

"Hey Mom," I say before shoveling a mouthful of reheated chicken and quinoa in my mouth.

"Hi honey, how are you doing?" Mom's warm voice

comes down the line. "I had a feeling in my gut that you might benefit from a chat."

I swallow and chuckle, shaking my head ruefully. "How do you do that?"

"Do what?" she asks, but there's laughter in her voice. She knows.

"Always know exactly when I'm in a shit mood."

"Mother's intuition. You've always worn your heart on your sleeve, Luca, and I can always sense when that heart is feeling a little bruised. So, what's going on?"

I exhale, letting my head fall back against the couch. Obviously, I can't tell her I'm fighting feelings for my employee. But I can talk to her about the other shit bothering me.

"Remember when I was a kid and upset about my leg. What was it you used to tell me?"

"Your abilities are stronger than your disability."

I smile, even though she can't see me. "Yeah. Guess I'm having trouble remembering that today."

"That wouldn't be because of the speech you have to give, would it?"

"You mean the one you emotionally blackmailed me into giving?" I reply wryly. "No. Well, maybe a little."

"Honey, I know it was a lot to ask you to step in last minute and give the keynote at the National ABS Conference. That organization has done a lot to support our family over the years, and they were desperate. I've always respected your choice to keep your limb difference and everything you've done for the community a secret. But don't you think it's time to step into the light? To stop hiding your accomplishments?"

I'm silent for a moment, maybe longer. Thinking of Charlie and Isla. Of my parents, of my own childhood. Growing up feeling so alone. Like no one understood what I was going through.

"I've never wanted to be treated differently just because I'm missing my leg."

"I think," Mom starts slowly, "that it's understandable to be worried about people's perceptions. And I think it's something everyone struggles with for different reasons. That doesn't make your reasons any more or less valid, but it does, hopefully, make you feel less alone in this struggle." She pauses. "Talking at the conference might be the soft launch you need, a safe space to share your story, so that maybe you feel more confident being open about it in general. Or with a special someone when the time comes."

The probing in that statement is anything but subtle. I'm certainly not going to tell her everything. Not yet. But...I can tell her this.

"One of my employees has a preteen son who has a missing arm. A birth defect like my leg." I smile. "He's a cool kid. And seems determined not to let his disability slow him down."

"Reminds me of someone else at that age."

I huff out a laugh. "Yeah. Guess so. Except he doesn't even bother trying to hide his limb. I was thinking of telling him and his mom. It seems wrong to hide it from them."

Mom makes a sound that could be agreement or could be probing me to tell her more. Either way, it works.

"I'm worried they'll be hurt I didn't tell them right away."

"It sounds like how they react to the news is important to you. Maybe *they* are important to you. Will she be at the conference?"

Fuck, she's way too perceptive. And there's that hopeful tone again. Then her question registers.

Shit, will Isla be at the conference? Is that how I want her to find out about my leg?

"I don't know," I answer as my mind whirls. The conference is in two days. And I'm heading to Vancouver tomorrow to meet with the owner of the Vancouver Tridents. There's no time to come clean with Isla before my speech. It's not exactly something I want to share over text.

Fuck.

Mom is oblivious to my turmoil, and I try to give her my attention once more.

"I'll just say one more thing, even though I've said it before. It bears repeating and maybe this time you'll listen," she teases. "Now, I know I'm your mother, and therefore biased. But you are an extraordinary man, and there's not a single thing about you that I would change. My only hope for you is that someday you can open your heart to the possibility that someone else might believe that, too."

Her words so closely echo Coral's from our last brunch, they blend together. If the two women who know me better than anyone else think I deserve love, then why the hell don't I?

17

ISLA

I WAS A SINGLE TEEN MOM. I raised a kid while finishing high school, going to university and earning my degree, and starting my career.

Being tired is a permanent state of being for me.

But this type of exhaustion, this mental and emotional drain that I'm currently experiencing, is an all-new low. And the cause of it? A six-foot-tall man who's at least ten years my senior, my boss, and the star of far too many of my recent fantasies.

If I thought it was hard to ignore my attraction to him when I first started working for the Thunder, it's nothing compared to how difficult it is now. Cracking open the door between us, only to slam it shut when we both realized just how bad of an idea it would be to explore things right now, absolutely sucks. Being around him, knowing how his lips feel on mine, how his hands hold my body, and then having to deny myself that pleasure day after day is pure torture.

Thank God the annual conference for parents and

caregivers of individuals with amniotic band syndrome is in Vancouver this year, making it easy for me to attend. In the past, the conference, which is hosted by a national charity to support people like Charlie and their families, has been out of town, so I've never attended in person. But this year, Mom pushed me to go. And now, the idea of having a few days away from the office, away from the temptation that is Luca Calloway in a suit, has me breathing a sigh of relief.

I need a break from the constant tension that simmers between us. I can't look at him without remembering the warmth of his breath on my skin, or the scratch of his stubble against my cheek when we kissed.

"Okay, I'll see you in a couple days. I love you, be good for Nana." I ruffle the hair on top of Charlie's head, earning a groan.

"Mo-oom, stop."

I give him an unrepentant grin. "Nope. I'm your mother. I'm gonna mess up your hair, tell you I love you, and remind you to be good for the rest of your life."

"Great," he mutters under his breath, but there's the tiniest of smiles on his face. "Love you, too." He drapes his one-half arm over my shoulders, turning his stump into my neck to "tickle" me the way he has since he was little.

"Bye, kid."

My mom pulls on a coat and walks me out to my car, which is already loaded with my suitcase and a briefcase with some work for me to do in the evenings.

"Try to have some fun while you're away. Go to the spa or out for dinner. Enjoy the break."

I nod along, even though she's said all of this before, and ignored my explanation of why that won't be happening.

"I know you, Isla Marie Forrester. You think you can't take the time, or spend the money, or whatever holds you back from doing something for yourself. But you can. You deserve to take some time for you."

I stop at my door and exhale slowly. "I'll try, Mom. But I have a lot of work to do in the evenings as well. I'm starting to look for other companies I might be able to get a job at once my contract with the Thunder is over."

She makes a *harrumph* sound that makes it clear how she feels about my plans. "You're not even thirty years old, Isla. Gorgeous, smart, kind, and single. Would it kill you to go and have some fun? You still have six months left on your contract. Plenty of time to find something else. But you only get so many opportunities to have a weekend by yourself in the city. Let loose a little!"

I bark out an incredulous laugh. "Are you suggesting I hook up with someone this weekend?"

Mom arches a brow at me. "So what if I am? Being a single mother doesn't mean you have to give up your dating life, you know. At this rate, your son will have a better social life than you do."

"Trust me, I'm all too aware of the social lives of teenagers," I reply wryly. "And I'll be doing everything I can to make sure my son doesn't follow in his sperm donor's footsteps."

"That doesn't mean you have to be celibate to set an example."

My head falls forward. "Mom. Can you please drop

it? I just want to go to the conference and enjoy a couple of nights in a hotel ordering room service and taking long baths. I'm not an old maid, there's plenty of time for me to start dating again in a few years."

Mom shakes her head sadly, but doesn't say anything more, just pulls me in to a hug. "Fine. Go. We'll be okay here."

"Thanks." I slide into my car, giving her a wave as I pull out of the driveway. I know I'm incredibly lucky to have parents like mine. When I told them I was pregnant at seventeen, they handled it the best they could. Their love and support of me and Charlie has never wavered. But in recent years, more specifically since Dad died, Mom's mission to get me to start dating has become more and more intense. She refuses to accept the fact that I haven't met anyone worth spending time with, time that could be spent with my son or working to provide a good life for us.

Well, I hadn't. Until I stumbled into a gorgeous man at a coffee shop, only to walk into a job interview and find him sitting across from me.

For the drive to the ferry terminal and the crossing to the mainland, I put on an audiobook and escape into the fictional world from one of my favourite authors, Starla Barrows. It's a perfect break from reality until the middle of the ferry crossing when it hits the first spicy scene. Suddenly, the interior of my car starts to feel warm, and I debate cracking a window. But that would mean anyone who might walk past could hear the deep tones of the male narrator explaining exactly what he wants to do to the female main character. I'm no prude and have no qualms letting it be known I read romance, but having strangers overhear the very sexy scene playing right now feels a bit uncomfortable.

Instead, I switch the audio to my headphones, put them on, and recline my car seat, settling in.

But then my eyes close, and I suddenly start picturing Luca in the role of the hero, and me as the heroine. Luca's hands are removing my clothing, piece by piece. Luca's voice is muttering what a good girl I am, how perfect my body feels under his touch. Luca's heated skin is rubbing against mine.

My eyes fly open on a gasp. Nope. Okay, no romance audiobooks right now. I press pause and pull off my headphones. Maybe Mom was right and I really do need to find a way to start dating again. If for no other reason than to get my boss off my mind and out of my fantasies.

Except, trying to picture being with anyone other than Luca, doesn't make me feel warm inside. It leaves me feeling cold and uninterested.

Which is a problem.

———

When I reach the hotel where the conference is being held, I check in and get a key to my room before making my way to the registration desk.

"Hello, I'm Isla Forrester." I give the smiling lady at registration my name, and she scans the list in front of her.

"Perfect, here's your welcome package and name tag. Tonight's welcome reception takes place immediately following the keynote speech, and drink tickets for the event are in the envelope. And just so you know, we had a last-minute change in our keynote speaker." The woman's eyes light up. "It's very exciting, however. We were able to get the developer of GaitSync, which revolutionized leg prostheses, to agree to speak. Apparently, he's very reclusive and this is his first time speaking publicly."

I nod along with her rambling. Leg prostheses aren't exactly something I keep up to date on, so I could always skip the speech and take a bubble bath instead.

"Anywho, do you have anyone joining you?"

"No." I shake my head. "Just me." I hadn't thought twice about coming alone, but her question makes me glance around at the other attendees. And everywhere I look, I see couples. Parents, grandparents, caregivers, loved ones, even adults with obvious limb differences and their partners are here. Everyone seems to be paired off, except me, even though I know that's likely not true. Still, what would it be like to not be here alone? To not be facing the challenges of parenting Charlie, advocating for him, supporting him with his disability all by myself?

Sure, my mom is a rockstar. She and my dad, when he was still alive, did everything they could to help me. But it's different. They aren't the ones responsible for making sure they know the most up-to-date research. They aren't the ones who have to worry about whether insurance will cover enough for the prosthesis their son wants. They aren't the ones lying awake at night worrying about his future, or what kinds of opportunities he will or won't have because of something that was out of all our control from before he was even born.

All of that falls on me and me alone. And most of the time, I think I manage that just fine. But it's times like this, when I'm surrounded by couples, people that parent and care for their loved ones as a team, or work together to support each other in whatever manner, that I wish I wasn't alone.

Maybe I need to start an online group for single parents or caregivers of kids with ABS. We don't have to be alone. I can't be the only one here by myself, even if it feels that way.

Yeah, like I have time for that. Well, maybe not now, but I could in the future. Once things are more settled, and I have a permanent job. I look around the lobby with fresh eyes, and this time, I notice a few other singles. I'm definitely not the only one.

I make my way on to the elevators that lead to the hotel rooms above the convention center, nodding politely at the two couples in the car talking amongst themselves. One pair gets off before me, their hands clasped together. The other, two older men, smile at me.

"Are you here for the ABS conference?" one of them asks, gesturing to the envelope I'm clutching in one hand that holds my registration package.

"Yes, my son was born with a missing arm," I answer, spying their conference lanyards.

The other man's eyes light up as he lifts his hand, and I see the missing digits. "It's such a wonderful experience to be around so many people who understand what we go through. Is your son with you?"

I shake my head. "No, just me."

"Well, be sure to find us if you want some company during any sessions or for lunch."

My smile comes easily. "Thank you, I'll take you up on that, I'm sure." The elevator opens on my floor, and I step off, gratified to be feeling slightly less alone.

That changes when I push open the door to my room and see the giant king-size bed. And all I can think about is how lonely that massive bed will be tonight, lying in it all by myself.

It doesn't take me long to unpack, and after sending some quick text messages to my mom and Charlie to check-in, I decide to wander back downstairs. There will be time for a bubble bath later. I might as well see what this reclusive inventor has to say.

I drape my own lanyard over my neck and head back for the elevators. The car is empty, and I step on before pulling up the agenda for the conference that I saved to my phone.

I scan the subjects of the different presentations and panels, my brain stuttering to a stop at the exact same time as the elevator comes to a stop on a floor below mine.

The door opens as I utter the name of the very last person I expected to see here. The same person staring back at me with a mixture of shock and trepidation written across his handsome face.

"Luca?"

18

LUCA

SHE'S HERE.

Isla is staring at me as if she's seeing a ghost. Her pert little mouth is open, those bright green eyes wide with surprise and holding no small amount of confusion. Cautiously, I step into the elevator, letting the doors close behind me.

"Hello Isla."

I want to curse my mother for putting me in this position, but I know I can't blame her. She might be the reason I'm here to share my story for the very first time publicly, but she's not the reason Isla is in the dark.

That's my fault.

She doesn't say anything in return, just continues staring at me in silence. The ride to the main floor is thankfully quick, and yet, at the same time, I wish it were longer so I could explain why I'm here when she has no clue I have the same condition as her son. Every spare second I had over the last forty-eight hours was spent thinking about what to say to her. And everything I came up with sounded wrong.

The door opens with a chime, and I gesture for her to step off the elevator first. She does, casting a furtive glance back at me.

"We'll talk, Isla. I promise, I'll explain," I whisper roughly, pleading with my eyes for her to give me a chance to do so. "Please, just find me after my speech."

Her eyes somehow widen farther. "Speech?"

I wince. But before I can say or do anything else, one of the event organizers walks up to me.

"Mr. Calloway, I'm so happy to meet you, thanks again for agreeing to step in at the last minute and speak to our attendees. If you'll follow me, I'll show you where we're setting up for your keynote."

I give the man a curt smile and nod. "Please, call me Luca. And I'm honoured to be here."

I look back at Isla as I follow after him, barely listening as he goes on about something to do with a brunch that's planned for all the conference speakers tomorrow.

Her arms are wrapped around her midsection, her shocked gaze tracking me from across the room.

Fuck. This is quite likely the worst possible way for her to discover my secret.

I'm led into the auditorium where I'll present, forcing myself to focus on the introductions to the rest of the foundation members who coordinated the conference.

In no time at all, I find myself standing to the side of a stage, listening to the MC talk about how honoured they are to have me here as a speaker.

It's funny. How can they be honoured when, until a few days ago, no one knew who I was to the ABS world?

The attention I used to receive when people found out about my missing limb was rarely positive. It might be pity disguised as empathy, it might be disgust, it might be ridicule. But growing up, it was never good.

Which is why I started hiding it. It was no one else's business what my leg looked like. That's what I told myself. And when GaitSync was ready for the public, I made it clear I wanted to remain anonymous as the designer. I'm proud of what I've done but drawing attention to that meant drawing attention to me. And I worked too hard to hide this part of myself.

It's only recently that I've started questioning why I still do that.

And part of the reason I've begun to question it is here in the audience.

Still, there's a big difference between opening up to the people in my life and sharing my story on a much bigger scale like this.

Mom owes me big time for this.

The MC turns to gesture at me and I hear the swell of applause that is my cue to step out onto the stage.

Here we go.

I take a deep breath. And with one final glance down at my printed notes, I begin. "Good afternoon, everyone. My name is Luca Calloway, and I was born with amniotic band syndrome, resulting in the absence of my left lower leg." I tug up the bottom of my pant leg, revealing my carbon fiber prosthesis. The crowd starts murmuring, and I wait for them to die down before I continue.

"When I was first asked to be a keynote speaker here today, my initial reaction was 'Who, me?' What could I possibly say or offer to all of you that would be of value? I'm just a computer geek who was sick and tired of having to go to so many damn appointments to get my leg fixed." I pause and smile for the first time. "Okay, that's a lie, my first reaction was 'Hell no, I hate public speaking.' But when your mom asks you to do something, you don't say no. Even at forty-two."

That earns me a chuckle from the audience.

I click a button that starts the slideshow I prepared. Photos of me from when I was a baby through childhood and adolescence, scroll through on the screen behind me.

"Now, you were told the speaker today was the designer of GaitSync. Which some of you might have heard of or might even have in your prosthesis. If you haven't, let me summarize. It's a computer chip that performs automatic gait analysis. In simple terms, it helps prosthetic limbs adapt to how you walk, making them more responsive, more intuitive, and ultimately, better. And yes, I designed it. I was nineteen when I told my dad it was total crap that they hadn't figured out a way to automatically analyze gait patterns and adjust prosthetic legs. I mean, I know prosthetists are our unsung heroes." The room erupts in a handful of cheers as I expected it would.

"In fact, mine is somewhere here today. Hey Doc." I grin and lift my hand to wave at the audience, not really sure where Tom is in the crowd, but knowing he's out there somewhere. "But who are the real experts in what people with lower limb differences need? The people *with* the lower limb differences. That's when my father told me something I never forgot."

I pause and press a button that stops the slideshow on a photo of me and Dad.

"He said nothing ever changes unless someone is brave enough to ask the first question. So I took my question to university where I studied engineering and robotics. My goal was not to fix something that was broken but to build something better. Why couldn't my leg learn how to help me, instead of me learning how to use my leg? It was years of long nights, failed experiments, and endless cups of coffee. But after six years, GaitSync was ready."

I start the slideshow again, and the photos continue to scroll by, this time with promotional images for Gait-Sync and ForeMotion, the prosthetic company that bought it, but also candid photos of people who are now using prosthetic limbs that use my technology. Those are the ones I'm most proud of. I grin at the photos, then sober when I look back at the crowd. This is the hard part.

"I've kept this part of my life private for years. And the reason I've done so is something I'm sure a lot of you are familiar with. I grew up like many of you, figuring things out as I went, navigating a world that wasn't always built for bodies like mine. I had to work extra hard to be seen as more than just the kid with the missing leg. When I was young, being different wasn't something I was proud of. It was something that was used to ridicule me. To put me down and make me feel like I was somehow less than everyone else. Hiding my leg, hiding that part of me, became automatic. And it stayed that way for too long. But someone I met recently has made me want to be brave and not hide my achievements. Meeting him reminded me of one important thing I think we all need to remember. The world will try to define you by what it thinks you lack. It's your job to remind it what you have. And what I have, what we all have, is resilience. Creativity. Determination" My gaze finds Isla in the crowd and my heart stutters. Her hand is covering her mouth, and I can't tell her reaction or emotions to my speech at all. This leaves me with only one option—to continue.

"This kid, he's smarter and stronger than I was at his age, and he doesn't hide his limb difference or let it hold him back. He's a huge part of why I said yes to speaking today, to sharing my story for the first time publicly. But he's not the hero of this story. Neither am I. At least, not by myself. We all are the heroes. Every one of us in this room and worldwide. Because we, the people living with ABS and the people who love and care for us, are the ones who need to be brave enough to ask the first question. Every single one of you sitting out there already has what it takes. What the world needs more of. Grit, compassion, ingenuity, and the courage to dream differently. So I want to leave you with this. Don't let anyone, not even yourself, tell you that your story is one of limitation. It's a story of transformation. Your challenges don't define you. What you do with them does. Thank you for letting me speak to you today, I hope you have a fantastic conference this weekend."

When the audience erupts in applause, all I feel is

relief that my speech is over, and a heavy sense of nerves over what I need to do next.

Find Isla.

———

"Thank you, I'm glad you enjoyed it." I shake yet another hand, give yet another smile. Fucking hell, I've only been at the reception for nearly an hour, and I've met more people than I can count. But I can't locate the one woman I need to find.

I know I should be grateful my speech apparently touched a lot of attendees, and I'll even go so far as to admit I feel a weight off my shoulders having my secret out in the open. It's gratifying, having people come up to me and sharing how GaitSync changed their lives. It feels good to see my work in action and hear from others I've helped.

Yet, I'm starting to feel impatient.

I need to find Isla. I need to explain myself. I don't know what she's thinking, learning I have ABS like that. Even though we were never really together, I feel shitty for keeping it from her, especially after I met Charlie.

"Luca, great speech. That was absolutely inspiring. Can I ask you a question about GaitSync?"

I stop searching the room for Isla and turn on my professional smile. "Sure. What's your question?" I take a sip from my drink as the woman in front of me launches into a complicated question about the programming component of GaitSync.

When I finally spot Isla chatting with a few other

attendees, I cut her off with an apology. "I'm so sorry, I have to go and take care of something. But if you find Tom Shivari, he knows as much about GaitSync as I do and can answer your question, I'm sure."

I move away, weaving through the crowd, hoping no one else stops me. And then, finally, I'm behind her. My hand reaches out to cup her elbow, and she whirls around, looking up at me with bright eyes and a cautious smile.

"Luca."

I don't even register the other people around us. The entire room fades away, and all I can see, feel, smell, and hear is her.

"Can we talk? Please?" My voice is low, urgent even. I don't know what I'll do if she's upset at me for keeping this from her.

"I think we should. But not here." She gestures to the room, full of noise and people. "You seem to be quite popular after that speech."

I rub the back of my neck. "Yeah. I'm so sorry you found out like that. I should have—"

"Luca, stop." Isla's hand squeezes my arm. I let it fall, and when she takes my hand in hers, I can't stop the tidal wave of relief that crashes over me. "You don't owe me an apology. I'm your employee, you had no reason to tell me your story."

I'm already shaking my head before she even finishes. "You're a hell of a lot more than my employee. And when I met Charlie, I could've said something." Someone calls my name, and I let out an annoyed growl. "Fuck. Can we go somewhere?"

Isla tugs her lower lip between her teeth, her gaze darting around the room. "We could...I guess we could go to a hotel room. Mine or yours, I mean. It's probably the only place we'll have privacy, the entire hotel is fully booked with conference people."

Being in a hotel room alone with Isla might be the worst idea ever if I'm to have any hope in hell of maintaining my boundaries.

But right now, those boundaries are the last thing on my mind.

19
LUCA

Standing beside Isla as I unlock my door is torture. I can smell her shampoo, fresh and floral. It would take nothing at all to reach out and grasp her hip in my hand. My head is not that far away, I could lean down and kiss the patch of skin bared at the top of her shirt.

I don't do any of those things. No matter how desperately I want to.

Instead, I gesture for her to go first into my dimly lit room. She walks in and immediately goes to the window.

"You have a good view."

I move to stand next to her, but my gaze isn't on the city skyline outside. It's on her. "I really do."

She turns her head and looks up at me. The silence stretches between us. Tense, and full of anticipation. But is it good anticipation or bad? I won't really know until I fucking talk to her.

"I'm sorry you found out about me this way."

She raises her eyebrows, and I wince. Maybe that wasn't the right opening line.

"I don't tell a lot of people about my leg. Not because I'm embarrassed by it or anything, just that, in my experience, it tends to take over. My disability becomes what people remember when they think of me. Instead of who I am as a person, or my achievements, or my role in whatever situation I'm in. I become the guy with the missing leg. That's all. Like my entire life can be summed up by what I don't have, instead of who I am."

Her hand reaches out tentatively, and lands on my upper arm. I take that as a good sign, and cover it with my own, squeezing gently.

"I'm not ashamed of my condition at all. And it's not that I thought for one second that you would be that way. Especially not after meeting Charlie. It's just become second nature to me not to share that part of my story. If it comes up somehow, or someone finds out, I try to downplay it and just move on. That's why there's nothing online about me having ABS, or my involvement designing GaitSync. The sale was private because I didn't want to draw any attention away from the good the product could do. But I know that wasn't fair to you. I've wanted to tell you for a while now, I just could never find the right way, or the right time. And then when things... changed between us..." I trail off, suddenly feeling warm and exposed.

I meant it when I said I trust Isla not to think of me any differently because of my leg. But the old wounds that still fester beneath the surface from people in my past who *have* judged me before are hard to ignore.

"Let's just say, I haven't always received the best

reactions from women when they discover my difference."

Isla sighs. "Let's sit down."

Together, we move to the small couch pressed against a wall. I sit in one corner, giving her space to sit wherever she wants. When she chooses to sit close to me, I mentally breathe a sigh of relief.

Toying with her hands in her lap, Isla says, "Things were already complicated between us, Luca. I understand not wanting to let me in any further. Letting me know something that not many other people know would be a level of connection that could turn against you. I get it. But I would never think of you as any different, or any less wonderful just because of a limb difference."

"I know you wouldn't," I say quickly, covering her hand in mine. "I know. I should have opened up to you a lot sooner."

She turns her hand over, lacing our fingers together, a smile playing at her lips as she looks down at our connection.

"You know, it's hard for me to let people in as well. Hard to trust that they won't hurt me or leave me." She lifts her gaze to meet mine. "Charlie's bio dad is the only guy I've been with, and the second he found out I was pregnant at seventeen, he bailed. A baby wasn't a part of his plan to become a professional football player."

She lets out a pained laugh. "And of course, it didn't matter that it takes two people to make a baby, he was the high school quarterback and I was the slut who got pregnant."

My blood boils hearing her call herself that.

"Isla," I start to say, but she squeezes my hand and nods.

"I know. It's not who I am. I'm Charlie's mom and I don't regret it." She lifts a hand and cups my cheek. "I just want you to know why I can understand being nervous to let someone in. To show your vulnerable parts to someone else. But" —she pauses, and I watch her take a deep breath in— "I want to be vulnerable with you. Hearing your speech, seeing this side of you, it makes me want to know more. I can't deny my attraction to you, Luca. Even if it's complicated. Even if it's scary."

I stare at her, my heart thudding in my chest. I can tell she's only given me part of her story. A rough sketch of how difficult it must have been for her. But the fact that she's letting me in, sharing so much of herself? It floors me.

"How can you be so amazing?" I'm not sure I meant to say that out loud, but when Isla blushes, and ducks her head down, I can't hold back from grasping her chin and tipping it back up so she's looking at me.

"I mean it. Thank you for trusting me with your story. I know now how hard it must be to let me in. I take that honour very seriously, Isla."

Moving slowly, I lean in and kiss her forehead lightly. When I draw back, I see her mouth slightly parted, her eyes wide, the green of her irises almost swallowed by the black of her pupils.

"I don't want to push you into anything you're not ready for. But I have to be honest with you. Being with you might be complicated, but not being with you is even worse. Now that I know what your lips feel like against mine, I'm finding it almost impossible to ignore the craving to feel you again."

"Luca." My name is a breathy plea falling from her lips, and it's the spark that reignites the embers that have been smouldering ever since I first kissed her at the gala.

She moves first, kissing me tentatively at first, then deeper, and everything in my world rights itself in an instant. Then, in one shocking move, Isla stands, pivots, and resettles herself straddling my lap, her pelvis pressed into mine. Her arms are around my neck, her fingers teasing my hair as we take the kiss deeper. She's the first rain after a drought. The first rays of sunshine bringing light to the day.

She's everything I've ever wanted and everything I never let myself dream of.

I tug her lip in between my teeth and she whimpers as I feel her body sag into mine even farther. Tightening my grip on her, I force myself to pull my mouth back.

"Isla. Are you sure about this?"

Her eyes are glazed with desire, and I watch her slowly blink as she registers my question.

"Are you?" She throws the question back at me.

"I've never been more sure of anything in my life. I want this. I want you. There's no question of that. But the reasons we put the brakes on are still there. I need to know you won't regret this later, because I don't think I could survive it if I hurt you."

My voice is gravely with unspoken emotion. How has

this woman come to mean so much to me in such a short amount of time?

She rakes her fingers through my hair again, a small smile cresting her lips. "I want this, want you, as well. And I trust you not to hurt me, Luca." Her tongue darts out to swipe her lower lip. "I'm nervous. I don't know how us being together will work, but I don't think I can resist you for much longer."

Oh fuck.

I stand up, needing to move to somewhere more comfortable. Somewhere it'll be easier to explore and feel each other. Isla's legs wrap around my waist, but not for long as I take a few steps to the bed and lower her down onto the soft surface.

"Take off your clothes, wonder woman." I nip her lip again, then step back and slowly start unbuttoning my shirt, staring at her. She's frozen, her lips slightly parted again as she greedily watches me. I stop halfway and tilt my head to the side. "I know you heard me," I say in a low voice.

"Oh fuck, that shouldn't be so hot," she breathes, her hands trembling as they go to the hem of her shirt and lift it over her head.

I chuckle and quickly finish opening my shirt. But when I go to push it off, Isla pops up on her knees and places her hands on mine.

"Let me?"

I nod and let her take over, and she slowly pushes my shirt off my shoulders and down my arms, her gaze trailing over the naked planes of my chest.

"Damn, guys have changed since I was a teenager."

My shirt falls to the floor, and I cup her cheek in my hand. "It's been a while for me, too. But you're in charge here. Completely, okay? Whatever you need or want, you tell me. Can you do that for me?"

She nods.

"Good girl."

I lean in and kiss her, letting my hands roam over her soft skin for a moment. God, she's all warm, soft curves, and she's here with *me*.

Her hands find my belt, and I smile into our kiss as she fumbles to get it open. We don't break our kiss, but I reach for the waist of her pants and quickly undo them. This time, it's Isla who pulls back, panting.

"Oh my God, I need you naked, like, *now*."

"The feeling is mutual," I grunt as I push down my pants. A part of me tenses, waiting for her reaction to seeing my prosthetic leg. But Isla doesn't even glance at it. Instead, she shimmies out of her pants and throws them to the floor before throwing her arms around my neck again. We kiss, messy and lust-fueled and desperate now. Like trying to stay away from each other has created a powder keg of need that's finally been ignited.

"Do I need to be aware of anything? Do you want to take your leg off or leave it on? I don't care either way, but I want you to be comfortable." Her little ramble is adorable and has me grinning at the combination of thoughtfulness and excitement in her voice.

"I'll take it off, if that's okay with you. But the only thing I want you to be thinking of is my plan to make you come as many times as I fucking can."

Her small moan brings me no shortage of satisfaction

as I move to the side of the bed and sit down before quickly removing my prosthetic, keeping the liner on underneath for now.

I've definitely found that with my missing limb, certain positions are easier and more enjoyable than others. Lucky for her, the easiest is also the best for her. And it lets me do something I've wanted to do for a long fucking time.

Once my prosthesis is off, I swing my legs up and get settled. Isla's looking at me through hooded eyes.

"C'mere. It'll be easiest if I'm on my back," I say gruffly.

She moves onto her hands and knees and crawls to me, her hips swaying in a hypnotic way. She doesn't even pause to look at my residual limb, and for that, I'm grateful. She comes to a stop next to me and places one hand on my stomach, just above the waistband of my underwear.

"Closer."

Her eyebrows raise and she doesn't move right away. Instead, her lips quirk up in a smirk. "Are you bossy in bed, Luca?"

In response, I surge upward and grab her hips, lifting her up to straddle me. With a startled cry, her hands find the headboard as I settle her high on my chest. My hands move around to grasp her ass, the flesh filling my palms perfectly.

"If I need to be. Now, I said closer." I push her lace-covered hips forward. "Let me taste you."

20

ISLA

All I can do is stare down between my legs at the rugged face of the man carefully pulling my panties to the side. Then his tongue swipes along my slit, warm and rough and oh, so fucking good.

"Luca," I moan, my head falling forward. "Holy shit." He does it again and again before picking up a rhythm that has me rocking my hips back and forth, feeling my orgasm build inside of me far faster than it ever has before.

No vibrator can compare to Luca Calloway's tongue. My brain goes fuzzy with the pleasure coursing through my body. I have one hand braced against the headboard and the other finds its way to Luca, gripping the strands of his hair tightly. He growls against my pussy and *ohmygod* I want to explode.

My hips start to rock against his mouth, chasing the orgasm that promises to be exquisite. "Please," I start to whimper, but I have no clue what I'm asking for. More? Less? Relief? God, I'm lost. "Luca, please, oh God."

I come apart seconds after he pushes two fingers inside of me. It's embarrassingly fast, but this is my first orgasm provided by someone other than myself in over a decade, so I guess it's okay.

When my legs start to tremble, I shuffle down his body before collapsing on his chest. I can feel his chuckle reverberate under my cheek.

"Is you passing out a good thing?" he asks, his deep voice rich with amusement and satisfaction.

I manage to lift my head and place a finger on his lips. "Shhh. I need a minute."

A warm hand lands on my back and starts to stroke up and down in soothing motions. "Take your time. I'm not going anywhere." He smiles at me, the expression soft and affectionate, and something about this moment feels so perfectly right. Like we were always going to end up here.

Like this moment was predetermined, and no matter how hard we tried to avoid it, there was no chance of putting it off any longer.

I move up slightly so I can press a soft kiss to his lips. "Minute's over." I smile against his mouth, feeling his lips turn up in return. Then I shriek with a giggle as he shows off some impressive core strength, raising both of us to sitting.

"Good," he rumbles, kissing me again, harder this time as his hands move up my back and quickly undo my bra strap. "Up," he grunts, lifting my hips. I go up onto my knees, and let him tug my panties down, but they're stopped partway by the fact that I'm still straddling him.

I flash him a wink and hop off the bed. "I'll take

care of these." I give my hips a shimmy as I push the underwear to the floor, loving the flare of heat in his gaze as it rakes over my now-naked body. My tongue slides across my lips as I zero in on the bulge under his briefs. I'd felt it when I was draped over him, but now I want to see it.

"You gonna take care of that, too?" His voice is gravelly and sends a shiver through me, but the smirk I see when I lift my gaze to his face? That's lethal.

I climb back onto the bed and crawl back up his legs, passing over his stump without a second thought. "Sure thing, boss."

It was meant to be teasing, flirtatious even. But apparently, Luca doesn't see it that way. His expression darkens as he stops me, his hand grasping the back of my neck as he shakes his head. "Not in here. Right now, I'm not your boss. You're in charge, remember? In here, I will always listen to you and always give you what you want. Tell me you believe that."

My heart dips and swoops as I nod. But there is one thing I have to clarify. "I believe you. But do you believe me when I say I still want you to be a little bit bossy?" I pinch my thumb and finger together to try and lighten the mood. "I kinda like it."

His face relaxes back into a knowing grin as he lifts his hips and pushes his underwear down just enough to free his cock. "Oh, I remember. How 'bout you take these off me now."

"I thought you'd never ask." I tug them down over his foot and toss them on the floor.

"Isla…"

I'm surprised to hear him sound almost hesitant, and look up at him, concerned.

"I'm sorry. I should've grabbed them before we got started and I could get up, obviously." He looks over at his suitcase. "There's condoms in the front of my bag. I swear I didn't pack them intentionally for this trip, they're still in there from the last trip I went on with my ex." He winces and rakes his fingers through his hair. "Fuck, I hope they haven't expired. And now I'm ruining the mood."

I hop off the bed and go to his suitcase, finding the strip of three condoms quickly and checking the date on them before going back to him. I drop them on the bed beside him and lean over to kiss him.

"Stop. You haven't ruined anything. Thank you for thinking of protection, and please don't apologize for needing me to get them. It doesn't bother me. And they're still good."

Luca rests his forehead against mine and lets out a soft sigh. "Thank you."

I don't mean to, but a snort bursts free from me, and I pull back, clapping my hand over my mouth in horror. But Luca just grins at me.

"Definitely not," I say when he pulls my hand down. But he nods and pulls me in for a kiss.

"Definitely yes. Now, where were we?"

I pick up the condoms and wave them at him. "Right about here." Then I tear one off and arch my brow. "May I?"

His lips tip up. "Please do."

I wrap my hand around the base of his cock and give

it a light squeeze. I fooled around with my ex, went down on him a couple of times, and I'm fairly certain I can figure out the basics. I *want* to do this with him. To him.

Luca makes me feel bold. Like I'm free to explore, and he won't judge my lack of experience. With him, I want to make up for the years I've been alone.

Leaning over, I lick a stripe up the underside before popping the head of him into my mouth.

Luca muffles a groan, his hand tangling in my hair as I swirl my tongue around his tip, then take him in deeper. I bob up and down, letting my saliva coat him so my hand slides easier. It's messy, but I'm assuming I'm doing it right from the sounds Luca makes.

"Fuck, Isla. I need you."

I lift my head off his cock, then put the condom wrapper between my teeth and tear it open. His dark eyes are heavy as I roll it down him. But when I straddle his hips again, and he takes his cock in hand to line it up with my entrance, an unexpected wave of nerves hits me.

"You okay?" he asks, his hand stroking down my arm. "We can slow down if you're not ready."

I breathe out a shaky laugh. "How can you tell how I'm feeling so freaking easily?" I drop down onto his upper thighs, my cheeks heating. "It's not that I'm not ready, or that I don't want this. It's just been a really, really long time."

"Can I ask how long, exactly?" he asks quietly.

I nod slowly. "Well, Charlie's almost thirteen. So..."

His eyes widen in understanding, no math required. "Isla."

"Now who's ruining the mood," I say, but my words come out unsteady.

"No, baby. You haven't. I'm honoured that after so long, I'm the lucky bastard that gets to be with you. We'll go slow, and if anything doesn't feel good, I want you to tell me, okay?"

I melt at his words. And simultaneously feel my nerves fade, the desire that was pulsing through me earlier coming back, stronger than ever. I can't honestly think of a better man to be with, now or ever.

Shifting forward, I kiss his lips, feeling the stubble against my face that was grazing between my thighs just a few minutes ago.

"Thank you."

It's all I can manage to say. Especially when a wicked grin covers his face. "In fact, I think I had better make sure you're ready."

He keeps those sinful grey eyes trained on my body as he moves his hand between my legs, finding my slit and sliding his fingers along my folds.

"Ohmygod," I gasp as his touch hits parts of my body that are still sensitive from the first orgasm he gave me.

"That's it. I want you nice and wet, baby."

His dirty words seem to have a direct line to my pussy as I feel it spasm, clenching around nothing.

"I am. Please, I need you. I need something."

"I've got you."

One finger dips in. Then a second. And a third. It's tight, but I know his cock will be even bigger. And I'm grateful he knew to prepare me.

"That's it. Fuck, you feel so good."

This time when my orgasm hits, it's a lot smaller than the first one. Still, it rolls through me in waves. But Luca doesn't give me time to recover, shifting me down his body slightly. When I feel his cock between my legs, I lift my hips, and he notches his tip to my pussy.

And with a deep inhale, I slowly start to lower myself down.

"Holy fuck," he breathes, his hands coming to grip my hips, helping to support me. It's a good thing, too, as I whimper at how thick he is, how full—almost too full—I feel. And he's only just barely inside of me. The stretch burns, but in a good way.

My hands land on his chest as I brace myself over him. I lift my hips back up slightly, then bear down, taking more of him.

"Christ, look at you. God, you take me so damn good, Isla. You're fucking perfect."

His words of praise make the last bit of resistance in me soften, and I lower down even farther.

"That's a good girl. Yes, Isla. *Fuck*," he groans when I finally take all of him.

For several minutes, he lets me control the movement, murmuring sweet words of praise as I rock back and forth, adjusting to the feel of him inside me. I'm so wet, so turned on from the two orgasms I've already had, that it doesn't take long for the pinch of pain I felt initially to fade into pure pleasure.

I've already come twice, so I'm certainly not expecting anything more. This feels good enough that I don't even care.

But then, there's no holding back the moan that falls

from my lips as he raises me slightly, then pulls me back down, hitting a different angle inside of me. "It's so good. *So good.*" I gasp, then whimper when he pushes up at the same time as pulling me down again over him. My legs are still a little shaky from earlier, but that doesn't seem to matter. Not when he takes over, moving my body for me, making me cry out with pleasure.

He might say I'm in charge, that he's not my boss in the bedroom. But right now, I am one hundred percent at his mercy, his to command and control, and I am completely okay with that.

Because another orgasm is coming, hard and fast. I don't have any hope of slowing things down or holding it off to prolong this. "Oh God, I'm coming. Right there, Luca. Right there. Oh!" I cry out as I burst into a thousand tiny pieces, barely hearing his groan as he finds his own release. My entire body is buzzing as I feel my core spasm around him. My movements eventually slow, and the trembling in my legs that I'd managed to ignore comes back. I'm exhausted. Drained in the best possible way.

Luca wraps his arms around me, pulling me into his chest, then rolling both of us onto the side, his cock slipping out of me. He starts to shift away, and I make a sound of protest.

He chuckles. "I'm just dealing with the condom."

He rolls back toward me a minute later, gathering me in his arms. Our legs tangle together as he runs his fingers down my hair. "Is this okay?"

I know he's asking about his residual limb, the soft

liner that I can feel against my skin, but all I can muster is a nod. His soft chuckle tells me it's enough, however.

"That was incredible," he says after a moment of silence. "Thank you."

A giggle escapes me as I tip my chin up to look at him. "Am I meant to say you're welcome? Because that feels backward, somehow. Shouldn't I be thanking you for not one, not two, but *three* orgasms?"

Luca lifts his head off the pillow and smirks down at me. "You know, you're right. You *should* thank me."

I laugh again, and his smile grows, even as he lightly smacks my ass. "Brat."

That just makes me laugh harder, and then he joins in, and the next thing I know, we're both losing it, clutching each other, lost in laughter.

When we eventually calm down, Luca tucks my hair behind my ear. "Would it be too forward of me to ask you to stay the night?"

I lean over and kiss him. "I was hoping you would. There's still two more condoms, after all."

In a flash, Luca has me on my back, and is holding himself over me, his dark hair falling into his eyes.

"Challenge accepted."

21

LUCA

Was last night real?

That's the first thought to cross my consciousness as I start to wake up. Then Isla shifts next to me, nestling her plump ass closer into the cradle of my body. Fuck yes, it was. Her slow, steady breaths tell me she's still asleep, and I take the opportunity to sink into the moment.

Last night was incredible. We used two of the condoms, Isla unleashing a side of me I haven't felt in ages. I didn't think about my leg, not once, after she grabbed the condoms for us. All I could think about, all I wanted to think about, was wringing as much pleasure from her as possible before we both fell into an exhausted sleep.

I've been with women that don't try very hard to hide their disdain for my limb difference, and I've been with women who don't make a big deal out of it. But last night was the first time I felt truly comfortable in bed with a woman. As if I could do whatever I chose to do, and if it didn't work because of my mobility challenges, it wouldn't matter. Isla's complete acceptance of who I am with no reservations was wildly freeing.

But now, in the gentle light of the morning after, I'm worried. Will the connection we had last night still be there when I do my morning care and put back on my prosthetic? Even if it is, what happens next? I'm heading home to Cedar Creek today, and Isla's staying for the conference. But when she returns, how will she want to handle things?

A muffled noise comes from the woman tucked into my arms, and I force my brain to stop spiralling as she slowly rolls over and blinks her eyes open.

"Hi," she says softly, a small smile creasing her face. Then she burrows in, tucking her head into my chest.

I chuckle and pull her in close. "Morning. What time is your first panel?"

Isla groans. "That depends on what time it is now."

"Still early, just after six," I reply.

She shifts back slightly and looks up at me with sleepy eyes. "Thank God. Breakfast isn't till eight."

I shift her onto her back and prop my upper body up on my elbow. She's breathtakingly beautiful, even first thing in the morning, her lips plump from being kissed for hours last night, her cheeks a light pink, possibly from my stubble. I lean down and press a kiss to the side of her neck, down the slope of her shoulder and farther, unable to resist her allure.

"So you're saying I have two hours to make you come for me again."

She half gasps, half moans, her hands sliding around to my back as I kiss my way down her torso.

"Y-yes, but I should probably shower, and you know, we keep saying we need to talk. Maybe now we really do?"

Fuck.

I'd been keeping my head firmly in the sand, trying to ignore that fact ever since she woke up. But she's right.

With a sigh, I lower my chin to rest on her stomach. Her breasts are right in front of me, teasing me with what I want but can't have. At least, not right now.

"Shower, I can agree to. Talking..." I pout. "Do we have to?"

Isla's light giggle is exactly the response I wanted. "Remind me, which one of us is older? Aren't you meant to the responsible, mature one?"

I scoff, moving back up to lay my head beside her. "Yeah, but you're a mom. That makes you infinitely more responsible than me."

She arches her brow. "Teen pregnancy makes me responsible. Noted."

That makes me grin. But at the same time, I wonder how she can't see in herself what I so easily do. She's responsible, she's kind, she's intelligent, and she's got her shit together. It's one of the many things I admire about her.

"All I'm saying is, we could be very responsible and use up that last condom. I am concerned about them expiring soon," I say solemnly.

"Mm-hmm," she says, toying with my hair. "We should do the right thing."

I push up on my hands and kiss her firmly, stroking her tongue with mine. I know we still have to talk. We can't put it off much longer. But right now, talking is the last thing I plan on doing with my mouth.

————

An hour and a half later, Isla walks out of the steamy bathroom with a very satisfied look on her face. Do I internally puff with pride, knowing I put it there? Hell fucking yes, I do.

She sashays over to where I'm seated on the edge of the bed, having just finished attaching my prosthesis. Bending over, her towel grazes my bare chest as she leans in and kisses me.

I groan against her lips. "Do you realize how much I want to tug this towel off you?"

With a giggle, she steps back. "Sorry," she says in an entirely unapologetic tone. She turns to where her clothes from last night are sitting on a chair and grimaces. "I'll have to wear these back to my room, I guess. I'm not willing to miss a single moment of this conference. Not even for you." She arches a look my way. "So stop looking like a sad puppy who just had his toy taken away."

I chuckle, but don't move. Somehow, watching her get dressed is just as intimate as watching her strip bare last night.

"Isla," I start, then pause when she turns to look at me. Do I really want to do this? Oh right, I'm the older one. I'm meant to be the responsible one. "I don't want to keep you from the conference, but we do need to talk about what happened here. About what we do next."

After taking a slow breath in and out, she walks over and sits beside me. She's wearing pants, but only her bra on top, and the lace is wildly distracting.

But this is important.

"We do." She looks down at my hands and covers one with her own. "I don't regret last night, Luca. But I'm also worried. All the reasons for not getting close to each other while I'm working for you are still there. All the reasons I'm scared of getting close to you still exist."

I flip my hand over and thread my fingers with hers, squeezing gently. "I know. And I'll go along with whatever you choose. But I have to say, if last night proved anything to me, it's that whatever this pull between us is, it's too strong for me to just set aside for six months. At least, not without considering if there's a way to make it work. As long as you feel okay about it, of course."

Isla nods, which I take as a good sign. "I feel the same way." She looks up at me, her vibrant green eyes shining. "I never expected this. Never expected you." She lets out a small laugh. "I honestly thought I'd just be a single mom until Charlie moved out or something, and then maybe I'd find time to have a social life again. He's been my entire focus. Hell, I haven't been on a date since high school. I'm not sure I even know how to be in a relationship, much less one as complicated as this."

I can't help it. My head dips down and I kiss her forehead, loving how easily she leans into me, trusting me to provide comfort.

She moves so her head is resting on my shoulder. It's only natural to kiss the top of her head again. I can't seem to stop kissing her. But then she lifts her head, shifting slightly away from me, and I know I'm not gonna like what she says next.

"Being a teen mom, facing that stigma, that was hard. I made it through, barely. But now it's not just me that I have to worry about, it's Charlie as well. It's his happiness and safety, giving him a stable home, that's what matters. And that's why being with you scares me. Because being known as the woman who slept with her boss, or worse, being accused of being the woman who slept with her boss to get a job? That would put me right back where I was as a teenager, facing judgment and criticism everywhere. My reputation, my career, my pride, it would all be at stake if people got the wrong idea about us. Charlie could suffer as well, if people decided to take their judgment out on him. And I can't let that happen."

I exhale slowly, thinking about what to say. I want to promise her that I won't let anything bad happen. That somehow, this will be different. That we aren't breaking any rules. But while that may be true, she wasn't breaking any rules when she got pregnant at seventeen. Like that situation, this one between us goes against the norm just enough to cause trouble. And I'm not dumb enough to deny the truth that women face far more criticism than men when it comes to this.

Add in the power imbalance and the age difference, and she has every right to be worried. There's nothing I can do to fully alleviate her fears. But this can't be all there is, one perfect night and then back to pretending there's nothing between us.

"Is there anything I can do to make it so you'll feel

safe enough to be with me?" I ask quietly. "Because I hear everything you're saying, and I respect your fears. But being with you feels right in a way I can't ignore. You're in control of how this goes. Just, please, tell me you're willing to try. "

"I feel the same way, Luca." Her hand lifts to cup my cheek, and I turn into it and press a kiss to her palm. "I can't walk away from this or you. Not anymore. I'm not asking you to do that, either. But keeping it a secret would help, I think. At least for now, maybe until I find a job after this contract, or I don't know. Until…"

"Until you can trust that I've got you, and that we're in this together. That I won't walk away and leave you to face the fallout alone."

Her quiet sob tells me I've finally figured it out. What she needed to hear from me was that I won't be like Charlie's sperm donor. I won't abandon her if things change and leave her to deal with everything by herself.

"I'm not him. And no matter what happens in the future for us, I swear to you, I won't let you handle any negativity that may surface on your own. If we do this, we do it together."

I wipe away her tears again, but she's smiling, and it's full of hope.

"Kiss me, Luca."

"Always."

22

ISLA

I STARE DOWN at his text as my ferry slowly approaches the dock. I decided to take an earlier boat home from the conference than I intended but didn't tell my mom or Charlie. They think I'm staying in Vancouver until this afternoon.

Instead, I'm meeting my secret boyfriend for a few hours.

Which might just be the wildest thing I've done since having a kid at seventeen. But I want to see him. The past two days were amazing. I had a great time at the conference, but the loneliness I was feeling when I first arrived only intensified after Luca left. Talking on the phone and one spicy video call was not enough, and as the minutes count down to seeing him again, my heart starts to beat louder and louder in my chest.

The boat comes to a stop and the ramp lowers, and I thank the ferry gods that I'm one of the first vehicles off.

My impatience to get to Luca is quite ridiculous, and I have to remind myself that getting a speeding ticket would be a bad thing as I zip along the highway toward Cedar Creek.

I pull up to his apartment building and find the visitor's parking he told me to use, right out front. That makes me nervous. What if someone recognizes my car?

"Like who, you dummy?" I mutter to myself under my breath as I gather my phone and keys into my purse. "You don't know anyone here well enough except Juni, and she'd probably celebrate."

Even once I'm ready to get out, I grip my steering wheel for a second and breathe. This makes it all real. If I go up to his apartment, there will be no chance of walking away from the other night and calling it a onetime thing. This is the cliff's edge, and I have to decide whether I'm going to step off or turn around and run away.

But if my life has proven anything to me, it's that I can do hard things. I can face down my fears and rise above. Because this connection I have with Luca is worth exploring.

Resolute in my decision, I get out of my car and walk up to the front door of the building, pressing the buzzer number he texted me earlier. The door opens, and I walk in, making my way to the elevator, where I press the PH for penthouse.

"How the heck did I end up dating a guy who lives in a penthouse," I mutter to myself. Yet, there's no denying the slight thrill I feel. I've never even *seen* a penthouse.

After the longest ride ever, the elevator doors open

directly into what is clearly his home, and I see Luca standing in front of me, a welcoming smile on his handsome face, hands stuffed in his pockets.

I step out, coming to stand right in front of him as the doors slide shut behind me, and we just stare at each other, smiling like fools for several seconds. Then whatever was holding us in place snaps, and I fling myself into his arms, kissing him with every fiber of my being.

We only break apart when he stumbles backward. "Oops, sorry," I say, but Luca shakes his head, stroking my hair.

"Don't apologize for being as excited to see me as I am to see you. C'mon, I'll make you a cup of tea." He takes my hand in his and leads me through a short entryway and into a giant, cavernous space.

White marble floors...maybe it's marble? What do I know?

White cabinets, white walls, white ceiling, white, white, white. It's bland, stark, boring, and nothing I expected from a penthouse apartment.

The only interesting feature is the wall of windows across from me, looking out over the city. But with the grey winter weather outside, even that isn't so appealing. There's a hall that I assume leads to bedrooms, and an interesting spiral staircase that leads to another door. A rooftop, perhaps?

I slowly turn around, looking for any sign of Luca anywhere in the space. But aside from a navy blue couch and a glass-topped coffee table with what looks to be an engineering magazine on top, there's nothing to indicate who lives here.

Until I reach the shelves that line one wall. There, I finally see a hint of the man I'm falling for.

It's just a handful of photos, but it's something, at least.

"How long have you lived here?" I ask, hoping he doesn't take offense.

With a chagrined laugh, he steps around me and moves to the open kitchen area. "Almost a year. I know it's kind of a blank space." He shrugs, and I see a hint of red climbing up his neck. "I never really bothered to decorate. In my last place, my ex did all the decorating. I guess I don't know what I'd want it to look like if I were to bother."

I instantly feel bad for mentally critiquing his home, and walk over to his side, sliding my arms around his waist. "It's fine, Luca. Not having art on your walls isn't going to push me away."

He turns to face me, draping his arms over mine, his hands resting on the small of my back as he drops a kiss to my forehead. "Good. Because that's the last thing I want to do."

The kettle on the stove starts to whistle and he turns, taking it off the heat and pouring it into two mugs. I tried to not have any expectations of what might happen when I came over here, but I have to admit, this was not what I had in mind. But I take the cup of aromatic Earl Grey tea and follow him to the couch that is the only pop of colour in the space.

He sinks down into one corner, and with his free hand, tugs me down right next to him. I tuck my feet under me and lean into his side, loving the weight of his arm as he drapes it around my shoulders.

"So, how was the rest of the conference?" he asks conversationally, and I can't help it, I giggle nervously. "What?" he says, shifting to set his mug of tea down.

I reluctantly move as well, putting down my mug and turning to face him. I've had to develop a level of confidence in life, and when I don't feel confident, I've become really good at faking it. This is one of those moments where I'm not sure if I truly feel brave enough to tell him what's got me confused, or if I need to fake it. Either way, here goes.

"I guess I'm a little surprised. When you suggested I come over before going to get Charlie, I didn't realize it would be for tea and a chat." I bite the inside of my lip as I watch for his reaction.

It's subtle at first. A slow nod of his head, the slightest crinkle at the side of his eyes formed when his lips tip up. When he speaks, all subtlety is gone and there's no mistaking the desire behind his words. "I was trying to be a gentleman. Show you that I'm interested in more than just sex with you. But if you think me offering you tea and asking about the conference is some sort of sign that I don't want you naked and writhing underneath me right this fucking second, then I guess I better show you how wrong you are."

Luca did his best to make me more than willing to throw caution to the wind and let myself fall even deeper for him, but after I picked up Charlie, and we went home, my brain kicked into overdrive. All throughout cooking dinner, cleaning up after, getting things ready for the morning, and getting my son into bed, I'm distracted. Caught up in wondering how tomorrow would go, whether we would truly be able to hide how things have changed in front of other people. Questioning if I was ready to face the music of being the "single mom who slept with her boss" and all the stereotyping that would come along with that label. Because it's inevitable. I know that. Eventually, people will find out about us. And then, it'll start. The sidelong looks, the whispered comments, the raised eyebrows.

From the moment I walked into his hotel room until now, I somehow managed to convince myself that it would be worth it. That being with Luca would over-shadow any negativity I might face. But now, in my home with my son sleeping down the hall, all of my doubts and fears seem so much bigger.

I don't fall asleep until close to 2 am, making my 6 am alarm clock offensive. Rolling over with a groan, I rub my hand over my face as I blink my eyes open. Like it or not, it's time to see what today brings.

Somehow, the universe likes me enough to grant me an easy morning. Charlie gets up with no complaining, his homework is done, thanks to Nana, and we're ready to leave on time.

"Bye kid, love you," I call out through the window as he slams the door closed with his hip.

"See ya, Mom."

It's the best I'm gonna get. I smile as I watch him

walk away, joining up with a couple of other boys who all greet him with high fives and fist bumps. And my gut churns.

He's happy here. He's settling in, making friends, finding activities and people that he enjoys. I should be thrilled, and I am. Yet, seeing how settled he is makes me once again wonder if I'm doing the right thing by exploring a relationship with Luca. After all, if it goes wrong, it has the potential to hurt not only me but my son, too.

My fingers are white around the steering wheel the entire drive from Charlie's school to the stadium. I pull into a parking spot and breathe deeply for a minute before unclenching my hands and getting out. The walk into the building feels both too long and too short. It's ridiculous to think everyone will somehow already know I slept with our boss. And yet, when I pass by one of the team trainers and they don't smile at me, instead of assuming they're distracted or focused, I imagine they're judging me.

And when Gabe greets me with "Good morning and welcome back. Luca wants to see you as soon as you're settled" my heart stops.

"Oh, okay. Did he say why?"

"He didn't, just told me to pass on the message. Hey, how was your conference?"

I blink several times as Gabe looks at me.

He's not acting differently, there's no need to panic. "It was fine. Informative." *In more ways than one.*

"That's great. There's nothing much to report around here. The new signage for the sponsors is up in the breezeway. We don't have any meetings today, so you can catch up on emails. But tomorrow, the website developer hopes to be done, so you'll have to review all of that and present a report to Luca about whether to approve it or not. Oh, and the ticket tier proposal you put together has been approved, so we need to know if we should go ahead and get those set up with a printer or if you think it should all be digital..."

Gabe keeps talking, but my attention starts to wander. I took this job to be a consultant. To offer ideas and suggestions, to come up with marketing plans and strategies. I never thought I'd be the one to start implementing things. Yet, here I am. Thanks to Luca's generosity with the budget, and the surprisingly quick and efficient way things have worked, we're past the point of planning and strategizing. There's less than a month until Christmas. Then, in the new year, the work will ramp up as we open to the public for spring training, charity games, and finally, the season opener. That's when my time with the Thunder will officially end.

Early April isn't that far off. Maybe it would be smarter to wait. To give me some time to make sure this won't impact Charlie in a bad way.

"Don't forget, Luca's waiting for you."

Gabe's voice penetrates through the haze of my thoughts. "Right. Yes, I'll go there now."

And ask him to be strong enough to press pause. Because I don't know if I will be.

23
LUCA

I'VE NEVER TRIED recreational drugs. I rarely drink. I've never picked up a cigarette.

And yet, right now, I think I know how a junkie feels when they're getting desperate for their next hit of whatever their vice is.

Isla is my vice. It hasn't even been twenty-four hours since I had her in my bed, in my arms. And I'm desperate to see her again.

When her delicate knock sounds on my door, my head snaps up from the computer screen I was trying to focus on. "Come on in," I call out, debating whether I should stand and go to greet her or stay seated.

Sitting would be safer. Less risk of me giving in to temptation and pulling her into my arms. Then she steps through the door, and I realize how hard this is going to be.

"Good morning, Isla," I manage to grind out, keeping my face neutral when I see Gabe following close behind. "Gabe, what can I do for you?" There. That sounded normal, right? Isla won't look me in the eye, she's fidgeting with her phone in her hands.

"Oh, is this not a meeting where you need me to take notes?" Gabe asks with a neutral tone, but there's some sort of glint in his eyes. Is it amusement? Is it suspicion?

I'm so caught up trying to decipher his expression, it takes me a second to formulate a response. Take notes? On what? How I kiss her? How I lift her up onto my desk so I can stand between her thighs and lick a path down her neck?

Fuck no, Gabe, I don't want you to take notes.

"Thanks, that won't be necessary. This is just a quick catch-up from last week." My voice is rough, but steady. And thank God, he seems oblivious to the tension that feels thick in the air because Gabe just nods.

"Understood."

Without being asked, he closes the door behind us. And then we're alone.

"Hey, wonder woman," I say with a smile, pushing back and standing. Fuck avoiding temptation.

But when I walk over to her, she puts a hand up, stopping me before I can touch her.

"What's wrong?"

"I don't know... I can't... We..."

Moving slowly, sensing she's spiraling and I have to stop it, I place my hands on her shoulders and squeeze gently. "Isla. Baby. Take a breath, let's talk."

She nods, but I can feel her shaky breath in and out under my hands. She lets me guide her to the chairs in front of my desk and we sit down. I take one of her hands in mine, letting my thumb rub back and forth over the back of her hand.

"You must think I'm ridiculous with how I keep flip-flopping," she starts, and I shake my head.

"Not at all. I think you're nervous and have every right to be. All I ask is that you talk to me, let me in, don't be nervous and alone."

She squeezes my hand back and I take that as a good sign.

"Last weekend felt like a dream. Having that time with you, away from real life, it was amazing. And yesterday, I was desperate to see you again, and then I didn't want to leave when I had to get Charlie. You make me feel so good, Luca. Being with you feels right, even as part of me says it should feel wrong. But I'm scared. The last time I let myself be reckless and impulsive, I ended up pregnant at seventeen. And yet, somehow, this time it feels even more risky. Charlie's finally happy here, and so am I. If things don't work out between you and me, I need to know I won't have to uproot my entire life because of it. I need to know Charlie won't get hurt, and if he gets attached to you, and then you leave..." she trails off.

I nod slowly. "I won't pretend to know how any of that feels. And I'll be honest, I'm not sure what I can say to reassure you that I have no intention of leaving, and even less of letting you handle any negative fallout from our relationship alone. If you want to press pause, now or at any time, we will. I want you, but more than that, I respect you. And I'm a patient man, especially when something is worth waiting for. And you, Isla Forrester, are worth waiting for."

She lets her head fall forward, landing on my chest, and I can't help it, I press a soft kiss to the top of her head. She might think she's being irritating, changing her mind and not knowing what to do, but if anything, it makes her maturity shine through. She's strong, and capable, and worried about jeopardizing her future. I have to respect that. Even if it's gonna hurt like hell to walk away now that I know how good it could be.

"I don't want to wait. Not when you say things like that, and I know you mean it." Lifting her head, Isla looks me in the eyes. "I want you, Luca. I promise to try and stop being so nervous if you'll keep being patient with me."

My smile breaks free. "Deal. Can I kiss you now?"

She nods. Our lips meet, and the world is set to right. I take it slowly at first, teasing her, savouring the feel of her in my arms again. But that doesn't last long. My restraint is a thin thread, ready to snap at any moment. And I'm not alone. Isla whimpers, pressing her mouth deeper against mine, her tongue seeking mine. Her hands come to the back of my head, tangling in my hair, holding me in place. Entirely unnecessary. It would take something drastic to make me move away from her right now.

"Why do you feel so perfect," I murmur as my lips trail down her jawline, the slope of her neck, and finally to the patch of soft skin bared by the collar of her blouse. I shift it to the side, continuing my path along every inch of her that isn't covered by her pesky clothes. "You've captivated me, mind and body."

Her fingers tighten, her grip almost painful. I smile against her skin. And lift my fingers to the top button on her blouse, pausing for a moment. She doesn't stop me, so I deftly undo it, freeing more of her for me to worship.

"Oh Luca," she moans softly as I kiss the mound of her breast. "I…"

"Me too, wonder woman. I want you so fucking badly."

She releases her hold on me, stands, and moves swiftly to straddle my legs, sitting in my lap. "We shouldn't be doing this here." Her lips find mine as her fingers again loop behind my neck. "Anyone could catch us." Another kiss and a roll of her hips that has me digging my hands into her lower back. "But I don't want to stop."

That last is a pained whisper and I realize I have to be the responsible one right now. Which, not gonna lie, feels really fucking good. My mature, put together Isla is a wanton mess, ready to throw everything out the window, just from a few kisses.

"Okay. We have to stop." I lean back slightly, moving my hands up her sides to cup her shoulders, squeezing gently. "I promised you I'd make sure we kept this a secret, and if we go any longer, I'm not going to be able to stop myself from bending you over this desk."

That was the wrong thing to say, judging by how Isla tips her head back with a soft moan. "I want that so badly."

"Someday. When the office is empty. I'll make it happen," I promise.

The look she gives me is full of heat. "You better." She shifts, standing up and glancing down to where my dick is obviously tenting my pants before giving me a smirk. "I'd apologize for that, but I'm not sorry."

Pushing myself up to stand, I capture her lips in one last punishing kiss. "Never apologize for what you do to me. I fucking love it."

A knock on my office door has me swearing under my breath and Isla stepping back quickly. "I'll open it while you get behind your desk," she whispers and I nod in agreement before moving as quickly as I can to sit down where my desk will hide the evidence.

Isla smooths her hair and takes a breath, squaring her shoulders before winking at me and saying loudly "Alright, that sounds like a plan. Thanks for the update." She opens my door to Dom, who's frowning down at his phone.

"Why was your office locked?" He looks up and sees Isla, his eyebrows raising as he looks to me then back to her. "Never mind. Hello, Isla. Hope your trip was good last week."

She nods and slips out around him. "It was, thanks."

After she disappears, Dom folds his arms over his chest. "Did I interrupt something important?"

I glare at him but don't answer. After several seconds, he sighs and sinks down into the chair that Isla was just sitting in. When she wasn't sitting on me, that is.

"I hope you know what you're doing."

"I'm not sure that's any of your business," I reply curtly.

Dom shakes his head, his expression a mixture of pity and concern. "Luca. I'm your partner, your friend. You dating one of our employees is absolutely my business. It might not be against some written rule, but it sure as hell is risky when we need her to finish her job."

I sag in my chair. He's right, and I'm not being entirely fair. "I'm not sure what to tell you. We like each other. And we tried to stay apart, but it just didn't work. So we're not going to deny things any longer. But we'll be careful and we're not going public yet. I'm handling it."

Dom's shoulders lift up and down as he takes in a long breath and lets it out. His jaw clenches as he stares at me, the pity in his gaze giving way to a hardened determination. "Okay, so how exactly are you *handling it*? Because messing around in your office isn't the smartest decision. People are gonna wonder what's happening when your office door has always been open and now it's closed and locked when she's in here. Not exactly subtle. How long are you keeping it a secret? Does her kid know about you? Cedar Creek's not a big city. If you're out together, someone's going to see something. Have you thought about that? How can you date her if you can't be seen with her in public?"

His barrage of questions sets my blood boiling. Not only with anger toward him, but with the fact that he's asking questions I don't have answers to. And I hate that uncertainty. "I don't fucking know, okay?" I explode in a harsh whisper. I lift my hand and rake it through my hair. "I don't know. It's new, and we're being careful. She's got a lot at stake and I'm not that selfish of an asshole that I'd ignore all of it and push her for more than she's ready for."

Dom leans back in his chair, his face relaxing into a slightly more understanding expression. "Alright, alright. I'm sorry I'm pushing you like this. But that's where the friend part of me comes in. I care about you, and you know I want to see you with someone instead of staying miserable and alone. And if you're happy with Isla, then that's awesome. I just don't want this to back-fire on either of you."

I nod, feeling my frustration start to recede. "I know you're coming from a good place. And you're not asking anything I shouldn't be asking myself. But truthfully, this really is new. We don't have it all figured out yet. She was at the conference last weekend. Her son has ABS. We ran into each other, and well..." I shrug. "I guess being away from real life was what tipped us over the line. I couldn't stay away from her any longer."

He exhales, lacing his fingers behind his head. "Damn. I didn't know that about her kid."

"Yeah. I did, which is why I really should've told her about me. But I didn't, so she found out when she saw me at the conference."

Dom whistles. "Was she pissed?"

I finally smile, thinking back to how amazing Isla was at handling the revelation. "No. Surprised, yes, but not mad. We talked a lot that night, but then one thing led to another, and now" —I spread my hands out—

"we're here. Do you think you can just step back and let me figure this out with her?"

"I will, just be careful. For both of you, okay?"

"Trust me, I will be."

24

ISLA

"How has your mother lived in Dogwood Cove for over a year and never taken you to Camille's for lunch?" Juniper shakes her head in disbelief as she navigates her car into a parking spot along the main street of Dogwood Cove. "They have the best sandwiches. And the bakery next door is probably the best one I've ever been to. Their apple nut muffins are to die for."

"She's mentioned a bakery with good muffins, but not Camille's," I reply as we get out. I immediately pull my jacket hood up against the cold. "Do they have good soup? This is soup weather." We hurry to the door of the very cute restaurant we decided to visit for lunch. Honestly, this entire town is cute. The town square with the white gazebo right across the street from the café looks like it was plucked out of a Hallmark movie. Stores and business line three of the four sides of the square, with a taller building, town hall, if I remember correctly, taking up the fourth. Even now, the first week of December, when the weather is cold and dreary, colour and life is everywhere. From Christmas lights on all of the street lamps, to winter and holiday-themed murals painted on the windows of many of the businesses. There's what looks like a sort of nativity scene set up by the gazebo, and a huge tree covered in giant decorations.

Inside, the café is about half full, but we find a table by the front window and sit down, peeling off our winter wear. It's warm and smells incredible in here, and I look around with wide eyes. "Okay, this place is fantastic." It's quirky and vibrant with bright colours splashed everywhere, an adorable chalkboard outlining the specials, a huge display case full of delicious-looking goodies, and subtle music playing in the background.

"Right?" Juni agrees just as a woman with dark hair comes over with two menus.

"Hey ladies, welcome to Camille's. I'm Mila, and you'll have to excuse me, but I'm normally in the bakery, not serving people. So if I drop something in your lap, it's on me," she says cheerfully. "Kidding." She grins at our surprised expressions. "I mean, I am normally in the bakery, but I won't spill anything."

"Good to know. Hey, aren't you the owner?" Juni asks. "I've been here a few times, and I feel like I heard someone say that once."

Mila nods. "Yep. Owner, baker, whatever else needs doing, that's me."

All of a sudden, realization dawns on me. "Wait. You're Mila Holt. From the Dogwood Cove Animal Shelter."

Her smile grows. "Yep, that's me. Have we met?"

"Not in person. Somehow, we missed each other at

the fundraiser gala. I'm Isla Forrester, from the Cedar Creek Thunder baseball team."

Mila's mouth falls open in surprise. "Oh my God! Get up here and hug me, woman!" I let her pull me out of my chair and into her embrace with a laugh. "How the heck did we miss each other that night? Oh wait, I know, because I was running around like crazy the entire time."

I laugh along with her and Juni. "It was a wonderful evening. It's so good to finally meet you in person after all those emails and phone calls."

"Definitely. Well, ladies, lunch is on me." Mila winks, then pulls out a notepad. "Do you know what you want or do you need a few minutes?"

I glance over at the chalkboard I'd seen on the way in. "I'm going to do the soup and sandwich special, please."

"Oh, same here." Juni hands our menus back. "Thanks, Mila."

"You got it, be right back with some water."

She walks away and Juni turns to me, leaning over the table. "Okay. So, spill the beans, girl. You came home from the conference saying you had big news, and it's been killing me to wait to hear it."

I can't hide my smile, but I do cast a quick look around to make sure no one can hear. Not that I recognize anyone in here aside from Mila, and she hasn't returned yet.

"When I went to Vancouver for the National ABS Foundation conference, you'll never guess who was there."

"Tom Hiddleston."

"No."

"Henry Cavill."

"No, it wasn't a British actor." I laugh, and Juni huffs.

"Well, then, I'm lost. Who?"

I lean forward. "Luca. He was the freaking keynote speaker."

Juni frowns in confusion. "Why was he the keynote —oh my God. Wait. What? Does he? No way."

I nod. "Yes way. He has amniotic band syndrome, on his leg. But he doesn't talk about it all that much, so keep that to yourself. I don't know if any of the guys on the team or in the office know. Okay?"

Juni mimes zipping her lips shut. "Got it. Secret. Locked away. So he was there, and?" She waggles her eyebrows at me. "Please tell me you finally did the dirty with boss man."

"Only if you never call it *the dirty* again," I say with a laugh. "And don't say boss man, like that. Charlie calls him that. Besides, I don't want anyone knowing. We're keeping it secret."

"Ooh, a clandestine romance. I like it." Juniper claps her hands together. "But not forever, right? Like, you're gonna tell everyone soon. I mean, it's not much of a romance if nobody knows about it."

"I know. But I'm worried if people find out, they're going to think I only got the job because of our relationship. And Charlie's never had to deal with me dating. Who knows what he'll think. He's met Luca, but will he think he's too old for me, or will he be upset?"

Juni scoffs. "Okay, first of all, if anyone tries to say you slept your way into the job, they can take a long walk off a short plank. You didn't even know him before that day. As for Charlie, he'd have to face reality someday. You're too hot to stay single forever. Besides, I thought you said he and Luca got along at that skills day or whatever."

"They did. But hanging out with a guy at a skills day and him dating your mom are two separate things. Besides, he's still not over losing my dad. What if he gets close to Luca, and then things don't work out?"

Her expression turns sympathetic. "Okay, let's not end your relationship before it even starts. Maybe you need to talk to Charlie. He's a pretty mature kid."

I sigh. "I know. I should. It's just, I never expected it to even get this far. We kissed a couple of times before the conference but decided not to let anything more happen until my contract was over. Then I saw him in Vancouver, and we were away from home and work and..." I trail off, my meaning clear.

"Oh, Isla," Juni murmurs. But the moment is interrupted by Mila, who sets down two glasses of water.

"Hey gals, sorry it took me so long to bring over your water. Your lunches will be out any minute."

"Thanks." I smile warmly at her, then look back to Juniper when Mila walks away. "It's okay, Juni. Everything will work out."

I hope...

———

Several hours later, we're back in Cedar Creek. After picking Charlie up from his friend's house, the three of us head home for pizza and a movie. Once Charlie disappears into his room with Gus, Juni corners me in the kitchen. I should've known this conversation wasn't over.

"Hear me out. What if you didn't keep it a secret?" She raises her hand as I open my mouth to protest. "No, wait. There's no rules keeping you two apart. You didn't sleep with him to get the job. Those are the facts. So does it really matter what anyone else thinks?"

"Yes!" I interrupt her, folding my arms across my chest as I lean against the counter. "What happens when my contract ends and I have to interview for a new job? What if my future employer thinks I'm a slut, or worse, thinks they're entitled to sex from me." I shudder.

"Then they're a fucking creep and you walk out of the interview and call the cops. C'mon, Isla. Be reasonable." Juni's firm, no-nonsense tone, combined with the pragmatic response, does bring me down a notch. "It would suck if people judged you for what you do in your personal life. And I get it, trust me, we women face that more often than not. You've experienced it firsthand. But what kind of life are you living if half of it is in the shadows?"

I arch my brow at her, fighting a smirk. "When did you become so poetical? Also, if we want to talk about hiding the truth from people, maybe you should turn that mirror around on yourself."

Juniper goes bright red, as I expected her to. "We aren't talking about me. And there's nothing to discuss, anyway."

"Well, there's nothing more to discuss about me and Luca, either," I fire back.

"What about Luca? Is he bringing some players to practice again? That was so cool." Charlie's voice startles both of us, Juni's eyes going wide as mine close and I count to five. *Please God, don't let him have overheard anything.*

"I'm not sure, kid. Aunt Juni and I were just talking about something I'm dealing with at work. That's all. So what did you and Miles get up to after school?" I ask, deftly changing the subject. I know I have to talk to Charlie about what's going on soon, but I am definitely not ready for that conversation yet.

His question does serve as further proof that my worries over him getting attached to Luca are valid. If Luca and I were to be together and they connected, and then Luca leaves?

My kid has suffered enough loss. I'm terrified of putting him through that again.

25

LUCA

"Fine, I admit, this was worth the money," Dom grumbles from beside me as we sip whiskey and watch the entire team and staff enjoy the holiday party we surprised them with.

"I'm glad you approve," I reply sarcastically, smirking into my glass.

He fought me on the open bar, and on the gifts I wanted to provide for everyone employed by the Thunder, but I pushed back. Every single person in here has worked their asses off to make my crazy plan a reality. Spring training will be here before we know it, and then the season. We might not be the big leagues, but it feels big all the same. The excitement for the Cedar Creek Thunder is growing every day, with more people following our social media accounts, advance ticket sales being far more successful than I anticipated, and community interest is climbing. I've been recognized several times when I've been out running errands, and while awkward at first, I fucking love that people seem happy with what I'm trying to achieve.

Gone are the days of a run-down stadium with less than half the seats filled at each game. Well, the stadium part is true. The seats being full? Time will tell.

And it's all thanks to one woman. The woman I'm trying to not be too obvious about searching the crowd for. I haven't seen Isla yet today, haven't had a moment alone with her in almost a week, and it's driving me fucking insane.

"If you think you're being subtle, you're not."

I turn and glare at Dom. "What?"

"You're glaring at every person who walks in the room that isn't Isla. Why don't you go and talk to some people instead? Distract yourself?" He gestures to the room filled with groups of players and staff mingling and chatting, while canned Christmas music plays in the background.

"I'm not glaring," I grumble under my breath, but when someone else walks through the doors of the room and it's not her, I feel myself deflate. *Fuck.*

"Sure, buddy." Dom claps me on the shoulder and sets his empty whiskey glass down. "You stand here and glare, I'm gonna go get some food."

I drain my tumbler and set it down as well, hating that he's right. I do need to mingle more and obsess over my missing marketing consultant less.

I make my way over to a cluster of players, including Griff, Foxxy, and Brady Dixon, the new pitcher we finally secured. "Gentlemen, having a good evening?" I ask and am met with cheers and slaps on my back.

"Absolutely. This is awesome. I've played for the Thunder for a bunch of seasons and we've never done anything more fancy than burgers and brews at a bar for a holiday party," Griff replies with a grin. "Getting all dressed up and fancy? Shit, it's kinda fun. And I look good in a suit." He spins on his heels as the other guys all laugh.

"Glad you're enjoying yourself." I grin back. "We'll have to sell out lots of games if we want to make it an annual thing, or Dom might have a heart attack."

Griff lifts his hand out to bump my fist. "You got it. Sold-out seats, here we come."

The other players all chime in with their agreement. Turning to Brady, I put out my hand. "Welcome to Cedar Creek, Brady. Sorry I haven't had a chance to connect with you. How are you settling in?"

He gives me a nod and a polite smile. "Good, thanks. This place reminds me of the town I grew up in, only better."

"Dixie's from Manitoba." Foxxy slaps him on the back with a smirk. "Didn't you say it was some tiny town full of sheep?"

Brady, or Dixie, I suppose I should call him, chuckles. "Yeah, that's about right. Cedar Creek's got a lot more going for it." This time, the smile he sends my way is much more relaxed. "I'm happy to be here."

"Good to hear. We're glad you joined us." Rafe still hasn't said what the reasons were for Dixie not wanting to join the major league, but their loss is our gain, I suppose. And if anyone understands secrets, it's me.

"Yeah, and you joined at the right time," Griff adds.

"Before Luca stepped in, things weren't so great around here. Those of us that have been on the team for a while had kind of accepted the truth that we stuck around just for the fun of playing baseball. I mean, the stadium was a disaster. Our gear was ancient. There was nothing enticing about watching us play in those ugly-ass old uniforms. It's no wonder we never had people in the stands."

"Dude, the uniforms were the worst! The new ones make my ass look awesome," one of the other guys, whose name I can't remember, chimes in, earning a laugh from everyone, myself included.

"It was weird. People in town knew we existed, but that was where it ended. It was like the town didn't really have any reasons to care. Not gonna lie, it fucking sucks to play to an empty home stadium, then go to an away game and see it packed to the rafters." Griff takes a sip of his drink, shaking his head.

"But it's different already." This comes from Foxxy. "We haven't even played, or opened the doors to the public, and I can tell, this season will be better. The guys on the search and rescue crew Griff and I work on have bought tickets for the home opener, and I've seen people wearing Thunder merch walking around town. Fuckin' merch. We never had that."

It baffles me how the previous owner let things slide. I make sure they're all paying attention when I say, "Listen, if any of you think of more things that could help make things better for you as players, or for the team, or for the town, please tell me, and I'll do whatever I can."

They all nod their agreement, but my attention is stolen by the woman who's just walked in.

More than my attention, Isla steals my very breath. The dark silver dress she's wearing has a subtle shine to it as it clings to curves I dream about every night. Her hair is swept over one shoulder and my chest aches with a longing to press my lips to the skin bared there. To feel her shiver and rest her cheek against my chest.

Fuck it.

"Excuse me, gentlemen. I see someone I need to catch up with. Enjoy the evening." I barely register their replies as I weave my way through the crowd, intent on reaching her side. What will I do then? No fucking clue. But I have to be near her.

"Luca. Hold up." Dom's voice is the only thing to bring me up short, partly because of the hint of warning I can hear. I turn to him with my jaw clenched.

"What?" I say in a clipped tone.

"Take a breath, man. Remember what I said about subtle? You're about as subtle as a fucking dump truck right now, crashing through everyone to get to her."

Thankfully, my friend is tactful enough to keep his voice pitched low, but I hear him loud and clear.

"Shit." I exhale. My hand grasps the back of my neck as I force myself to look at Dom, and not in Isla's direction.

"She's got you bad," he comments wryly. "Are you sure you can handle keeping this secret?"

"We have to. Until she's ready."

He nods slowly. "Alright. I'm guessing you need a minute to catch up with your marketing consultant on the community open house that's coming up, right?" he says just loudly enough for those around us to overhear.

"You're the fucking best," I reply in a whisper, full of gratitude. Dom gives me a nod and a subtle eye roll.

"Go."

I don't need to be told twice. Pivoting on my good leg, I resume my quest to get to Isla. Only now, it's not just to be near her. Dom gave me the perfect excuse to get her alone.

It takes a second to find her, but I do, standing by the bar, chatting with a few of the other admin staff. I make my way there, feeling the anticipation build. Dating in secret is not for the faint of heart. Add in her responsibilities as a mother, and it's proving to be a huge challenge to find time together, even with working in the same office. The need I have to kiss her is insane.

Finally, I reach the group. "Evening, everyone. Sorry to be rude, but I need to borrow Isla for a minute." I put on an apologetic expression. "I know it's mean of me to talk shop at a party, but something's come up with the open house."

Isla's eyes widen but she remains silent. Thankfully, the other two people standing with her seem to buy my ridiculous excuse. I gesture toward the hall with my hand. "It'll just take a few minutes."

"Sure, that's fine," she says quietly. Then, giving the others a smile, she follows me out of the banquet room. We walk down the hall without talking, keeping a respectable distance between us. The first empty room I find happens to be some sort of storage room, judging by the stacks of chairs and folded-up tables. But I don't give a fuck. My need for her is borderline desperate at this point.

The second the door snicks shut behind us, I press her up against it, my hands gripping her waist tightly as I push my lips against hers. She whimpers, looping her arms around my neck and holding me just as tightly. Her fervor matches mine, and for a second, my mind ponders whether I could do more than just kiss her in here. But reality intrudes. Between my leg and the fact that there's a room full of people waiting for our return, a few stolen kisses is the best I can hope for.

Better make it worth it.

There's no space left between us as I lift one hand to cup her jaw, my thumb grazing her soft cheek. I do what I wanted to back in the banquet hall and rain kisses down her neck, finding the bare skin of her shoulder. Her fingers curl into the back of my neck, anchoring me there. I take a deep breath in, letting the soft scent of her fill my senses.

Moving back to her mouth, I tease the seam of her lips. They part, ever so slightly, and I feel the invitation, the desire curling even deeper between us. I deepen the kiss, letting it say all the things I know deep down I'm feeling, but equally know I can't yet say with words.

Voices filter in through the door, and we break apart, both of us breathing heavily. I look into Isla's eyes and see the same thought written across her face.

"Just one more," I whisper, and she nods eagerly before pressing her mouth to mine.

But one more will never be enough. I'm not sure anything will be.

26

ISLA

"Hey Mom."

I look up as Charlie walks into my office. "Crap."

He drops into a chair with a smirk. "Exactly what every kid loves to hear from his only parent."

I cover my face with my palm and let out a groan. "Sorry kid, I won't lie, I halfway forgot you were coming for lunch. I'm super behind on work and didn't realize it was already that time." My son straightens and shrugs. "It's okay. I can just play vids on my phone."

"Vids?"

That earns me an epic eye roll. "Video games, Mom, geez."

I chuckle. "Sorry, I don't speak preteen."

"Isla are you—oh, sorry."

I look up from the email I'm trying to finish typing again, and this time it's Luca darkening my doorway. "Hi." Do I sound breathless? God, I hope I don't. Not that Charlie is paying any attention to me. No, he's actually lifted his head from his phone and is looking at Luca as well.

"Hey Charlie, didn't realize you were coming in today. I'll come back later."

"No, it's fine, what do you need?" I say, and I guess Luca hears something in my voice, because a concerned expression covers his face as he steps into my office.

"I was just going to ask what your plans were for lunch, but it looks like you're busy."

"We were meant to go for lunch, but she's gotta finish work," Charlie pipes up, his nose back in his phone.

Luca glances from my son to me. Seeming to reach a conclusion, he places his hands in his pockets and speaks to Charlie. "Want to come with me for a tour of the stadium while she finishes whatever she needs to do?"

To my surprise, Charlie immediately pockets his phone and stands. "Totally."

"You don't have to do that, Luca," I protest, but Charlie shoots me a glare, and Luca just chuckles.

"I've got some time. And he should know his way around the stadium. Who knows, maybe he'll be playing here one day."

"That would be so awesome," Charlie says, his voice full of awe. "Do you think there are any players around today?"

Luca shrugs. "Maybe, I'm not sure. But we can check out the locker room and the dugout. Maybe throw some balls around outside if it's not too cold while we wait."

"Cool." Charlie turns to me. "C'mon, Mom. This way you have time to work. And we can order food later."

I open my mouth to say that'll work when Luca interjects, shooting me a subtle wink. "How 'bout we take care of ordering something for all three of us so your mom has more time? I won't intrude on lunch, but I was going to order in some sushi, if that's cool?"

"I love sushi. And you can eat with us, right, Mom?"

There's not a chance I'll say no, not when the two of them have identical hopeful expressions on their faces. Even if I should be worried about them growing closer, I can't help but feel all warm and fuzzy about it. It gives me hope that Charlie will accept our relationship easily when I find the guts to tell him.

"Of course, he can join us. You two have fun."

Luca dips his head in a nod before gesturing to the door. "Come on, Charlie, let's go see if any of the guys are in the gym."

The two of them turn and walk out of my office, Charlie already peppering Luca with questions. I manage to return my focus back to my unfinished work. An hour later, they reappear, both grinning ear to ear.

"Hey Mom, we ordered sushi. And Luca showed me everything. It's really cold outside, so we didn't stay on the field for long, but he said I could throw the first pitch at a game sometime if I want to."

"That's awesome, kid." I smile at my son, who's dropped back into a chair, and immediately pulls out his phone.

I mouth the words *thank you* to Luca, earning a warm look in return. I wish I could do more than that. I wish I could hug him and tell him how much it means to me that he's willing to connect with my son.

When lunch arrives, and the three of us are crowded around the table in Luca's office, I listen to the two of them talk about baseball with huge grins on their faces. They don't stop chattering about next spring and the upcoming major league season, and whether or not the Vancouver Tridents have a chance of taking the championship again.

Until there's a break in conversation, when Charlie drops a potential bomb.

"You haven't asked about my arm."

His statement comes out so casual, so matter-of-fact, and yet it makes me grateful I don't have food in my mouth to choke on.

My gaze flies to Luca, but he's calm, a small smile on his face. "No, I haven't. I guess it never occurred to me, it's not really my business. Everyone's bodies are different in some way."

Charlie studies him, and I hold my breath, waiting to see what he'll say.

"True. But normally people are nosy and ask. I've been like this my whole life, so I've been asked a lot."

Luca glances at me, his gaze dropping ever so briefly down to his leg, then back up to me, and I give a subtle nod.

"I can understand that," he says casually before reaching down and pulling up his pant leg, revealing his prosthetic. "Mine is easier to cover up, but I've still been asked a lot of times, too."

"Holy shit!" Charlie exclaims, his mouth falling open.

"Charlie, language!" I say, but honestly, his reaction is exactly what I expected.

"Sorry, Mom," he replies immediately, still staring at Luca's leg. He finally glances up at me, eyes wide. "Did you know?"

I wince, but nod. "I did, but it wasn't my business to tell anyone."

Thankfully, he doesn't seem to care. "Yeah, I get it." He turns back to Luca. "I haven't met a lot of other people missing arms and legs. How did you lose yours?"

"I was born like this. Amniotic band syndrome."

Charlie's eyes are huge, like saucers now. "Woah. Same as me! That's so freaking cool. Not that you're missing your leg, but that it's the same reason."

"That is pretty cool." Luca tilts his head to the side, letting his pants fall back down to cover his prosthesis. "You know, any time you want to talk about it, I'm here. I wish I had known someone else with ABS when I was younger."

My heart cracks wide open. Not only did Luca just share his story voluntarily, but he respected Charlie's space by letting him share his own. And then that offer. For a man who likes to keep things private, who doesn't seek attention or accolades, despite doing incredible things, to offer that kind of support to my son?

It just makes me fall for him even more.

———

We wake up the next morning to a winter wonderland.

Sort of.

The thing with this part of Canada is, we're never fully prepared for the first snowstorm. Bad ones, the kind that close schools and make driving dangerous, don't happen that often on Vancouver Island, so when they do? It shuts down everything.

There's an email waiting in my inbox when I check it at 7 am, informing all staff that the stadium offices are closed, and everyone can work from home. A second email confirms that Charlie has no school, so I mentally shift gears to a snow day for the two of us.

I let the preteen sleep, and with a fresh cup of tea in hand, settle into the armchair by the front window where I can look out at the snowy landscape while sorting out my day. Gus comes into the room and lets out a small meow of discontent. Of course, this is the chair he likes to sit in all day as if it's his personal throne.

"Sorry, it's my chair today," I whisper, and he turns his back to me and stalks off, I assume returning to Charlie's room.

I manage to get an entire hour of work done before Charlie comes stumbling in, bleary eyed.

"Hey Mom. It snowed last night."

I laugh quietly. "Sure did. School's canceled and I'm not going into the office."

His face lights up. "Sweet. I'm gonna go get some breakfast."

He shuffles off to the kitchen, running his hand through his hair, making it stand straight up. Gus trots behind him, weaving in between his legs, and Charlie leans down and scoops him up, draping the damn cat over one shoulder.

"Feed Gus," I call out, earning a "'kay" in reply.

Turning back to my computer, I reply to a couple

more emails from my team to make sure everyone knows what to try and tackle today.

I've just hit send when my phone vibrates with a new text message on the table next to me. Scooping it up, my heart skips a beat to see Luca's name.

LUCA: Morning wonder woman. Are you and Charlie okay with the snow? Need me to come bring supplies, or shovel the driveway?

ISLA: You're sweet to offer, but we're fine I promise.

Charlie walks back into the living room and I drop my phone face down on my lap.

"Can I play some video games for a bit? Then maybe go outside with Miles? He says there's a good hill for sledding close by."

"Sure, brush your teeth and make your bed before you start, okay?"

He flashes me a thumbs-up before moving much quicker now to his bedroom. Once he's gone, I pick up my phone again and see another message from Luca.

LUCA: So there's not an innocent reason for me to stop by and see you. Damnit.

ISLA: LOL. Only if you're doing the same for all your other employees...

LUCA: Definitely not. Special treatment is for beautiful marketing consultants only.

LUCA: Still wish I could see you. We haven't had any time together. I miss you.

LUCA: And now that I sound like a needy idiot, I'll see myself out.

ISLA: No don't. You're not the only needy one, I miss you too. Trust me, I really do. But Charlie's here, and he still doesn't know about us.

I watch the three dots bounce while biting my thumbnail. Somehow, I know what he's going to say. I just don't know how I'll reply.

LUCA: When do you think you'll tell him? I don't want to pressure you, honestly. But it would make things at least a little easier if he knew, wouldn't it?

ISLA: It would, I know. And I will tell him soon. It's just not easy. He's never seen me in a relationship before and I'm not sure how he'll take it.

LUCA: I understand. And it's your call. You're his mom. But selfishly I hope you tell him soon. He's a good kid, I'd like to spend more time with him. And you.

ISLA: Thank you. For understanding and for saying he's a good kid. I promise I'll find a way to tell him soon.

LUCA: Well, maybe we can talk later today? Video call? I'm sure we have something "work related" to discuss… ;)

ISLA: Charlie's going out sledding with friends in a couple of hours. I'll call you then.

LUCA: Can't wait, baby.

27
LUCA

I'm a patient man. A calm, relatively steady one, who doesn't get anxious or overthink things often. Which is why the fucking obsessive level of overthinking I'm doing about me and Isla is driving me insane.

I've barely slept these last few nights, going around and around in my brain, wondering if the reason she won't tell Charlie about us is because she's not sure about us herself. I mean, part of me can understand that. It's not like we've had any time to progress our relationship, what with how busy we both are at work, plus the whole sneaking around thing. Telling her son would help with that, but only so much.

The problem is, even with how hard it is to get Isla alone, every chance I do, I find myself falling for her even more. She's making me see the possibility of a future where I'm not alone. Where I can open myself up to a partner, a family, love. She's making me question why I ever thought I *couldn't* have that. Or was it just that I resigned myself to it, with no real reason behind it except not finding the right person.

Because the right person was a single mom a decade or so younger than me.

"Luca? Can I ask a huge favour?"

My head snaps up at the frazzled voice of the woman weaving her way into my heart.

"Of course. What can I do?" I take in the dark circles under her eyes, the pen sticking out of her messy bun, and the nervous way she's twisting her fingers together.

"Okay, so this is borderline inappropriate for me to ask, but Juniper is busy, my mom can't get here in time and you're the only other person he knows."

I get up and move to stand in front of her, mindful of the open door to the rest of the offices and where I place my hands. The sides of her shoulders feel innocuous enough.

"What do you need, Isla?" I ask calmly, staring into her eyes. I feel her sag under my touch and ache to pull her into my arms for a real hug.

"Charlie just got home from school, and now he wants to go skating with some friends downtown. I guess there's an outdoor rink or something? But he needs a ride and I'm nowhere near done with the plans for the open house and the printer needs final files for the autograph posters before 4 pm and—"

I interrupt before she can go any further. "I got it, wonder woman. I'll drive him. No problem. Where is he?"

Gratitude is etched across her face as she breathes an audible sigh of relief. "Thank you. You're saving my butt.

He's at home. But I'll tell him to get ready as soon as you leave."

"Great. I'll head over there now and pick him up. Need me to pick him up again later? Or are you going to be able to head home at a reasonable time?" I let my hands fall from her shoulders when Gabe walks past, and stuff them in my pockets instead.

"I'll make sure I leave in time to pick him up." Stepping forward, Isla lifts a hand and rests it on my chest, looking up at me with warmth, gratitude, and wistful desire. "Seriously, Luca, thank you for doing this."

I decide to chance it. Checking over her shoulder that no one is in view, I bend down and peck a fast kiss to her lips. "Anytime. I'm glad you asked me." Then I step back before I give in to the temptation to take it a hell of a lot further. "Go and text Charlie, tell him I'll be there in fifteen minutes."

———

I may have put on a brave face with Isla, making it seem like hanging out with Charlie on my own was no big deal, but that was a lie. I'm nervous as hell as I pull up to their place. He's waiting outside, his coat folded over his arm.

"How's it going?" I say by way of greeting once he's slid into my car.

"Fine. Thanks for the ride."

I might not have much experience with preteens, but I was one myself. So I know the short answers and standoffish tone are normal when they're with someone they don't know very well.

"Not a problem," I reply calmly as I pull out onto the road. "So, ice skating, huh? I used to skate at that rink."

That earns me the reaction I'd hoped for, a shocked look on his face when his head whips around to look at me. "You went skating? But your leg."

I shrug, keeping my eyes forward. "Why should that stop me? Your missing arm hasn't stopped you from joining Little League, has it?"

"No."

I let him sit with that for a second. Isla mentioned to me once that Charlie doesn't have an arm prosthesis yet because he hated the feeling and look of one. He'd *rather have no arm than a plastic robot arm* were his words, if I remember correctly.

Can't say I blame the kid. When I was younger, prosthetic legs were hideous things that looked like overgrown doll legs. They've come a long way in appearance and technology, just as I've come to realize I don't give a fuck what it looks like, as long as my prosthesis lets me do what I want to do. But that anxiety about physical appearance is hard to let go of. Especially when you're young.

"Trust me, skating with my leg wasn't easy. I fell a *lot*. I only went a few times before I got tired of being covered in bruises from hitting the ice."

Charlie snorts, then looks away quickly. He's still staring out the window when he speaks again. "I asked my mom if we could talk to a prosthetist about getting an arm. There's a guy here in town, apparently."

"Yeah, Doc is awesome. He's been my prosthetist for years." Once again, my casual demeanor pays off and Charlie turns to stare at me again. "Tom Shivari? He's not a doctor, though."

I laugh this time. "True. I've always called him Doc. It's kind of a joke between us. He's cool, though, and knows his stuff."

"Do you still see him?"

"Yup. Any time I need something adjusted. Which isn't that often anymore. Did your mom tell you what I did before I bought the baseball team?"

"No."

My lips turn up. I've never wanted to be anyone's hero, but damn it, I'm allowed to be proud of what I've done. And if it can help a kid like Charlie, then I'm going to share it.

"I designed a microchip that analyzes gait patterns in amputees in real time. It can help them adjust things quickly so less appointments and prosthetic adjustments are needed."

"That's so freaking cool." The awe in his voice makes my smile grow.

"Thanks. Doc, I mean Tom, was the guy who helped me test it out on myself. Like I said, he knows his stuff."

"Would you...would you come to my appointment with him?"

I try to hide the flare of surprise at his question. Before I can respond, he continues.

"It's just, my mom is super nervous about it. I think because I was such a pain about prosthetics when I was younger, so she's worried this is gonna be bad. It would be cool to have someone who gets it to come with us so, like, you can ask the questions we might not think of. But I get it if you're busy." He looks down at his lap, having mumbled the last part.

"If you want me there, and your mom's okay with it, I'll be there."

"Cool."

I'm honoured Charlie trusts me enough to ask that of me. But also scared as anything. What if I let him down? What if I'm not the guy he needs? Sure, it's just an appointment, but it means a hell of a lot more.

"So, you and my mom. What's that about?"

I am in no way prepared for that question, but I manage to hide my shock fairly well, I think. "What makes you ask that?"

Out of the corner of my eye, I see him shrug. "I dunno, exactly. But ever since we moved here, she's been happy. More happy than I've seen her. And you guys are, like, *always* together. And I know you text each other. She thinks I don't know it's you, but I'm not stupid. And she left her phone unlocked one time and I saw your name. She smiles when she texts, and I think it's you."

I blow out a slow breath. Fuck, I wish I knew what Isla would want me to say. Or what—if anything—she's told Charlie. But from the way he's phrasing things, I'm going to assume she still hasn't talked to him.

"Your mom is a wonderful woman. She's doing great work at the Thunder."

Charlie scoffs. "Dude. I'm not talking about her work."

I pull up to a stoplight and sense him turn to look at

me. When I glance over, the fiercely protective look on his face makes me want to smile, but I don't.

"Are you dating my mom?"

How do I respond without crossing the line? Isla should be the one to talk to him, but I don't want to lie, either. Damn it, this is hard. I think quickly and then hope like hell he accepts my response.

"I want to. I like her a lot. I like you, too," I add, starting to drive again, now that the light is green. We're almost to the ice rink now. "More than that, I respect your mom. Which is why she should be the one to talk to you about what's between us. I'll say this. I like her, I respect her, and I swear, I'll do whatever I can to make her happy."

"*Keep* making her happy."

I look over quickly again to see the smallest smile on his face.

"I think you're already making her happy, so if you keep doing that, then we're cool."

I pull up in front of Cedar Creek's outdoor ice rink and put the car in park before turning to face Charlie.

"Good to know. Thanks, Charlie." I offer up a smile of my own.

"Thanks for the ride, Luca. See ya."

I watch him climb out of my car and walk up to a couple of boys standing near the benches close to the skate rental shack. Then I draw in a full breath and try to wrap my head around what just transpired.

One thing is for certain. Charlie is way more perceptive than Isla seems to realize. And she's been avoiding the conversation about our relationship for no reason, seeing as he's already figured most of it out.

I pick up my phone and open up my text messages.

> LUCA: I know you're busy wonder woman, but just a heads up. Your kid is smarter than we've given him credit for, and he's figured out we're dating.

> ISLA: WHAT?! Omg. Tell me you're joking.

> LUCA: Sorry, I'm not. He just gave me the talk. Keep my mom happy or else.

> ISLA: Oh lord. I'm sorry.

> LUCA: For what? Having a son that loves you and has your back? Don't apologize. He's a great kid.

> ISLA: I'm still not sure about telling everyone else though.

> LUCA: I know. I'm not pressuring you. When you're ready, we'll go public.

> LUCA: But at least you don't have to worry about how he'll take it.

> ISLA: That's true. But I do still have to have a talk with him about us. Make sure he's really okay, and see if he has any questions or worries.

> LUCA: Good luck baby. I think it'll go fine.

28

ISLA

"DEEP BREATHS. You can do hard things," I whisper under my breath as I wait for Charlie outside the skating rink a couple of hours later. Maybe I shouldn't have been so shocked when Luca said Charlie had figured out we were dating. He's a smart kid, intuitive and observant.

Still, I had hoped to check-in with him about the very idea of his mom dating before it actually happened.

Too late for that now.

The passenger door opens, bringing in a gust of cold air and a red-cheeked preteen. "Hey Mom."

"Hi. How was skating?"

"Cool. Hard, but fun, I guess." He's staring down at his phone, scrolling through something with his thumb.

"Charlie." I put one hand on his leg to get his attention. "Can we talk?"

He makes a disgruntled sound but looks up at me. "Is it about Luca? Cuz I'm cool with you two. It's fine."

I blink several times. "Okay, I'm glad you're 'cool,' but I still want to talk about it. This is the first time in your life I've dated someone, and I really want to make sure you're comfortable with me having a man in my life."

The look of horror that covers his face is comical. "Oh my God. Mom. Please don't call it that. Having a man in your life?" He scrunches up his face. "That just sounds so weird. You have a boyfriend. Whatever. I dunno why you haven't had one before."

"Because you have always been the only man in my life, honey," I say, layering on the cheesy sweetness, and earning a full body shudder that has me laughing.

"Gross. Just don't, like, kiss and stuff in front of me and it'll be fine. Can we stop talking about it now? Please?"

"For now. But I need you to promise me something," I say once I've stopped giggling.

"What."

"If you feel weird about it, or have questions, or get annoyed, or anything, really. Please come to me. Talk to me. You're still my number one guy." I risk his annoyance by ruffling his sweaty hair. "Your opinion matters a lot, kid."

A half smile tips his lips up. "It's cool, Mom. I like Luca, and he makes you happy." He glances down at his phone again. "Hey, can we order pizza tonight?"

And I guess that's that.

"Sure."

———

Now that Charlie knows about us, Luca suggested the three of us start spending more time together. Which is why today, on the first day of Charlie's winter break from school, we're driving to the stadium in the evening for some time in the batting cages. Charlie made a comment about wanting to work on his one-handed batting, and when I mentioned it to Luca, he suggested this.

Not gonna lie, it made my heart squeeze that he is so quick to include my son's needs and wants into our plans.

"Okay, this is really freaking cool," Charlie says as we step into the newly refurbished space on the bottom floor of the stadium.

"Thanks. I gotta admit, it was a little bit self-serving. I love using batting cages to get some energy out myself and wanted to be able to do that here." Luca comes to stand next to me, his hands in his pockets. He looks down at me with a soft smile. "Hey, wonder woman."

Charlie glances back at us from one of the batting tees. "No gross mushy stuff, got it?" He points his finger at us with narrowed eyes. "We're here to hit some baseballs."

Luca grins, lifts one arm, and drapes it over my shoulders. "How about a compromise? You head over to the rack and choose a bat while I give your mom a kiss. Then no more mushy stuff."

I choke, but Charlie tips his head toward Luca, then pivots on his feet and jogs over to the rack of shiny new bats.

"Hope that was okay to say. I really want to kiss you." Luca has stepped in front of me and is moving his hand to cup my cheek.

"Then why are you wasting time talking?" I reply impishly.

He's still chuckling when his lips land on mine. The kiss is short, chaste, but still fills me with butterflies.

"Time's up."

We break apart at Charlie's shout, and I turn to see him tugging on a helmet.

"C'mon, boss man. Turn on the pitching machine."

"You got it." Luca winks at me, then jogs over to the machine in front of Charlie.

Is it really this simple? To open my life, my son, my heart to a man? I guess when that man is Luca Calloway, yeah. It is.

29

ISLA

"Are you sure you want me to leave Gus?" I ask under my breath as my mom walks me to her door. "I can take him home tonight."

Mom waves her hand in dismissal of my offer. "It's fine, you and I both know the devil cat will be happier with Charlie."

I giggle quietly. Mom has experienced the wrath of Gus more than once, hence his nickname from my otherwise peaceful, animal-loving mother.

"Okay. Thanks." I lean in and hug her tightly, then call out to my son. "Hey kid, I'm leaving, can I get a hug?"

A minute later, he comes out from the kitchen, chewing on another one of Nana's gingerbread cookies.

"Promise me you'll eat a vegetable with your cookie?" I ask with an exasperated tone. My smile softens the request, and sure enough, Charlie just gives me wide grin, a couple of crumbs falling from his mouth. "Gross, kid."

"Bye Mom, love you." He throws his arms around me, one hand splaying on my back and the end of his other squeezing as tightly as he can.

"Love you, too. Be good, have fun tomorrow, and I'll see you both for dinner."

I kiss the top of his head, give my mother another hug as well, then head out to my car.

We came down to Dogwood Cove to spend Christmas with my mom, and the past couple of days have been lovely. On Christmas Eve, we got sandwiches at Camille's, then went to a Christmas tree farm and cuddled some baby animals, and we all ate far too many cookies. Christmas Day was lazy, as we opened gifts, ate even more cookies, then had a delicious dinner together.

And later that night, when Mom and Charlie were in bed, I video called Luca and opened the small box he snuck into my bag. The selection of gourmet teas and stunning porcelain cup was a beautiful present, and I felt guilty for not getting him anything in return. Until I thought of a perfect gift I could give him.

Which is why on Boxing Day, I told Mom a little white lie about wanting to go back a day early to have a little time for myself. She didn't question me and asked Charlie if he wanted to go to the movies with her and then spend one more night with her.

I wait until I'm safely on the highway headed toward Cedar Creek before I call Luca.

"Hey, wonder woman, how's your visit going?" His warm voice slides over me, making me shiver in the best possible type of anticipation.

"It was great, but I'm on my way back to Cedar Creek now."

"Oh?" There's no mistaking the pique of interest in his tone. "Is Charlie in the car with you?"

"Nope. He stayed behind with my mom."

There's a second of silence before Luca speaks again, his voice even lower. "Are you saying you're going home alone?"

"Yes."

"And are you wanting to stay alone?"

"Definitely not."

Luca groans. "Thank God. I'll be there soon, baby. Drive safely."

The rest of my drive goes by quickly, thank God. And as soon as I'm home, I spring into action. A quick tidy up around the house, and a shower to tidy up myself, is all I have time for. I've just shrugged on the one lingerie set I have, a barely-there satin and lace teddy with a matching satin robe that I tie around my waist, when there's a knock on the front door.

My heart thuds in my chest as I make my way there and undo the lock. I open it slowly and am greeted by Luca's warm gaze sweeping up and down my body before zeroing in on my face, his eyes hooded with lust.

"Christ, woman. Do you always answer your door looking like every man's wet dream?"

I step back to let him in before the cold air outside can turn my nipples any harder. "Nope. Just when I know it's the only man whose wet dream I want to be." I sashay ahead of him, putting an extra sway to my hips.

When I hear his muffled groan as his bag hits the floor, I smile like the cat that got the cream.

Seconds later, arms encircle my waist and he tucks his head into the crook of my neck, his lips finding my skin and pressing kisses everywhere he can. His hands start to roam up and down my body, and I arch back into his chest.

"Merry Christmas, Luca," I murmur, then gasp when he covers my breasts, his fingers and thumbs coming to pinch my already hard nipples. I reach behind me, grasping him behind his neck, twisting my head so I can find his lips and kiss him deeply. I'm greedy for his touch, his kiss, everything he'll give me. We haven't had sex since the conference weekend, and while fooling around in the office has a forbidden appeal, neither one of us has felt comfortable letting it go too far. All of that means I'm desperate for him.

So desperate that I can't wait any longer. Dropping my hands from where I was holding onto his hair, I drag him forward a few steps to my couch before turning in his arms and pressing myself against him. "I need you. Now. Please."

Luca presses a bruising kiss to my lips before slipping his hand under my robe. Finding me bare and wet, he groans, dropping his head to my shoulder. "Fucking hell, Isla. I need you, too. Four weeks is way too goddamn long to not have you."

My hands find the waist of his pants. Dark grey sweatpants that I'll admire his ass in later. Right now, they have to go. "Can we do it here? Like this?" I gasp as I push them down, only getting as far as the top of his prosthetic before his strong hands grip my hips and lift me up slightly onto the back of the couch.

"We're gonna find out," he says through gritted teeth. His eyes are wild with desire and I know without asking that mine are the same. I fumble with his underwear but manage to get them pushed down far enough to free his cock, which I instantly grab with my hands. "Damn baby, hold on," he says, chuckling, covering my hands with his. "Gotta get a condom."

Maybe I should be embarrassed by the whimper that escapes me, or the words I say next, because do I really need to make it so obvious how I'm feeling? But I don't care.

"We don't need one. I mean, I'm on a birth control shot. And you already know there hasn't been anyone but you." I hold my breath, waiting for him to respond.

Cupping my face, his expression softens into something so kind, so gentle, so...loving. "I haven't been with anyone else since my ex. And I got a full checkup a few months ago, so I'm good. But are you sure? After Charlie, I didn't want to assume you'd be okay without extra protection."

My heart swells so big, I swear it's going to burst out of my chest. This amazing man, even now, when we're nearly consumed with lust, thought of my past, my accidental pregnancy as a teenager, and wanted to make sure I was comfortable.

"I'm okay with it." I tug him back between my spread legs. "What I'm not okay with is you going anywhere that isn't right here." I lean forward, closing the small distance between us, and kiss him, intending to keep it light. But Luca clearly isn't having that. His tongue spears between my lips as he grinds his hips into mine. If it's an awkward or challenging position with his leg, he doesn't let on as he rocks into me, pressing against my core in a deliciously teasing way.

Once again, I push down his underwear, feeling his lips turn up underneath mine. This time, he doesn't stop me when I wrap my hand around his length, squeezing it lightly. He doesn't stop me when I notch him to my entrance. He doesn't stop me when I roll my hips forward, taking him inside.

No. He doesn't stop. He takes over, his hand coming to my thigh, gripping it tightly as he thrusts into me. I cry out against his kiss, feeling overcome by the sensation of him filling me. And yet, along with that overwhelming feeling is the undeniable sense of being settled, exactly where I'm meant to be.

"Fuck, you feel like heaven," Luca whispers when we stop kissing to breathe. "I missed you. Not just this," — he punctuates it with a push of his hips— "but you. Holding you. Being free to be with you."

I know what he's saying. And I feel the same.

But then he tilts my hips up, driving forward at a new angle and any coherent thoughts fly out of my head. My hands fall back, scrambling for purchase on the couch behind me. He won't let me fall. I know that. I can give myself over to the pleasure he's wringing from my body, one slide of his cock at a time.

"Oh God, Luca," I whine as he keeps moving, rocking himself in and out of me, igniting nerve endings I never knew existed. "I'm so close."

"Wait for me." His voice makes it clear that's a command, not a request. And my body responds, holding me in this place, this precipice where I know the fall will be delicious, but the anticipation is just as good.

He thrusts in a few more times before moving his thumb to my clit. "Now, baby. Now."

I detonate.

I scream out his name, my body shaking as I clench around him. I fling myself forward to hold onto his shoulders as we both ride out our orgasms, tangled in each other's arms. His shoulders are heaving with every breath as I feel the warmth of his release inside of me.

And as I slowly return to earth, relaxing into his body, he gently pulls my robe back up to my shoulders, kissing my skin as he covers me up.

I place my hands on his cheeks, tilting his head up to kiss me properly. His cock twitches inside of me and I can't avoid the giggle that escapes me.

"Really? Already? I thought older men needed more time."

He growls at me as he draws out. "Careful, Forrester."

I giggle again, but it quickly turns to a grimace as I feel the wetness between my legs. Before I can say anything, Luca whips off his shirt, moving it to clean me up before tossing it over by his bag and pulling up his own pants.

I slide off the couch and drape my arms around his neck, tugging him down for another kiss. I wish I never had to stop kissing him.

When I pull back, I look up at him with an innocent

expression. "So, serious question. How much time does a man your age need before he can go again?"

Somehow, I break free of his arms and dance out of range as his face goes from amused to surprised. Then he takes off, following me down the hall to my bedroom where I let him sweep me up into his arms.

"When there's a woman like you waiting? No time at all."

30
LUCA

"I thought you said you didn't need recovery time," Isla teases between gasps of air.

Sassy little brat...

As soon as her legs relax from the death grip they have around my head, I look up at her with a smirk. "Are you really gonna tell me that was not an enjoyable way to pass the short amount of time I needed?"

She slaps her hand over her eyes and giggles as I kiss my way up her body, eventually settling on my side next to her. I decided to remove my prosthesis when we made it to her bed, and any misgivings I had about it being awkward, or her being fazed by it, were quickly dismissed.

Isla has never once looked at me as anything less than a man. A whole, complete man. And that's an addictive thing for a guy who's fought demons in his head his entire life that have tried to convince him otherwise.

I draw circles across her warm skin with my fingers,

watching her smile up at me. How the hell did I get this lucky? I'm about to open my mouth and ask that very cheesy question when Isla pushes me onto my back and props her elbows on my chest, her head resting in her hands.

"You're spoiling me with orgasms," she says with a satisfied-sounding sigh.

I stroke her hair back from where it's falling into her face, loving how she tips her cheek into my palm. So trusting, so open. "It's not spoiling when it's what you deserve."

Her eyes, which had been drifting shut at my caress, snap back open. "Good point. I think it's time you get what you deserve, as well."

I stare at her, transfixed, as she shimmies down my body, copying my earlier move of kissing her way across the planes of my stomach, down past the V of my hips, and then, as she tongues the tip of my cock, I groan, "Fuuuck." She looks up at me with mischief and lust in her eyes.

"We'll do that again, too," she says conversationally, and I choke out a laugh as she takes my entire length into her hot, wet mouth.

My head falls back against the pillow as I lose myself to the heaven that is Isla. But when I lift my head again and see her hand snaked between her legs, I snap back to awareness.

"Stop."

Isla freezes, turning wide eyes up at me. She slowly lifts her mouth from my dick. "What's wrong?"

"That pussy is mine to touch." I reach down and take

her arm, pulling it up toward me so I can suck the taste of her off her fingers. "Mine to taste." Then, sitting up, I lift her up enough to drag her up my body, and guide her to turn around so her delicious ass is in my face. I lean in and nip at her flesh before nudging her legs apart. "Mine."

My tongue swipes up her slit. And even though I just finished eating this perfect pussy not even five minutes ago, I'm hungry for more. I lick and suck like a starving man at a feast. Isla catches on immediately and returns to sucking my leaking dick. The vibrations that come when she moans with a mouthful of me are fucking transcendent. And dangerous for my ability to outlast her.

"Shit. I'm gonna come," I grind out before biting the crease between her ass and thigh again. I try counting to ten, I try recalling the code for GaitSync, I try anything I can to stave it off, but it's impossible. Especially when Isla doesn't let up, sucking and licking and pumping up and down on my cock until I explode into her mouth with a roar.

I come so damn hard, I don't even realize she's climbed off me until I feel her settle back in against my side. The sound of protest I make has her laughing, but my bones feel like Jell-o, and I can't bring myself to react.

"I wasn't done with you," I say, my voice thick.

"Don't worry, I wasn't planning on stopping anytime soon." Nails lightly rake up and down my chest, swirling around my nipples. "We have all night." She kisses my jaw, then my mouth. I reach up and cup the back of her head, holding her to me, pouring my heart into the kiss.

All night. It won't be enough. Already, I know that.

Isla moves to straddle me, plastering her body against mine. I push up slightly with my hips, rubbing my cock against her. I'm ready to go again, or at least I will be soon, especially with her writhing on top of me.

I move my hands to her hips and Isla lifts herself just enough to grab my cock and line it up with her entrance. Pushing up to her knees, she slowly lowers down onto me with a soft moan.

"Oh," she sighs as she starts to move. She rocks her hips slowly, clearly focusing on her own pleasure this time, and I am entirely here for it. Her movements are languid, her eyes half closed as she smiles down at me. "Your cock feels so amazing."

"Yeah? Good. I want you to use me, baby. Make yourself come on my cock. Can you do that for me?" I rumble, running my hands up and down her smooth thighs.

Her smile grows as she lets her head fall and continues rocking back and forth, leaning backward to rest her hands on my thighs. I bring one hand to where we're joined, rolling my thumb over her clit, making her gasp.

"Yes, just like that."

I keep it up, playing with her clit until she's panting on top of me, leaning forward this time, her hands planted on my chest as she bounces up and down on my dick. My hand is getting crushed between us but I'll be damned if I'm gonna stop before she comes.

"Luca," she whimpers. "Oh God. Oh God. Oh. Oh!" I feel her pussy squeeze around me and manage to tug my hand free so I can grip her hips tightly and somewhat take over, thrusting up and into her, using my leg to get as much leverage as possible. My orgasm comes seconds after hers, and her pussy is still fluttering around my cock as I let go inside of her.

The feel of her boneless body collapsing onto my chest is quite possibly the best feeling in the world. All too soon, she climbs off me carefully, padding into the bathroom to clean up. I hear the toilet flush, and the sink run, and then she's back, climbing onto the bed and curling up beside me.

"I don't quite know how it's possible, but that was even better than the first time," she says in a satisfied, sleepy voice.

"The first time tonight or the first time ever," I say with a tired chuckle as I tuck her in close. "Either way, I agree."

"I never knew sex could feel like that. Like with you, I know I'm exactly where I belong." She buries her face into my chest. "I'm sorry, that was so cheesy."

Can she feel how my pulse just sped up? I shift enough so I can tip her chin up before pressing a soft kiss to her forehead. "That wasn't cheesy. It was perfect. And it's the same way I feel when I'm with you." I kiss her again, breathing in the scent of her shampoo. "It's never been like this for me, either. I don't have to think about anything when I'm with you, I can just be. I can just *feel*. And that's a gift, Isla. One I treasure."

Her shining eyes and small smile say everything. It's the reassurance that I'm not alone in how I feel. In falling hard and fast and only want more. I start talking again before I lose my courage.

"I want you, Isla. I want this. I want to get to know

Charlie more. I want to hold your hand and walk down the street and take you out for dinner. I'm all in. And it's okay if you're not ready for all of that yet, I'll keep waiting. But I need you to know, I'm serious about us."

She doesn't answer right away, but when she does…

"I want all of that, too. I want you, Luca."

Any tiredness I might have been feeling disappears at her quiet, confident statement. I stroke my fingers down her cheek, staring at her with pure wonder. This amazing woman wants *me*.

"Rose and thorn for being in a relationship with me." I'm half joking when I say it, but underneath, I can still feel a shred of vulnerability. I need to know she really means it.

Isla just giggles, shaking her head slightly. "Everything you are, the way you make me feel, the way you are with Charlie, it's all roses and no thorns." She lifts herself up just enough to kiss me sweetly.

I drink her in. Then, there's no more hesitation in me when I swiftly move over top of her and show her with my body just what hearing that makes me feel.

Sleep is overrated, anyway.

31
ISLA

January brings with it a bitter cold front. Yet, all it takes is one look from Luca and I'm burning up inside. We're still keeping things quiet at work and in public, but we've had two more batting cage dates with Charlie. Watching the two of them interact has only made my feelings grow stronger.

Of course, their growing connection hasn't eased my worry that Charlie could be devastated if things don't work out with Luca and me.

But there's no more denying the fact that I'm falling in love with Luca, even if I'm not ready to say that yet. We text all the time, sneaking whatever stolen moments we can find while we're at work. And when we're not together, I'm constantly thinking of him.

Today is the first time I've hallucinated about him, though.

Charlie and I are sitting in the waiting room of the prosthetist we're seeing to discuss arm options when the door opens, and in walks Luca.

When Charlie jumps up and walks over to give him a fist bump, I blink back to reality. Not a hallucination. He's actually here.

"Hi," I say, careful to keep my hands at my sides and not reach out for a hug the way I want to. The warm expression on his face, coupled with the subtle wink, sends a flush of heat through me. "What are you doing here?" My eyes widen as something clicks into place. "Wait. Tom is your prosthetist. You mentioned him in your speech. Of course he is, it's not like there's a lot of them around here."

As I ramble, Charlie is looking at me like I just grew a second head, and Luca's wearing an amused smile.

"Yeah, I've been seeing Doc since I was a lot younger. He's the best. And I'm here because Charlie asked me to come." He turns and arches a brow at my son. "But I thought we agreed he would give you a heads-up."

Charlie has the decency to look chagrined as he turns to me. "Sorry. I totally forgot. But it's cool, right? I figured since Luca knows a lot about prostheses he might know things to ask that we wouldn't. And he knows Tom. Doc." He turns a grin to Luca. "Thanks for coming."

Luca's face softens. "No problem." Turning to me, he tilts his head to the side slightly. "Is it okay that I'm here?"

"Of course, it is," I say, fighting back the sting of tears. Blinking rapidly, I turn to Charlie. "But a heads-up would've been nice."

"Charlie Forrester?" An older South Asian man steps out into the waiting room, looking around. When his gaze lands on Luca, he lights up before he frowns slightly, obviously confused. "Luca, we don't have an appointment today, do we?"

Luca slings his arm over Charlie's shoulder. "Nope. I'm here with my buddy Charlie and his mom today. Moral support. Someone's gotta make sure you do your job right."

Tom, at least I assume it's Tom, laughs loudly, shaking his head. "Yeah, okay. Well, Charlie, come on back." Then, turning to me, he sticks out a hand. "Tom Shivari. You must be Isla?"

"Yes, nice to meet you. If it makes you feel any better, I only just found out about our third wheel myself."

Tom laughs again. "Excellent, someone else to keep Luca in line."

If Charlie's at all nervous about the consultation with Tom, he doesn't show it. Instead, my son wows me with how prepared he is. How did I not know he'd done so much research about prosthetic arms? Way more than what he and Juni showed me when he first brought this up.

He asks about different materials, hand attachments, considerations for balance, and so much more. Luca interjects a few times, and I simply sit there and try to absorb it all.

Then Tom asks Charlie a question that I would have assumed had a simple answer. And once again, my kid surprises the heck out of me.

"I'm impressed with how much thought you've put into this, Charlie. From the history your mom gave me, it seems you tried a prosthetic arm when you were much younger but didn't have a great experience. Can I ask what's changed and why you feel ready to try again? It will help me know what I need to do to support you being successful this time around if I know not only what went wrong last time, but also how it might be different this time."

Taking a deep breath in, Charlie fixes his gaze on the floor. His leg bounces, and it's the first sign that he's feeling anything but confident and excited.

"I've always loved baseball. Me, my mom, and my Poppa, we used to watch a ton of games on TV or go to live ones whenever we could. I'd watch the players and picture myself out on the field. With two arms."

I watch him swallow, and my hand flies over to Luca, who's sitting beside me, clutching his hand in mine, desperate for support. He squeezes it back, and I immediately feel settled enough to keep listening.

"I know there's guys who play with disabilities. Jim Abbott is my favourite player because he only had one hand, like me. I watch the Paralympic baseball games every time. But those guys have really good prosthetics. Like, crazy expensive good. And I was scared that I'd suck at baseball, even with an arm. So I decided not to bother. No arm, no risk of sucking at the sport I love."

My heart cracks in two. I knew he struggled with his confidence, he always has. I've done my best to help him find things he can excel at and encouraged him every step of the way to not let his disability hold him back from achieving anything in life.

How did I miss the fact that it was holding him back from what he loved most of all?

"Then we moved here and my friends convinced me

to come hang out at their practices. And the coach helped me figure out some stuff, ways I could still do things and sorta play one-handed." Finally, a smile comes back to his face. "But I know I could be even better if I had an arm. And now there's attachments that can hold a glove or a bat. I dunno if we can afford it, but I wanna try."

My son spins in his seat and looks at me with a pleading expression. "I'll help pay for the attachments, Mom. I'll find a job or do whatever. I just—"

Luca interrupts, looking at Tom. "How much are we talking, Doc? There was that hockey player you worked with a couple of years ago, that was in the news. Didn't you help him get set up with an arm that held a hockey stick? There's got to be something similar for baseball."

Tom nods, looking back to Charlie. "There are lots of options for athletes. But Charlie is right to bring up the cost. They're not cheap."

"What if cost isn't an issue?" Luca's voice is firm, and I know what he's about to say next, which is why I cut in.

"Tom, let's go ahead with measurements and get the process started for something today. I'm sure any prosthesis will be a lot better than what we tried when you were younger." I look at Charlie, who nods and gives me a small smile. "And then maybe we can get some quotes for the attachments for baseball. I'll take a look at our insurance coverage and we can figure out what we can do. Sound like a plan?"

Charlie's up and out of his chair in a flash, flinging himself into my arms. "Thanks, Mom." I hug him back, closing my eyes and sending a silent prayer out to the universe that somehow, I can find a way to make this happen for him.

"There are some charities that provide funding for families needing medical devices," Tom says gently. "I can apply for them on your behalf."

I shoot him a grateful look. "That would be wonderful, thank you."

"My pleasure. Okay Charlie, let's get started."

As we walk out of Tom's office some time later, Luca hangs back with me as Charlie heads to the car.

"Isla, let me pay for whatever Charlie needs."

I shoot him a quelling look. "That's generous, but unnecessary. I can take care of my son's needs."

He shifts on his feet. "I know you can, you're fucking wonder woman. But I have the money. I can do this for you."

We come to a stop outside, a few feet away from the car. Keeping my voice down I say, "I know you can, and I appreciate that you want to help. But I can't just accept you spending that kind of money." *No matter how much I want to.*

He gives me a look that tells me he won't let it go quite that easily, but I just stare right back at him.

The tension is only broken when Charlie opens the car door and shouts at us. "I'm hungry, can we go get burgers?"

———

"Lunch is on me," Luca announces when we slide into a

booth at Dot's Diner, giving me a look that all but dares me to protest.

I don't. Instead, I smile and say, "Thank you."

"I'm starved," Charlie says, scanning the menu. "I could eat one of everything."

"That sounds familiar."

I look up to see Dottie standing next to the table. "The appetite of boys is a thing to behold."

She laughs, leaning down to give me a quick hug. "That it is. I take it this is Charlie? And who might you be?" she says, looking to Luca. Then her brow furrows. "Wait a second. Luca Calloway? I heard you were back in town."

Luca stands and puts out his hand. "That's me. I'm sorry, I don't remember if we've met."

Dot waves him off after shaking his hand. "You wouldn't, it's fine. But I've seen your face in the paper a few times recently. And I think you went to school with my son Troy Barbieri. I think you're the same age. He's working in the kitchen for me now."

Luca's face breaks into a grin. "Troy's here? Yeah, I remember him. We used to hang out quite a bit."

Dot smiles warmly. "I'll let him know to come say hi. Now, what can I get y'all to eat?"

We place our orders, and Dot walks off with a promise to bring Charlie a milkshake on the house.

"Mom, what is she wearing?" Charlie whispers under his breath.

"It's called a poodle skirt. Dot likes them."

His eyebrows raise in a typical preteen expression that

clearly shows he thinks it looks weird, but thankfully, he doesn't say anything else about Dot's clothing. And when she comes back with water for all of us and a strawberry milkshake for Charlie, he gives her a very polite "thank you."

"Charlie, what do you think would be the hardest thing to do in baseball with a prosthetic arm?" Luca asks suddenly. He's leaning forward across the table, staring at my son intently.

"Um." Charlie takes a slurp of the milkshake. "I mean, throwing is the obvious answer 'cause it takes so many different muscles and stuff. But I can throw pretty good with my natural arm, so that's no big deal to me. I guess, probably batting. Even if you learn to swing one-handed, it's hard to get enough strength and speed. Coach Rhett taught me how, and I tried a bunch, but it's hard to always know exactly what isn't working and how to fix it."

Luca nods, then leans back. "Right. Feedback. Just like gait analysis. Huh."

"What are you thinking?" I ask.

"Nothing."

"Calloway, holy shit. It is you." An absolutely giant man approaches the booth with a wide grin.

Luca pushes back from the table, and the two men engage in a backslapping hug that makes their old friendship obvious.

"Troy. It's good to see you, man."

The two of them immediately start talking about high school memories, and Charlie tugs on my arm. "Mom, I see a couple friends over at the counter. Can I go say hi?"

"Of course. Just keep an eye out for when the food arrives so you can come back to eat."

"'Kay." He slides out of the booth and walks over to the two boys sitting on stools with milkshakes in front of them. I watch them for a minute, my heart feeling all warm and fuzzy seeing my son happy.

The thought that I might have to dash his hopes if the prosthesis he wants is too expensive douses those feelings.

"What's going on in that beautiful head of yours? You were smiling, then suddenly you stopped."

I look up to see Luca sitting across from me again. "Nothing," I reply too quickly, and Luca's expression tells me he sees right through me.

"Will you at least consider letting me help?" he says quietly.

I look down at the table, focusing my gaze on a small scratch in the bright-white laminate. "I don't know," I answer honestly. "I love that you want to help Charlie, but..." I trail off as a warm hand reaches over and covers mine, squeezes it quickly, then retreats.

"I'll back off for now. But please think about it?"

Lifting my gaze to meet his, I nod.

"I will."

Dottie's cheery voice is the perfect interruption. "Alright, who's hungry?"

32

ISLA

"Isla…"

My attention snaps back into focus from the constant worrying about how I'll pay for Charlie's arm. The quote Tom gave me made my gut churn, and I've spent the last week looking at options for taking out a loan, as well as learning more about the charities that offer funding for this sort of thing.

Gabe is standing in front of my desk, and it's clear that isn't the first time he's said my name, which makes a blush creep up my neck.

"Sorry. What did you need?"

"Are you solving the world's problems or simply lost in a really good daydream? Either way, I just wanted to check-in before I head home." He holds up one hand and starts checking things off as he continues. "The press release for the charity game is in your inbox to be reviewed and approved. We've got the Dogwood Cove Animal Shelter and the Cedar Creek Wildlife Rescue on board. I have to say, the idea of making it an animal adoption event at the same time was genius, and your friend from the rescue organization is bringing some animals that can't be rereleased into the wild as well. And the social media campaign is ready to go, pending your approval."

I manage a small smile. "Thanks for the update, Gabe. Have a great night." He turns and leaves my office, and my mind immediately goes back to running the numbers on how the heck I can manage to pay for Charlie's prosthesis.

If I had a permanent job, one with extended medical benefits, this would be easier. But my contract with the Thunder is up in just under four months, and I have yet to decide what to do next.

Luca has hinted strongly at wanting to hire me as the permanent head of marketing. But the idea of dating my boss long-term makes me incredibly uncomfortable. The problem is, the Cedar Creek job market is not exactly booming. Not for someone with my education and skills, at least.

My thoughts circle back once more to Luca's offer to pay for Charlie's arm. I honestly don't know what to do. Do I want my child to have the very best? Yes. Do I want to owe the man I'm dating for making that happen? Definitely not.

Just then, my phone starts to vibrate with an incoming call. Seeing that it's the prosthetist's office, I answer quickly.

"Hello?"

"Isla? It's Tom Shivari. I have some news." He sounds

excited, and my brow furrows as I wonder what it could be.

"Okay, I'm all ears."

"One of the charities I applied to for funding just emailed me, and they accepted your application. More than that, they're covering the entire cost of Charlie's arm and the attachments he needs to play baseball."

"What?" I cry, sitting up in my chair. My hand is trembling as I lift it to cover my mouth.

"It's a charity that focuses on inclusivity in youth sports. I'm looking at the acceptance letter now, Isla, hang on. I'll forward it to you."

A few seconds later, it pops up in my inbox, and I open the email. My eyes are blurry with tears as I read the message that confirms Let's Play Canada is paying for Charlie's prosthesis.

"Oh my God," I whisper.

"So, no worries on getting the deposit to me. I'll get everything going on my end and let you know when we've got an idea on timing. How does that sound?"

"Amazing. Thank you, Tom. Thank you so much." I can't keep the emotion out of my voice.

Tom's warm chuckle comes down the line. "You're welcome, Isla, but all I did was fill out the application. This is great news, though. I'm sure Charlie will be thrilled."

"He definitely will be."

We hang up a minute later, and I look up the phone number for the charity. My heart is racing as I dial it.

"Thanks for calling Let's Play Canada, this is Stacey, how may I direct your call?"

I take a deep breath. "Hi, my name is Isla Forrester. I was just told that your charity is covering the cost of my son Charlie's prosthetic and I wanted to say thank you."

The woman on the end of the phone makes a delighted sound. "Oh hi, Isla, thank you so much for calling. We were thrilled to be able to fund your son's request. Actually," —she laughs lightly— "we were able to approve all of our recent requests with full funding, thanks to a new donor who stepped forward."

My jaw drops. "Really? That's incredible."

"It truly is. With their donation, we've provided funding to over twenty families in the Vancouver Island area. That was the donor's only request, that funding stay local to where he lives."

As soon as she says that, I know exactly who the donor is.

I swallow, my throat suddenly dry. "I'm so happy for all of those families, and again, thank you for approving my son's application."

"It was truly our pleasure, Isla. Take care."

The call ends, and I let my phone fall into my lap, only to have it drop to the floor when I abruptly stand. Leaving it where it is, I walk swiftly down the hall to Luca's office.

"How much money did you donate?"

He looks up from his computer. I watch his face go from confusion, to understanding, to a cautious sort of hopefulness, all in the span of a few seconds.

"To what, exactly?" he asks, and I choke out a laugh.

"Don't be obtuse. You know what I'm talking about."

He pushes away from his desk, stands, and moves

slowly around to the front of it. Not coming close or touching me, as if he knows I'm a bundle of emotions that could explode at any time but not having a clue as to whether or not those emotions are happy or upset.

"I made an anonymous donation to a charity that supports an initiative near and dear to my heart."

"You donated enough money to pay for the funding requests of over twenty families, Luca," I whisper, feeling tears build behind my eyes again. "That's a lot."

He takes a cautious step forward and lifts his thumb to brush away the first droplet to break free. "I have a lot of money and I wanted to do some good with it. And I hoped this would be a way to help you and Charlie that you could accept."

There's no stopping the tears now. Pride be damned, I can't be mad at him for this. I lift up on my toes and press a kiss to his cheek. "Thank you," I whisper.

When I lower back down, I lean in and wrap my arms around his waist. I can feel the thump-thump-thump of his heartbeat beneath my cheek as I just breathe him in. This incredible, kind, generous, and thoughtful man, who has made my son's dream come true and helped so many others at the same time.

And my heart fills with an emotion I've never felt before.

I'm in love with Luca Calloway.

The song playing from his speakers changes into something instrumental, slow and moody. Luca's hand trails down my spine to rest at the small of my back as he takes my other hand in his and lifts it to his lips for a kiss.

"Dance with me?"

A small laugh escapes me as my gaze darts toward his still-open office door. Letting him hold me the way he has been was risky enough. But dancing? Then again, it's late enough that the office is probably empty. It's highly likely we're the only two people in the building, aside from the nighttime cleaning staff.

"Don't think about it, just dance."

I blow out a shaky breath. "Okay."

We slowly start moving. It's nothing fancy, just a swaying motion, side to side. But gradually, I feel my body relax again, and when he rests his cheek on the top of my head, it's natural for me to soften into his chest. Our hands are clutched close together, resting over his heart as he moves us around in a circle. The low music, dim lighting, and steady rhythm of his heartbeat makes the rest of the world disappear. It's just us, suspended in this one perfect moment.

The song ends, moving into another, this time with a slow, seductive rhythm. Luca's grip on my back tightens almost imperceptibly, his fingertips digging in just above the curve of my ass. I shift against the bulge in his pants, which has been growing thicker and harder as we dance.

There hasn't been an opportunity for us to be intimate in a couple of weeks. Between my responsibilities with Charlie, and his with the team, finding time for just the two of us is a challenge, to say the least. I know how much I'm missing the feel of him holding me, being inside of me, and I know he misses it, too.

Which is why I dig deep to find the courage to seize this opportunity. Breaking free of his hold, I ignore his look of confusion and turn, walking to his door, which I close and turn the lock. When I spin around to face him, he's leaning back against his desk, a knowing look heating his gaze.

"Why, Ms. Forrester. Are you wanting to engage in some scandalous workplace behaviour?"

I arch my brow and put an extra sway in my hips as I close the distance between us. "Is it still scandalous if there's no one around to catch us?"

As soon as I'm within reach, he's snagging me by the waist and pulling me flush with his body. "Does it matter?"

I'm already shaking my head when he dips down to kiss me, long and deep, erasing any lingering thoughts except one.

I want him.

Luca spins me around, then lifts me up so my ass lands on his desk. "I've dreamed about having you here, spread out over my desk." His hands run up my thighs, bunching the fabric of the skirt I'm really glad I chose to wear today. "If you would accept my offer of a permanent job here, think of all the opportunities." He waggles his eyebrows, but instead of laughing like he probably expects me to do, I shake my head.

"Luca, we've talked about this. I can't be in a relationship with you and work for you permanently. You know that I already feel uncomfortable about it even now, and my contract ends in a few months. If I took the permanent position, you'd always be my boss, and I... we..." I trail off, unable to put it into words. If I stay working here, I would have to end our relationship.

"Okay. Okay, I'm sorry." He cradles my face in his

hands. "I'll stop bringing it up. I don't want to lose you or what we have. I'm just not good at feeling helpless." He sighs. "And I'm incredibly jealous of the lucky company that ends up snatching you up."

I cover his hands with mine, sliding my face sideways so I can kiss his palm. "I appreciate you wanting to help. But I won't change my mind on this. I'm choosing to be with you, which means my time working for you is up in April."

He gives me a chagrined smile. "Understood. Now, have I totally ruined the mood?"

I move my head from side to side slowly. "No, I think we can bring it back." I wind my arms around his neck and pull him in for another deep kiss. My head automatically falls to the side when he starts to trail his lips down my neck.

Then he starts to crouch, and I stop him with a hand to his chest. "Wait. I have an idea." I hop off the desk and quickly walk around to the other side before sitting on top of it again. Then, tossing a coy glance over my shoulder, I put my heel on his desk chair and push it out.

The emotions that flash across his features stun me. Surprise, awe, gratitude, lust, and dare I say it, something akin to love?

"Have I told you how much I admire your forward-thinking mind?" he says in a conversational tone as he rounds the desk himself, unbuttoning his shirt as he goes. He takes a seat, but the chair is pushed away from the desk. Leaning back, he finishes removing his shirt, all the while looking at me with a stare that has me burning up inside. "So creative, detail-oriented, and always thinking of the impact on others."

Out of nowhere, he lunges forward, grabbing the edge of the desk and pulling himself in close. A hand reaches behind my neck and tugs me down to meet his lips for another kiss. Then he goes for the hem of my skirt.

"Lift your hips."

I do, just enough for him to shimmy my skirt up so it bunches around my waist. Luca groans when he sees what I can only assume is a dark patch on my pale green underwear.

"You're so fucking wet for me, aren't you? Needy, desperate, and so ready."

I'm whimpering and nodding with every stroke of his thumbs on my inner thighs. "Yes. Please, Luca."

He reaches for my panties, and in a move I thought was only in books and movies, tears them from my body before dipping his head down and licking a path up my slit, making me cry out. My orgasm is hovering just out of reach, and I know it won't take much to bring it closer. Sure enough, as soon as Luca sucks my clit into his mouth, his teeth just barely grazing over the already sensitized nerves, I come undone, my arms shaking as I call out his name.

Despite the intensity of my release, I recover quickly. Because as wonderful as that was, I need more. I throw myself forward, fully trusting him to catch me as I land in his lap, my legs straddling his waist. My upper body is still clothed but his is bare, and I pepper kisses all over his chest while I frantically try to undo his pants.

Luca meets my intensity, his own fingers deftly undoing the buttons on my blouse and pushing it down my arms, forcing me to abandon my work so I can shrug it off. But I get his pants open, and then I'm the one to give the instruction as I climb off his lap.

"Lift."

He quickly shoves his pants down before pulling me back onto him, right over his rock-hard cock.

"I want to take my time with you, baby, but I can't wait right now."

"I know, I need you. Now," I pant, lifting myself just enough to lower back down, letting his cock fill me.

"Fuck." He drops his head to my shoulder as we breathe together. Then I start to move. Rocking my hips back and forth, I glide over his shaft. Luca grunts out my name, his fingers digging into my hips. My own hands are roaming all over his chest, his strong shoulders, the soft strands of his hair, memorizing the feel of every inch of him until it's burned into my soul.

This time, he reaches his climax first, thrusting up into me with a roar, but it isn't long before I feel my core tighten and then my head falls back as I moan.

We stay where we are, connected in the most intimate way possible for several long moments after. My head is resting on his shoulder, my fingers idly drawing circles over his skin.

The realization of just how strongly I feel for him comes back to me. I know, without a doubt, that Luca will never push me for more than I'm ready for. I have to be brave. I have to prioritize my own happiness for once.

"I think we should tell the team about us this weekend when they come in for the photo shoot."

His hand, which was lazily stroking up and down my spine, stills. "Really?"

I nod, which, even if he can't see, he can feel. "Yeah." Lifting my head, I dig deep, finding that well of strength and courage that has gotten me through so much in my life. "You matter to me, Luca. A lot. My feelings are strong and only getting stronger. I'm still scared about how people might judge me, but I need to stop letting that stand in the way. I want to be with you. You said it that night, just after Christmas, that you're all in. Well, I am, too. It's time we let everyone know."

33

LUCA

"You're sure you're ready for this?" I ask Isla under my breath as we leave my office, heading down to the locker room to meet with everyone before the players take part in a photo shoot for a baseball season calendar that will double as a fundraiser for the Cedar Creek Wildlife Rescue. Apparently, the team will have photos taken all over the stadium, including outside, despite the dusting of snow, with all kinds of rescued wild animals, including baby otters that Isla is far too excited about. Isla and her friend Juniper claim the six-month calendar will be a test, if it sells well then she's urged me to consider making it an annual collaboration.

Isla narrows her eyes at me and lets out a small huff. "That's the fourth time you've asked me in the last two days. And what has my answer been each time?"

I duck my head. Okay, so maybe I'm going overboard with wanting to make sure she's truly comfortable telling everyone about our relationship.

Isla's hand comes to just above my elbow and she

squeezes it gently, leaning into my side. "Are you sure you're ready? Because it's not all about me, Luca. If you'd rather wait..."

I cut her off with a shake of my head. "No, not at all. I can't wait until I don't have to hold back from touching you or kissing you." We come to a stop at the elevator bank, and I turn to face her. "I'm ready for the world to know how I feel about you."

I love her.

It's way too soon to say anything, though, so I keep that part to myself. The elevator doors open and we step inside. The short trip down two floors to where everyone is waiting for us seems to take forever. Or maybe that's just my impatience. We came up with a loose plan and asked all the players to meet down in the locker room for a quick check-in before the photo shoot. I'll announce our relationship and make it clear that things started well after Isla's hiring, and that her work for the team has nothing to do with us being together. Not that her work can't stand on its own, but she asked me to say that, wanting there to be no misunderstanding.

I only hope no one reacts poorly. I've got a lot of faith in the team but you never know. And Isla has faced more than her share of condemnation for things she doesn't deserve. For that matter, so have I. And I'm definitely not wanting to experience that ever again.

The hum of chatter reaches our ears as soon as we step out of the elevator. But even over that, I hear Isla draw in a shaky breath. Reaching down, I take her hand, threading our fingers together. *Here we go.*

I push open the door to the crowded locker room,

and we make our way to the front of the room where Rafe and Levi are standing. Levi notices our hands first, his only reaction being the raising of his eyebrows.

"Hey everyone, thanks for coming in a little early," I project my voice loud enough to cut through the chatter. It doesn't take long for everyone to fall silent. "I appreciate you all coming in today for the photo shoot, it should be a good time."

"You gonna be Mr. April, Luca?" Cal calls out from the crowd, earning a few chuckles. While a part of me is surprised that's the first comment, and not something about the fact that Isla and I are still holding hands, I push that thought away, and grin good-naturedly. "Nah, I don't want to steal the limelight from all of you."

The laughter is louder this time and I have to raise my free hand to get them to settle down. "Before you cuddle up with a raccoon in front of the camera, Isla and I wanted to let you all know something. I believe in always being upfront and honest, especially with those of you who have given so much to this team." I glance down to the woman at my side. "Isla and I have been seeing each other outside of the office."

I pause, waiting for the outburst. But it never comes. When I look around the room, all I see are small smiles on everyone's faces. Strange, but not in a bad way. I continue with the script Isla and I agreed on. "I hope you all know that integrity is very important to me, so let me be perfectly clear. She was hired well before there was anything between us. There were no blurred lines, no gray areas. Nothing inappropriate or unethical happened in the hiring process. But over the last few months, we started to develop feelings for each other. I don't have to tell any of you how amazing she is, and I don't need anyone telling her how much she's settling by being with me."

Finally I see a response, but it's definitely not anything I was expecting. The team is all smiles, *smug* smiles, even. Then Foxxy yells from the back of the room, "I called it, pay up, Griff!"

The room erupts into laughter and cheers.

"'Bout time you came clean."

"Congrats Luca, you're a lucky man."

"Don't let him get away with shit, Isla!"

"Finally! I fucking hate keeping shit a secret!"

Everyone starts laughing again and I peer through the rows of players to figure out who said that but can't figure it out.

What the fuck?

Clearing my throat, I turn to Isla and see her biting her lip like she's trying not to smile. She's obviously figured out the situation while I'm still putting the pieces together.

"Okay. What's going on?"

No one answers right away until Rafe steps forward, a look of amusement clear on his face.

"I think the guys appreciate you keeping them informed, but ah, well, I'm afraid you were mistaken if you thought it was a secret that you two were dating."

My jaw drops. "Seriously?"

Rafe winces, rubbing the back of his neck. "Yeah."

I look out at the players, most of whom are nodding. "You all knew." When I glance down at Isla, she doesn't look to be freaking out by this revelation. If anything, she seems relieved.

And I guess I am, too. So much for our concern about their reaction.

With a rueful grin, I say, "Well, alright then. Isla and I are dating. End of conversation unless anyone has a question."

Cal's hand shoots up. "Why'd you think you had to keep it a secret? We like you, we like Isla, and we're all adults. You two dating is no big deal."

The other guys all nod in agreement.

Isla steps forward to answer. "That was my decision. I didn't want to complicate anything, and dating the boss isn't always well received." She grins back at me. "Obviously, I was worried about nothing."

"Does this mean you're going to head up the marketing department permanently?" someone asks.

It's subtle, but I notice Isla's wince. She's still resisting me when I try to convince her to accept a permanent role here. I understand why, even if I don't like it.

"I'm not sure yet," she hedges.

"You better," Griff calls out. "We need you to make us look good."

"How about you win some games and make your-selves look good?" Isla fires back, and the guys all laugh. "Speaking of looking good, it's photo shoot time, boys."

34

ISLA

"Stop being a baby, Cal, it's just a bird!"

I bite my lip to stop from laughing as I watch Juniper glare impatiently at Cal, who's staring in horror at the large, yet remarkably calm, owl perched on the gloved hand of a volunteer from the wildlife rescue.

"Easy for you to say, June Bug," he mutters. "If that thing takes my eye out, I'll never forgive you."

I turn away as I hear someone call my name, still laughing to myself. Who would've guessed Cal "Pretty Boy" Prescott was afraid of owls.

Brady Dixon, Griff, Foxxy, and a couple of the other players are gathered in a close circle. At least these guys don't look scared.

"We need you to decide who gets which animal," Griff announces when I walk up.

Placing my hands on my hips, I arch a brow at them. "Are you seriously saying that as grown men, you can't come to an agreement?"

They look back and forth amongst themselves, but

no one says anything until Brady steps forward. I don't know the quiet newcomer all that well, but he seems like a good-natured and polite guy.

"The problem is, we all want the otters." He gives me a wry grin. "They're babies."

"Fucking adorable babies," Rowdy, one of the outfielders, pipes up.

"But you said we all had to have different animals," Griff adds. "So only one of us gets the otters. I said Foxxy should go with the fox, because, well, duh."

Foxxy narrows his gaze at his best friend. "Yeah? Well then, you should go with the raccoon since you're both fucking snack bandits."

The group erupts into a debate over who gets which animal, and all I can do is shake my head in disbelief for a couple of minutes as I come up with a plan on the fly.

Grown-ass men arguing over otters. They are pretty cute, I have to admit, but this is ridiculous.

"Okay, enough!" I clap my hands to get their attention. "Here's how it's gonna go. Foxxy, yes, you're with the pair of foxes in the dugout. The marketing potential for that is endless. Rowdy, you get the squirrels, be as silly with them as you want. They're inside, in the locker room. Griff, go and see Juniper, she's got a hawk that needs someone who can be calm. And" —I look at the remaining three players— "Brady is with the otters. Lucky, go put on some eye black, you're with the raccoon, also in the locker room, and Hiro..." I fix him with a hopeful look. "How do you feel about eagles?"

He shrugs. "Fine, as long as it doesn't bite my head off."

"Great. Go with Griff to find Juniper, she's with the birds of prey."

Hiro and Griff head off to find my best friend and Cal, and I turn to the others. "Well, you know your assignments, get going."

"And they call *me* lucky." Lucky throws his arm over Brady's shoulders good-naturedly. "Of course, the new guy gets the baby otters. Betcha didn't expect this when you signed on with the Thunder."

Brady chuckles. "Definitely not. I thought I'd be playing ball, not playing with otters." He grins up at me. "Thanks Isla, but why'd you choose me?"

I shrug. "Actually, Lucky's right. It wasn't about me choosing you, you did just get lucky. Rowdy's goofy enough to have fun with the squirrels. Foxxy was a given. I've seen photos of Lucky's eye black and knew that would be a great photo, so it was between you, Griff, and Hiro, and I went alphabetical. Dixon comes before Voss and Tanaka."

The guys all disperse, and I take a minute to regroup. With multiple different shooting locations set up throughout the stadium and facilities, there's a lot of moving parts today.

The photos with the birds will take place on the field, the otters and ducks are naturally in the medical treatment area, where the large tubs that will eventually be ice baths have been filled with slightly warmer water. The dugout and the locker room have also been commandeered for other photo setups.

As long as I don't have to break up any more arguments over who gets which animal, we should be good to go.

"Have I told you how sexy it is when you take charge?" Luca's voice is warm and low in my ear as his arms slide around my waist, tugging me back.

"Not recently," I tease, letting my body relax into his arms. "But let's save that conversation for later. We've got wild animals to wrangle."

"Do you mean the players, or the actual animals?" Luca retorts and I giggle.

"Both."

35
ISLA

"I DUNNO WHY YOU'RE NERVOUS." Charlie doesn't even look up from his phone. "You guys have been dating or whatever for a while now, what's different about tonight?"

I finally find the pair of shoes I've been hunting for in a box in the back of my closet and hold them up in triumph. Then, scooting backward, I turn and lean against the wall, pushing my hair out of my face.

"I'm not nervous. I'm…" I pause and consider what word to use. Because the truth is, I am nervous. It's our first date since telling everyone we were seeing each other just two days ago. "I want to have a good time."

Charlie finally glances over at me from where he's sprawled on my bed and raises one eyebrow. He mastered the trick a couple of years ago and loves to pull it on me. "And those shoes are gonna make it a good time? Okay." The eye roll he tries to hide isn't lost on me.

"It's not about the shoes. Those are just because they're cute and go with my outfit." I stand up and walk over to the bed, sitting down next to him. "And I'm not nervous."

Fake it till you make it, right?

Charlie rolls off my bed and moves to the doorway of my room. "Whatever you say. Can I order some pizza?"

"I already told you, Aunt Juni's bringing over dinner."

He tilts his head to the side, considering that. "Right. 'Kay. Then can I go play some vids?"

"Sure."

He hops off my bed and leaves my room, and I turn my attention to picking the right pair of earrings.

An hour later, Charlie's still in his room playing video games and Juniper is watching me put the finishing touches to my makeup. Luca's due to pick me up any minute, and the nerves I thought I'd laid to rest are back. Only this time, I have a far too knowing best friend watching me.

"Okay, how do I look?" I turn away from the mirror and twist back and forth for Juni's inspection.

"Absolutely stunning. Just don't forget to breathe." She stands and places her hands on my shoulders. "Enjoy tonight. You deserve a romantic date with your handsome man. And if you decide not to come home, that's just fine. Charlie and I are all good here."

It's tempting to take her up on that offer. Going back to Luca's place, making love and falling asleep in his arms, sounds dreamy. And not so realistic. I shake my head.

"That's not exactly the kind of impression I want to set with Charlie. Every time I go on a date, I stay out all night? Nope."

"It's not every time, but it could be this time."

I fix Juni with a look. "Stop. I'll be home by midnight. Luca and Charlie need to have some more time to get to know each other before sleepovers happen."

"Fine, be all responsible and stuff," she huffs.

Just then, there's a knock on the door, and Juni's eyes light up. "He's here. Quick, let me see your teeth."

After checking that I don't have any lipstick on them, and my breath is fresh and minty, I hurry to the door and open it.

Luca's standing in the doorway, wearing similar clothes to what I see him in at the office: charcoal slacks and a light grey shirt. But the top two buttons are open, baring a bit more skin, and his demeanor is less professional, more relaxed, and entirely too sexy.

He steps forward, cupping my chin and kissing me sweetly. "Hey, wonder woman, you look gorgeous."

"Thanks," I whisper, stepping back so he can come inside.

"Hey Juniper, how are you?" he greets my friend warmly.

"Good, thanks. You two have big plans for tonight?"

Luca turns to me with a soft smile. "Sort of, but they're a surprise for Isla."

"Hi boss man!" Charlie comes barreling in, stopping just short of the couch. "Hey Mom, Miles wants to know if I can go to the movies with him and some guys from the team tomorrow afternoon."

"I'm sure that'll be fine, let's talk about it more in the morning."

"Okay. Have fun tonight. Bye Mom, bye Luca." He turns and leaves as quickly as he came in.

"Love you," I call out, earning a muffled "love you" in return before his bedroom door closes.

"Don't worry, I'll make sure he gets off the video games and out here to play Monopoly with me soon." Juni starts ushering us toward the door. "You kids go and have fun."

"You'll want a warm coat, maybe some gloves." Luca stops me when I go to get my lighter jacket. I look at him questioningly, but he just shrugs. "Surprise, remember? But warmth is important."

I move to pull down my winter coat, grabbing a pair of faux suede gloves as well. Glancing down at the booties I spent way too long hunting for, I ask Luca, "Are my shoes okay or do I need snow boots?"

He chuckles and says, "Those will be fine."

Once we're in his car, driving toward the highway that leads out of town instead of toward the waterfront like I expected, I break down and ask, "Okay, where are we going?"

Lifting one hand from the steering wheel, Luca rests it on my leg. "Don't you like surprises?"

"Not really," I reply honestly.

"Okay, I'll tell you part of it. But can you trust me enough to let me keep some of it a surprise?"

I relax back into the heated seat. "Fine." I don't really want to ruin whatever he has planned, but I truly don't like not knowing what to expect.

"We're heading up the mountain for dinner. That's why you needed a warm coat. We'll be inside to eat, but I thought we could check out the stars while we're up there. There's meant to be a meteor shower later."

"Oh," I say softly, absolutely enchanted by the idea. "That sounds incredible."

He flashes me a quick grin and squeezes my leg. "Good. I'm glad. There's more, but I'm holding onto the details for later. Is that okay?"

"Yes." I cover his hand with my own and settle back. It's more than okay, it's perfect. The lodge up at the top of the small ski hill just outside of town has a restaurant I've wanted to go to but haven't yet. From what I hear, it's small, intimate, and romantic. I should've known Luca would think of something that is both public and private. We aren't hiding anything, but he's easing me into this by having our first date somewhere that's not too crowded.

Not much later, we pull into the parking lot up on the mountain. With it being early February, there's still plenty of snow up here. The ground is a dirty white, and I don't argue when Luca tells me to wait for him.

He opens my door, helping me out and immediately into my coat, which I do up with a shiver. "It's so much colder up here," I say, stating the obvious.

"I've got a blanket in the back for stargazing later, and we'll take some hot chocolate or tea out with us. And if it's too cold, we can skip that part."

I lean into his side. "Luca. I'll be fine, your date night planning skills are top-notch."

He exhales a small laugh. "Good. I want tonight to be perfect."

"It doesn't need to be perfect. It's already more than good enough because I'm here with you."

He pulls us to a stop just outside the door to the lodge and tips my chin up so he can kiss me.

"Nice line, Forrester."

"Well, I am good at knowing how to appeal to an audience," I tease. "A good one-liner is marketing 101."

His throaty chuckle follows us inside the warm, cozy lodge. We're escorted to a table next to the window, with a perfect view of the mountain and the twinkling lights of the town below.

Once we've given the waiter our drink order, I reach over and take his hand. "Thank you, Luca. This is incredible."

He doesn't answer right away, instead, he stares into my eyes. Then, less than a minute later, Luca blurts out, "Isla, I'm in love with you."

The horror that flashes across his expression is comical simply because it's so opposite of the calm, confident man he usually is. "Shit. I didn't mean to say that. I mean, I did, but not like this." He's adorably flustered, and as stunned as I am by his confession, I hope he can see the truth shining through the emotional tears building behind my eyes.

"I love you, too."

His shoulders drop in an exhale as he gives me a shaky smile, so at odds with the mature, steady man I've fallen for. "Thank fuck for that. I had it all planned. Later, under the stars, I was going to tell you. I've wanted to for a while, but I wanted it to be—"

"Perfect?" I interrupt, sniffing away my tears. "What did I tell you earlier? It doesn't need to be perfect."

Luca's up and moving around the table in an instant, and without a care for who might see or what they might think of our display. I stand to meet him for a long, slow kiss.

"I love you," he murmurs against my lips.

The sound of a throat clearing nearby has us parting to see the subtly smiling waiter with our drinks. "Sorry to interrupt." He sets the glasses down and then swiftly retreats, leaving us staring at each other, giddy and punch-drunk in love.

I let Luca guide me to sit back down, then, to my surprise, instead of taking his seat across the table, he moves his chair around beside mine, his back facing the rest of the dining room. Draping his arm over the back of my chair, he takes his other hand and gently cups my chin, leaning in and kissing me again.

"Good thing we're not trying to keep this a secret any longer. I'm pretty sure everyone saw that," I whisper, letting my head fall to his shoulder.

"A billboard downtown would've been more subtle," Luca cracks and we both start laughing quietly.

When our amusement settles, I lift my head, raking my fingers through his hair until my hand rests on the back of his neck. Staring into his eyes, I can see his love for me. And it makes my heart so full, it feels like it could burst.

"This was better than a billboard."

36
LUCA

I PULL into the driveway of Isla and Charlie's house, cut the engine, and sit in silence for a few seconds. It's funny, looking back at how just a year ago, I thought I was content with my life. I'm sure I was happy in Toronto, with my ex, her friends who became my friends, and the apartment we shared downtown. But that life was *her* life, and I've since realized I was really just a visitor.

But I had my research lab with my mentor from my postgrad degree and everything I needed at my fingertips to design and build whatever I wanted. Even after Gait-Sync was in its final stages, I was in the lab every day just tinkering, trying to come up with another idea. Another project to fill my time and occupy my mind. I can see now, that's all my life was. A series of moments, trying to pass the time, subconsciously hoping inspiration would strike or something would click, and I'd finally feel like I belonged wherever I was.

Not in a hundred years would I have expected to

finally feel that sense of belonging in a much smaller city on the opposite side of the country, surrounded by mountains. Much less with a single mom a decade younger than me who sets my soul on fire in a way I've never experienced before.

Even the last time I was in a serious relationship, I never envisioned a future where I'd end my day at an actual home. There was never talk of a family, buying a house, or moving out of the city. Yet, here I am, about to have dinner with Isla and Charlie at their home for the first time. We've spent plenty of time together over the last several weeks but never here.

They're a family. One that I'm lucky enough to get to be a part of, in whatever small way I can. And what really surprises me is just how much I want that. I'm not just in love with Isla, I'm in love with the possibility she represents. A future I hadn't ever dreamed of, and a future I could easily see myself being perfectly happy living. With her, Charlie, and hell, maybe even another kid if I'm not too damn old.

At that sobering thought, I exhale.

Kids. Family. Home.

The door to the house opens, warm light spilling out. It's Charlie, and he's raising his...right arm!

I get out of my car as fast as I can. "You got your arm!"

"Yeah! And Tom got the batting attachment. You gotta come out back and see." His obvious excitement bleeds into every word and I'm so fucking happy for him.

I follow Charlie back into the house where music is

playing, some candles are lit on the coffee table in the living room, and an enticing, savory aroma fills the air.

"Damn, what's your mom cooking? It smells incredible," I ask Charlie as I close the door behind me.

"Dunno what it's called, some chicken thing with these weird, shriveled tomatoes. It's good, though."

"They're not shriveled, they're sun-dried," Isla says, walking into the room barefoot. She comes right up to me, and to my surprise, kisses my cheek. "Hi."

"Okay, so remember, that's as much kissing as you're allowed to do in front of me. Got it?"

At Charlie's disgruntled statement, Isla spins and smiles sweetly. "Listen kid, you're gonna have to get used to a little bit of kissing. Especially if you're going to insist on dragging poor Luca right back outside into the freezing cold to hit some balls before dinner. It's still February, you know."

Charlie huffs and rolls his eyes. "Fine. Oh, did you warn him about—"

A loud hissing sound interrupts Charlie and all three of us turn to see a very large cat with its back arched, tail puffed, and yellow eyes staring into my soul.

"Gus," Charlie finishes. But before he can move, the cat suddenly relaxes its posture, then saunters over and weaves between my legs, even rubbing its head on my prosthesis underneath my jeans.

"Um, Mom? Is Gus okay?" Charlie whispers.

When I look at Isla, her mouth is open in shock. "I... I...I don't know." She turns to me, eyes wide. "That cat hates everyone except Charlie. Even me. What is happening right now?"

I give up on fighting my smile and shrug. "Guess I've been accepted."

Isla's the first one to start laughing, then Charlie and I join in. And it's quite possibly one of the best moments of my adult life.

Eventually, Gus stops lavishing me with attention and wanders off, his tail in the air.

"C'mon out back, Luca. Mom set up a net so I can practice my swing with some wiffle balls."

I dutifully follow Charlie through the kitchen, where Isla has returned to the stove and is putting on some vegetables to cook. In the backyard, sure enough, there's a tall net set up with a batting tee in front of it.

I zip up my jacket for protection against the cold, damp air as Charlie picks up a bat and clicks it into the attachment on the end of his prosthesis before taking a batting stance. He swings, connecting with the light-weight white ball and sending it flying into the net. He does it a few more times, each time hitting the ball on the tee, but I notice how he's having to compensate with his posture and adjust his prosthesis every time.

After four or five swings, he turns to me, a hesitant smile on his face as he rubs his elbow with his hand. "It's pretty cool, right? I don't know how to make it so it doesn't slip if I swing hard, though. I can hit the wiffle balls, but a real baseball would need more power, and I can't seem to get that."

I nod thoughtfully, my mind spinning with disjointed ideas and thoughts. "Do you have a real ball here? Can we try a soft toss approach so I can see?"

Charlie nods and jogs over to the patio where he grabs a couple of baseballs out of a bucket. He hands them to me and takes his stance again. Moving into position, I look at him. "Don't worry about power the first couple of times. Just let me see you swing at an actual toss instead of a tee."

"Got it."

I throw the ball. He swings and misses, just barely. The second toss, he chips the ball with the edge of his bat. I watch him take a deep breath in and out before retrieving the balls and bringing them back to me.

I grab some of the wiffle balls as well, just so we can do more tries without pausing to get the balls. "Keep trying. I see what you mean about the prosthetic slipping. It could be the grip or the angle that you're swinging."

"Or I just don't know what I'm doing 'cause I'm not used to swinging with two arms." Charlie sounds frustrated but also determined. "I know I need to keep practicing, but it's hard not knowing what I'm doing wrong. Tom said we could mimic batting at our next appointment, but it won't be the same as doing it for real."

That's when it hits me. I designed GaitSync so I could have real-time feedback on my gait and adjust as needed to avoid pressure sores and overuse issues. What if there was something similar, but for arms? Specifically, for athletes who need to understand how to adjust speed, torque, and pressure. Amputees can't rely on real sensory feedback from their skin and muscles, so we need the technology in our prostheses to give it to us.

My idea snaps into place. I can see it clearly. All the steps needed to develop the right type of microchip. Or if something similar already exists for professional athletes, how to adapt it for kids like Charlie.

I can do this. I can build this for him. But not here. I need the lab back in Toronto, at the university. I need my old mentor from university and the access he has as a professor to all the equipment and materials.

Most of all, I need time. The early days of developing GaitSync were long, solitary, and often sleepless. Fine, it didn't have to be that way, but the technology would've taken years longer to produce if I hadn't given it every-thing I had. Back then, I didn't have anything else competing for my time. Even when I was with my ex, I still spent anywhere from ten to fourteen hours a day in the lab. But now? Now, I have the Thunder. I have my parents. I have Isla and Charlie.

Except...the Thunder doesn't *really* need me. At least, not in person. I can join meetings via video conferencing, and Dom can manage anything here. My parents are good. And leaving would be for Charlie, so surely he and Isla would understand. Besides, it wouldn't be forever. Once I have the basic design sorted out, I could try and set something up on the West Coast to continue the work.

I'm so lost in my spiral of planning that I don't realize Charlie's still talking until he taps my arm.

"Dude, you okay?"

"What? Yeah. Sorry, I was thinking about some-thing," I say, giving myself a mental shake.

"No kidding," Charlie agrees, then he looks down,

scuffing the ground with his foot. "So, um, did you hear what I asked?"

Shit. "No man, sorry. I didn't. Can you ask me again?"

I watch his throat bob up and down as he swallows. Whatever he asked, it's important. I make sure I'm giving him my full attention.

He sucks in a breath and says, "There's a preseason exhibition game coming up in a couple weeks and Coach said I could pitch an inning. I've been working a lot on my left-hand pitching, and it's getting pretty good. Will you come watch?"

I'm sure I'm grinning like a fool when he stops talking. "Charlie, that's awesome. Of course, I'll be there. I'm honoured you asked."

He ducks his head down again, and I see his cheeks darken. "Cool. That's cool. Thanks."

"Hey, you two, dinner is ready."

The moment is interrupted by Isla's voice. I turn and see her standing in the doorway, backlit by the glow from the house. And I'm taken aback by the simple beauty of the moment. I want more of this. So much more.

"Coming," Charlie says before looking back at me. "Thanks again, Luca. For, like, tonight and um, you know. The game."

We move toward the house and I say, "Any time. And I mean it when I say that if you ever need to talk about your arm, or your prosthesis, or any of that stuff with someone who gets it, just call."

Charlie screws up his face in a grimace. "Old people call. How 'bout I text?"

I nudge him with my shoulder and growl, "You calling me old, kid?"

He laughs as we enter the kitchen. "I mean, your hair. My nana says only old people have grey hair!"

"Nana said what?"

I move over to Isla and kiss the side of her head. "Apparently your mother would think I'm very old."

Isla bites her lip, her eyes dancing. "I mean..."

"Brat," I mutter teasingly.

"I'm gonna go take off my arm," Charlie announces, hurrying out of the room.

As soon as he's gone, I spin Isla into my arms, dipping my head and kissing her properly for the first time all evening.

"Thank you for spending some time with him," she says after we break apart. Except I'm not done, and I close the distance, kissing her again.

"You don't have to thank me. I like Charlie. He's a great kid."

She leans back, and I chase after her lips, needing more. "I know he is. And I want to thank you. Because you're giving him something I can't. Someone who understands what his life is like. And that means more than I can say."

That sobers me instantly. How many times when I was growing up did I wish I had someone who understood how hard it could be, missing a limb? The idea of being that person for Charlie fills me with so much satisfaction, it surprises me. I never wanted to be anyone's hero. I'm not some inspirational story. But maybe I could be some kind of role model, or at the very least, a support for Charlie. Someone who gets it, who's willing to listen, not with sympathy, but with understanding.

And maybe I can use my knowledge and resources to help him do everything and anything he wants in life.

That's even better than being a hero.

37

ISLA

I TRAIL behind Luca and Charlie as they talk nonstop about who knows what. We're on the boardwalk, down at Cedar Creek's pier for the annual Maritime Fair. The market that's set up is busy, with music from buskers filling the air, along with the delicious aromas of fried food and treats. It's crowded, but not too much, the weather surprisingly mild for early March, with clear skies and sunshine instead of cold, dreary rain.

Charlie says something that makes the two of them laugh, and I smile fondly at the sight. Luca's dark-haired head is tipped down to be closer to Charlie's lighter-coloured one. Charlie's wearing his prosthesis today with a regular hand attachment he's not bothering to hide. And I know that's in part because of Luca. When he was over for dinner the other night, they talked for a long while after Charlie showed off his new batting attachment. And since then, I know they've exchanged several text messages. I love that Charlie has Luca in his life. Someone to connect with, someone to look up to, someone to help normalize his experience having a limb difference.

I'm used to facing judgment: as a pregnant teenager, as a single young mom, and as the mom of a child with a physical disability. I tried to shield Charlie from that judgment, but it was inevitable that he'd face it, too. And while he's mostly taken it in stride, I know firsthand how much it hurts to be looked down on for something you can't control. It's why I'm protective of him. Life has thrown curveballs at my son since day one, and I couldn't stop all of them from hitting and hurting him.

This relationship with Luca doesn't seem to be another one of those curveballs. It's obvious that Luca fits in our life a way I never expected anyone to. He's not just playing a role, he seems to truly love being with us and the life we live as a family.

How did my life become so freaking amazing?

"Because you are so freaking amazing."

Luca's murmur catches me off guard. I didn't realize I had spoken out loud, and I definitely wasn't aware he had come back to stand near me.

"Charlie needed the restroom," he continues, dipping his head down to kiss me. "And I hope you know you deserve all the happiness anyone could have."

Charlie bounds back up to us before I can respond. "C'mon Luca, let's go check out the trading card stall."

He drags Luca away, and I move to catch up. Listening to the two of them, I definitely do not fully understand all the numbers and names they're rapid-fire talking about with the man behind the tables, only catching about fifty percent. Then Charlie turns to Luca.

"Someday the Thunder's cards could be something people collect."

Luca whirls around to face me, almost stumbling in his haste. "We don't have trading cards!"

I can't avoid bursting out in a laugh at the horror on his face. "No, we don't."

"Seriously, Mom?" Now Charlie is looking at me with pure disappointment. "What kind of marketing plan for a baseball team doesn't include trading cards?" He shakes his head. "Epic fail, Mom. Epic."

"Can we get some designed before the season starts? Shit. How did we miss this?" Luca's spiraling, right in front of us, and so I step forward and kiss him gently on the lips.

"Relax, Luca. If you really want them, then first thing Monday morning, we can get in touch with the company that did the graphic design work for the logo and signage. I'm sure they can help. But you have to talk to Dom."

Luca blows out a breath. "Right. Okay. Damn, I can't believe we didn't think about trading cards."

Biting my lower lip, I debate whether or not I should remind him that player cards were in my original marketing plan, but we chose to move ahead with other items instead. Of course, knowing Luca, he won't let something silly like a budget hold him back.

Just like he didn't with the equipment he put in the recovery room for the players. Who ever heard of an independent league team having state-of-the-art cryotherapy systems, anyway?

I stayed out of that argument between him and Dom.

It doesn't have anything to do with marketing, so I had nothing to say. But the trading cards, I suppose I could've pushed for, but it was early on and I didn't want to ruffle feathers.

"C'mon, let's go and get some food." I urge the two of them away with a wave of thanks to the trading card vendor.

Over fresh fish tacos, to no surprise, the conversation between my boyfriend and my son turns back to baseball. This time, they're discussing the major league teams, specifically, the Vancouver Tridents.

"Coach Rhett thinks they can go all the way again this year. He says the rookies they've signed are solid, but he wouldn't tell us who they are."

Luca chuckles. "Yeah, because he's probably not meant to know, seeing as he's not on the team anymore."

Charlie nods. "But his best friend is married to the coach's daughter or something."

Luca shoots me a glance and a smirk. "True. There's lots of relationships on the team, from what I've heard." Turning back to Charlie as I fight a blush, he masterfully redirects the conversation. "Hey, how's it going with your batting at practice these days?" I watch my son closely to see his response. When I've asked how his practices has gone now that he has his prosthesis, I haven't gotten much more of an answer than "fine."

His head ducks down, and he picks at a fry on his plate. "It's okay, I guess. It's getting easier to catch and throw, for sure. But batting is still hard, one-handed or with my prosthesis. Coach Rhett is trying to figure out how to help, but I'm the first kid with one arm to join the league, so they don't really know what to do. I guess I can always just be a designated runner instead of a batter."

"Hey, the league had to deal with me and my missing leg. This is fixable. We'll get you hitting more accurately," Luca says with so much confidence, Charlie lifts his head with a hopeful expression.

"Do you really think so? I mean, I can, you saw me the other night. But it's hard. And I'm inconsistent. I can't figure out what I need to fix because it seems to change each time."

"You will. We will. Maybe Doc can come out to some practices, or Rhett and Doc can talk. There's gotta be a way to get everyone on the same page about what you need to be successful."

Part of me wants to caution Luca against putting unrealistic ideas in Charlie's head. Asking a prosthetist to speak with a Little League coach just so my son can be more successful at a recreational sport feels a little over-the-top. But then I see the hope shining on Charlie's face. And I keep quiet, not wanting to make that go away.

The rest of our time at the festival feels like a dream. A happy dream where I have a partner in this life, someone to help with Charlie, to love him and me the way we both deserve.

Later, back at our house over pizza for me and Char-lie, and a salad for Luca that we teased him about endlessly, we played a cutthroat game of Monopoly. Luca and Charlie laughed together as they both took me for all my money.

Things can't possibly get any better than this. When

we're cleaning up after Luca sweeps the board, taking me and Charlie for every penny, I feel arms snake around my waist as I put the leftovers in the fridge.

"Thank you for a perfect day." Lips press against my neck, and I smile, my eyes drifting shut.

"You're only saying that because you won Monopoly," I tease, turning in Luca's arms and wrapping mine around his neck.

He starts to gently sway back and forth, as if we're dancing to silent music. "No. I'm saying it because I haven't felt like this before. Like every moment keeps getting better."

I press my lips to his in response.

"Ew. Gross, guys, not in the kitchen," Charlie gripes, moving to the freezer as we break apart, grinning like idiots at each other. "You like ice cream, Luca? Or is that another thing you don't eat 'cuz you're a weirdo health nut."

"Charlie," I chide, stepping out of Luca's arms. "Don't be rude."

But Luca just laughs. "Sorry to disappoint, but no, I don't eat ice cream. I take my weirdo health nut status seriously."

"Not even if it was Nutella flavoured?" I can't help but tease.

Luca's mouth falls open. But there's a twinkle in his eyes. "Wait. There's Nutella ice cream?"

I lift my hand and pat his cheek. "Oh yes. There's Nutella ice cream. And Nutella cookies, Nutella frosting..."

Luca sweeps me into his arms with a groan. "Stop. Just stop. This is torture."

"And that's my cue to get outta here. Night Mom, night Luca."

Luca turns us so I can grin at my son. "Goodnight kid. Love you."

Charlie has already left the kitchen when Luca's head dips down and kisses the side of my neck. "And I love you, Isla Forrester."

38
ISLA

"Cross your fingers and toes for me," I say to Juniper as we walk up to the restaurant where the Cedar Creek Business Owners Association is holding their semi-annual luncheon.

Knowing how desperate I'm starting to feel about my job situation, Juni suggested I join her as her guest today, and I eagerly accepted. I need to network, to get my face and name out there, and make it clear I'm looking for a permanent position in Cedar Creek.

"It'll work out. Gotta have faith. You and Charlie are staying in Cedar Creek."

I wish I could muster up that much confidence, but the truth is, I'm worried. Luca's brought up the idea of me staying at the Thunder a couple more times. But as much as I want to do that, not only because of the job security, but because I'm loving my work there, I just can't do it.

I can't work for the man I'm in love with. Not long-term. Which means I've got to find another job, and fast.

It's already March, and the early April end date for my contract is coming up in a matter of a few short weeks.

But an hour of small talk later, and my hopes are sinking faster than the Titanic.

Sure, I've met plenty of local business owners, even handed out some of my cards. But no one seems to be looking for a marketer. Well, no one except for a doggie daycare that wants to branch out and do grooming and boarding and wanted to discuss me helping them with their social media campaign.

It's another short-term contract with lower pay. I'd love to help them out, but it's hardly a solution to my problem.

As if my mood couldn't get any worse, right then, I see Miranda Mulaney standing near a group of older men, her red lips parted in a wide, fake-looking smile.

The moment she sees me, her eyes narrow into slits, even as she continues whatever conversation she's in the middle of.

Whatever, she can glare at me all she wants. There's absolutely no reason we should have to interact at all. And even if we do, what was a ploy to get her to leave Luca alone the day we first met is now reality. She can't touch me.

Turning my back on her, I make my way over to a pair of women I recognize as owning one of the local fitness studios. I highly doubt they need someone like me since Juniper looked into the classes and found out they're so popular there's often a waitlist, but still. A connection is a connection.

But that's a dead end as well. They're lovely

women, and I'm grateful to accept the free one-week pass they offer for me to come and try out some classes, but a marketing expert is not something they need.

It's not something anyone in this town needs, apparently.

Except for the man I'm dating.

As Juniper and I walk out of the restaurant after the luncheon is over, my mood is gloomy.

"Okay. We're going to Dot's for milkshakes, no arguing." She threads her arm through mine and leads me to her car.

"I don't know, Juni. I should just go home. Charlie's got his big game tomorrow, and I'm tired and—"

"Stop. You're spiraling, babe. Let's sit for a few minutes over creamy chocolate shakes and make a plan."

By now, we've reached her car, but I don't open my door, instead staring at her over the hood of the car. "What plan is there to make? There's literally no work for me in this town. I've sent out resumes and queries to dozens of businesses between here and Dogwood Cove. No one is hiring right now."

"You could always come and work with me, I could use some help."

I laugh, but it's hollow sounding. "I love you, Juniper, but caring for injured owls and rescuing raccoons is not my area of expertise."

Juniper just shrugs and opens her door. "It wasn't mine, either. I was going to be a nurse, remember?"

Heaving a sigh, I follow her into the car, letting my head thump against the headrest before I answer. "Yeah, but you can't stand the sight of vomit, so that was never going to work out."

"True. And I'm happier with my animals," she says brightly, steering her car into traffic, in the direction of the diner.

I let her keep up a stream of chatter the entire way there. I really should insist she take me home, Lord knows I'm not good company right now.

The job search has been the primary thing on my mind, that's for sure. But then, out of the blue, Luca announced two days ago that he needed to go to Toronto for something. He was pretty evasive and vague when I asked why, saying something about seeing his old mentor.

It still annoys me that he wouldn't tell me the whole truth. He left early this morning, and all I've heard since then is a quick text to let me know he arrived safely. Adding onto my annoyance with life in general, my period showed up today, two days early.

I'm a real treat to be around.

Maybe that's why I'm not getting anywhere on the job front, maybe everyone can sense I'm a hormonal grumpy beast right now.

"Earth to Isla, we're here."

I blink and look at Juni, then out the window, where sure enough, we're parked in front of Dot's Diner.

"Sorry," I say as we get out of the car. "My head is a mess right now."

Juniper joins me on the sidewalk and bumps me with her hip. "It's all good. C'mon, milkshakes are on me."

Inside, the bright colours and sounds of the diner do

little to improve my mood. I let Juni guide me over to a booth and take a seat.

"Hi girlies, what can I get for ya?" Dot's smiling face falls as soon as she looks at me. "Uh-oh. Isla, hon, what's got you so glum?"

"Job woes, man trouble, and Aunt Flo visiting." Juni ticks them off, one by one, in a concise summary of my current predicament. "We need chocolate shakes with extra whipped cream."

"I'm on it." Dot's hand lightly squeezes my arm as she bustles away. She's back before long, setting down two large old-fashioned fountain glasses, full to the brim with creamy chocolate milkshakes.

"Thanks, Dottie," I say, mustering a smile.

"On the house, hon. Now, tell me about these job woes and man trouble. Let's see if Aunt Dot can help."

"Unless you tell me you need a marketing professional on a long-term basis, there's no helping the job situation. And the man trouble is more of a man frustration."

Dottie hums. "I'll keep my ears open for a job. I hear a lot of things and meet a lot of people, you know."

"It's true, Dot knows everything about everybody," Juni chimes in, winking at Dot.

"You say that like it's a bad thing," Dot retorts with an easy smile. "Anywho. Man frustration is something I'm quite familiar with. Before my Frank died, he used to drive me round the bend. What's that Luca done now?"

"Nothing, really," I admit. "He just went out of town this morning and didn't tell me why."

"That's not nothing. Communication is important. But do you trust him?"

My nod comes instantly.

"Then trust he has a good reason to go. And trust that him not telling you could be as simple as the fact that men can be complete idiots and don't always think about the need to keep their partner informed."

Juniper starts to giggle, and I find myself eventually joining in. Luca may be an incredibly mature, confident man most of the time, but I've certainly seen the other side of him. Would I call him an idiot? Of course not. Occasionally oblivious and impulsive? Definitely.

"Thanks Dottie, that helps." I smile up at the older woman. It's crazy, but I do actually feel a little bit better. I don't exactly have a lot of experience being in a relationship, so hearing from someone who does goes a long way to helping me understand everything.

"Anytime. Now, if you want my advice, which, to be frank, you're gonna get even if you don't want it, you need to talk to him. Tell him how you feel. Ask him to explain. It'll be good for both of you." Her gaze drops to the wedding band on her left hand. "Especially if he's a keeper like he seems to be. Those are the ones worth the extra work."

Dot's sage advice, bittersweet as it is, knowing she's grieving the man she loves, stays with me all afternoon. When Juni eventually drops me at the stadium so I can grab some things to work on over the weekend, my thoughts are with Luca. I just saw him this morning, but I already miss him.

"See you tomorrow at Charlie's game," she calls out

with a wave. It's just a fun pre-season match up between the two Little League teams, more of a practice than anything, but it's Charlie's first time pitching, so he's been vibrating with excitement all week. It's too bad Luca's trip couldn't be delayed, I'm sure Charlie would have loved for him to be there tomorrow. But when he told me he was leaving town, it didn't occur to me to mention the game. Not when he already had flights booked and everything.

But Juni and I will be there for Charlie, and she said Cal might join us. Hopefully, a Thunder player cheering him on is an okay substitute for Luca. As I walk past his office with the door closed, I blush, remembering our stolen moments in there. Passing Gabe's desk, my gaze lands on a piece of paper sticking out of a folder. A piece of paper that has my name on it.

I come to a stop. Gabe's computer is on, so he's obviously still here, even though he isn't at his desk at the moment for me to ask what's in the folder. Indecision wars within me. I shouldn't snoop, but what could that be?

"Isla, hi."

I turn to see Gabe walking up. His gaze drops down to the folder, and then his eyes widen before he scoops it up and tucks it under his arm.

"What is that, Gabe?"

"Just some papers for Luca."

That's an evasive answer if I ever heard one. "Why was my name on it?" I cross my arms over my chest.

Gabe looks at me, his expression carefully neutral. "I think that's something you should take up with Luca."

"Gabe," I say, unable to keep the pleading from my voice. "What is it?"

His lips turn up ever so slightly. "I don't want to ruin the surprise."

I swallow. "I hate surprises, Gabe. Please, I won't tell him you showed me."

He studies me for a second before I see him relent. "For what it's worth, I think it's fantastic." Opening the folder, he turns it to me.

I skim it quickly, seeing just enough to set my blood boiling and my heart cracking.

Fantastic is not the word I would use.

39
LUCA

I should've told Isla why I was going to Toronto. A part of me knows this. But I wanted the microchip to be a surprise. A good one, hopefully. And after my very promising meeting with my old mentor, I feel even more certain I can do this.

I haven't felt this spark of innovation in years. Not since the initial concept for GaitSync came to me back in university. It's exhilarating. And terrifying. Because initial concepts are just that—the starting point for something great. But the number of starting points that never make it any further is massive.

But in the day and a half that I've been back in Toronto, I've already made headway. Yes, the project is going to take a lot of work, but the idea has potential. At the lab where I created GaitSync, I hammered out a lot of details I had been missing in the design. Now I'm filled with energy, despite it being late here on the East Coast. I could have easily kept working, but my old mentor pushed me out the door, saying he had to go home to his family.

Family.

I'm not sure when I stopped picturing my parents when I thought of that word and started picturing Isla and Charlie instead, but it feels right. I know that down to my very soul. And I miss the people I hope to call my future family.

Back at my hotel, I pick up a to-go order from the restaurant on the main floor and take it up to my room to check in with Isla and Charlie. I'm finally going to tell them what I'm working on before I spend a few more hours developing the design. My plan is to be here for a week to take advantage of my mentor and the access to equipment he can give me, then I can head back to Cedar Creek with a list of what I'll need to set up a functional lab over there so I can keep working close to home.

And while I'm working on the microchip for Charlie, Gabe is helping me with a surprise for Isla. A solution to her job problem, and the perfect way to free up my time so I can focus.

I set my dinner down and open my computer to start a video chat, only to have my phone ring with a call from Rhett Darlington. Something nudges at the back of my mind, but I can't figure out what. So I answer his call.

"Rhett, what can I do for you?"

"Hi Luca, I just wanted to touch base about the upcomin' charity game."

Right. Now his call makes sense. "Of course. We've had phenomenal ticket sales for it already. Were you able to talk to the Little League board about my proposal?"

"Yep, and they are in full support. That was what I wanted to update you on."

I frown slightly, feeling confused, and still, there's the annoying thought that I'm missing something important. "I appreciate the update, but you could've just sent an email. Was there something else?"

Rhett exhales down the line. "Actually, yes. Damn, this is awkward, Luca. But I know you're gettin' close to the kid, so I thought you should know. Charlie was pretty devastated you weren't there today. He did a great job pitchin'..."

The rest of whatever Rhett says turns to a buzzing sound in my ears as my heart falls to the floor.

Fuck, fuck, fuck.

The game was today? No. I swear, I checked my personal calendar before I booked my flights and there was nothing on it this week.

"Are you saying the exhibition game was today?" I put Rhett on speaker as I check my phone. "Shit. I had it down as next week." I groan, covering my face with my hand.

Rhett makes a sympathetic sound. "Damn, I'm sorry man. Yeah, it was today."

"Rhett, I gotta go. If we need to talk about the charity game anymore, just send me an email and we'll plan a meeting."

I don't even wait for his reply before ending the call and immediately dialing Isla on my computer. Her beautiful face fills my screen a moment later, but there's an icy expression in place of the happy warmth I'm used to.

"Isla, I'm so sorry, I feel like such a dumbass. I can't

believe I missed Charlie's game. It was in my calendar for next week. I fucked up, and I feel absolutely awful. Rhett just called me and told me he did great. Is he there so I can apologize to him as well?"

"He's in his room," she says stiffly and my stomach drops even further. "I didn't realize you were meant to be at the game, but that explains his mood. I thought he'd be so proud, seeing as he struck out two players, but he's been grumpy ever since we left the field."

I run my hand over my face. "Shit. He asked me to be there, and I completely messed up."

If anything, Isla's face grows even colder. She's a mama bear and I just hurt her cub. "Well then, when you're home, you can apologize to him."

I lift my gaze. "I know this doesn't make up for missing the game, but I'm in Ontario because of him. I had an idea for a microchip that could help Charlie with his prosthetic and what he wants it to do." I launch into the simplest explanation I can come up with for the development that will help Charlie adjust in real time when he's batting by providing vibration feedback through his prosthesis. By the time I finish, Isla's staring at me, her beautiful face a mixture of emotions, that iciness finally thawing.

"You left for Charlie."

I nod emphatically. "I would've said something but the problem with this sort of technology is that even the best of ideas don't always work out. I didn't want to get his hopes up by telling him what I wanted to try and create if I didn't know it was a possibility. I worked out the rough design and came up with a plan for the next steps, which I can do here. Everything I need is getting delivered back home next week, and my realtor is looking for a space for me to work in Cedar Creek right now."

I exhale. "But none of that is as important as the fact that I hurt Charlie. And you. I'm sorry. Do you think you both can forgive me?"

Isla sighs, her gaze turning down. "Charlie will get over you missing the game. And I know he'll be thrilled about the microchip. When you get home, you can explain everything to him." She looks back up, and any hope I was feeling falls when I see the hurt still on her face. "But I need you to explain why Gabe had paperwork on his desk naming me as marketing director for the Thunder. I told you, I didn't want to work for you after my contract ends. I thought I was clear, I can't do that and date you. I don't understand why you won't accept that. How could you just do this when you know it's not what I want?"

Fucking hell. As if tonight could get any worse. "Isla, you weren't meant to see that."

Her head falls back as she shakes it. "Of course. Let me guess, it was a surprise."

The sarcasm and pain in her voice is unfamiliar to me. And I hate it. "I can explain. Just give me a chance to explain."

She lowers her head and looks at me. And even through the screen, I can see tears welling in her green eyes. "We can talk when you get home. I...I need to go, Luca."

My computer screen goes black before I can tell her I'm sorry, or that I love her, or anything else.

"Fuck," I yell, slamming my computer shut.

I came to Toronto thinking everything was good. Great, even. I'm working on making Charlie's dreams come true and giving Isla what she wants and deserves. And somehow, it's all crashing down around me.

All because I was a fucking idiot who thought keeping shit to myself and making it a surprise for them both was a good idea.

I mentally berate myself for a while longer before picking up my phone and opening my messages with Charlie.

> LUCA: Charlie, I'm so sorry about today. I had it in my calendar wrong. I would never have missed your game otherwise. Can we talk when I'm back, so I can apologize again? I want to explain why I'm out of town.

It takes a while before he responds. It's only one word, but it's a lifeline I'm happy to cling to.

> CHARLIE: sure.

That's one Forrester hopefully on the road to forgiving me, time to focus on the other. I open a text thread with Gabe and Dom. After quickly typing a brief summary of my fuckup, I explain exactly what I need them to do, and emphasize the need for it to be done quickly.

Gabe responds first.

GABE: On it boss. And I'm sorry. It's my fault. She saw the paperwork on my desk, and I didn't realize she wouldn't know the whole picture.

LUCA: It's okay. I should've told her what I was planning from the start.

DOM: Coral says you're a dumbass and need to learn to communicate.

GABE: I would concur. Minus the insult since you're still my boss - for now.

LUCA: Just get everything I need done, please.

DOM: We will. It'll all work out, Luca.

I fucking hope so.

40

LUCA

It wasn't easy convincing myself to stay in Toronto and finish my work here instead of flying home to Cedar Creek immediately following the imploding of all my plans. But I'm determined to make this microchip a reality, and I had full trust in Gabe and Dom to set everything up for me.

I'm still home a day earlier than I intended, however, when I finally drive back into town. And my heart is set on one thing: getting my wonder woman to forgive me. Which means fixing things with her son first.

It was surprisingly easy to get Charlie to agree to meet me for lunch today, made even more so by him having a day off from school. Even though secrets and surprises are what got me in this mess, I couldn't avoid one more. Which is why I asked him not to tell his mom about our meeting.

I pick him up at their house, knowing Isla is at work. The drive to the pizza parlour he wanted to eat at is quiet and tense. Charlie answers my few questions with the shortest responses possible, staring out the window the whole way there. By the time I pull into a parking spot, my nerves are shot.

I turn the engine off but make no move to get out of the car. After several seconds of silence, Charlie turns to me at last.

"Are we gonna eat?"

I nod. "We are, but I'm really hoping that when we sit down and have some food, you're no longer hating my guts for missing the game."

His head turns back to face the window. "Whatever. It's fine. I'm not mad."

"No, I guess maybe you're not, and I could understand if you're still hurt. I feel really bad about not seeing you pitch, Charlie. I made a stupid mistake and I missed something important to you."

"So why were you in Toronto, anyway?"

I consider it a good thing that he's at least willing to ask questions and not shutting me out, even if his tone is still borderline belligerent.

It's hard to temper my expression. He's hurting, and letting my excitement bleed through too early could backfire. "Remember the night I came over for dinner and you had just got your attachment for your prosthesis?" He nods. "You had some really good insight into why it wasn't working exactly the way you wanted it to. And I could see how easy it would be to feel frustrated by the limitations of the attachment the way it was. I know Doc is awesome, and I'm sure he's got lots of ideas, but that night, you gave me an idea."

Charlie's face makes it clear he's waiting for me to get to the point, so I hurry on. "You know I told you about GaitSync? Well, that night I thought of something, another microchip, but one for arm prostheses. Something that could give real-time feedback via vibrations to help you know exactly how to adjust your movements to better mimic the natural feedback people get through their hands and wrists. It's not just for athletes like you, but for anyone who wants more precision and control over how their arm works. Instead of having to wait to work with someone like Doc on the changes."

"That sounds cool," Charlie says slowly, and I can hear the fragile thread of interest in his voice. "But what does all that have to do with you going away?"

"I wanted to get back to Toronto, where my old lab and my former mentor were to see if we could hammer out an actual design concept for the microchip. I didn't want to tell you or your mom about the idea until I knew it was possible."

I take a chance and rest my hand on his shoulder. Thank fuck, he doesn't pull away. "Please trust me when I say, I wouldn't have gone if I hadn't put the date of your game in my calendar wrong. I never would've left town and missed the game on purpose. I'm really sorry, Charlie. I let you down, and I feel absolutely terrible about that. There's no good excuse; I screwed up and I hurt you. The thing is, that happens in life. Everybody screws up sometimes. There's no avoiding it. So I'm here, doing the best I can by explaining what happened and asking if you can forgive me."

His stare is unflinching, and I don't let myself look

away. Then, underneath my hand, I feel his body let go of some of the tension. "Yeah. I guess I can. That chip thing sounds pretty cool."

I sag back in my seat and let my smile break free. "I think it will be. There's still a lot of work to do, but I've got a plan so I can do it from here now."

"You don't wanna work on it at your old lab?"

"Are you and your mom going to move to Toronto?"

Charlie makes a face. "I hope not, but if she doesn't find a job, then who knows."

"Well, if you two are here, then I want to be here. You and your mom are the most important things in my life now. And I'll do whatever it takes to prove that to you both and hopefully earn a spot in your life for a very long time."

There's the barest hint of a smile on his face. "Cool. Mom deserves that. Someone who puts her first, I mean. And you're a cool guy. So I guess I'd be okay with you sticking around." That fraction of a smile falls. "But she's been really upset all week. And I don't think it's 'cause of my game."

I purse my lips and exhale. "It's not. It's because I screwed up with her, too. But I'm fixing it, I swear. In fact, I could use your help with the finishing touches, if you're willing?"

He studies me with a narrowed gaze for several seconds before nodding. "I'll help. But Luca, you gotta stop screwing up. This is strike one." He winks.

I choke out a laugh. "Deal, kid."

———

The next day, everything is ready. The charity game between the Cedar Creek Thunder and the Cedar Creek Little League team is in two days. I know for a fact Isla is still taking today off as planned, back before I screwed everything up and she thought I was coming home today.

I also know my assistant is an underpaid genius, because he somehow got her to agree to pop by the offices this morning on the pretense of there being a critical issue with one of the banners that was delivered recently.

Do I like tricking her, especially in a way that I know is stressing her out? Of course not. But for the plan Charlie and I came up with over pizza, she had to come to the offices alone. Well, sort of alone.

And that brings me to now. Waiting impatiently in the executive offices at the stadium.

"You're gonna wear a hole in that brand-new carpet and trust me when I say, we don't have the budget to replace it with your recent restructuring."

I pivot on my good foot and glare at Dom. "Don't make me regret putting you in charge."

He just laughs, leaning against the door frame to my former office. "No going back now. The ink is dry and the paperwork filed, my friend."

I smile, even as my fingers tap out an impatient pattern on my leg. "No going back. Just don't sink the damn ship, okay?"

He tips his fingers in a mock salute, just as I get the text I've been waiting for. "They're here."

Dom flashes me a thumbs-up, then heads back to his office while I stand in front of the elevators. A couple of minutes later they open, but only Charlie emerges. "Where's your mom?" I ask as he walks over to me, holding out his hand.

"On the concourse, trying to find the banner. She thinks I'm still in the car. Lemme see it?" I hand over the thin piece of metal, and he grins down at it. "Cool."

His phone dings with a text, and he hands me back the plaque to pull it out of his pocket.

"It's Mom, she wants to know where I am."

"Tell her you're inside, and you think you found the banner."

He thumbs out the text, then pockets the phone.

"She's on her way." We take up our positions in front of the elevator doors, Charlie with his hand now behind his back, once again holding the piece of metal.

The doors open with a ding, and Isla steps out. "Charlie? Where's the—oh, Luca. What are you doing here? I thought your flight didn't get in till noon. Wait, do you know where the banner is with the typo? I can't believe that happened." She tugs at her ponytail, and I can't take her being so stressed out a second longer.

I step forward and take her hand in mine, squeezing. "Breathe, wonder woman. There is no banner with a typo. I'm sorry, but I had Gabe lie to you to get you here."

She stares at me in confusion. "What?"

I look back at Charlie and give him a subtle nod. He brings his hand round to the front and holds up the name plate I gave him moments ago.

Her face falls as she reads it. "What is that, Luca?"

I take it from Charlie and hold it out to her. "I know I have a lot to explain. When you saw the paperwork on Gabe's desk, you jumped to the right conclusion, but you didn't know everything. So this is exactly what it looks like. A name plate for an office door that says Isla Forrester, Marketing Director." I look up at her with a hopeful smile.

"It's yours, Mom," Charlie says excitedly. "Cool, right?"

But she's shaking her head, her expression making her frustration clear and I know if I don't explain everything, I'll lose her. Suddenly, the elaborate plan Charlie and I came up with seems like a mistake. I should've just told her.

"Luca, why are you still forcing this on me? I won't work for you and be in a relationship with you any longer."

I take her hand and plead with her. "Please. Just come with me? Everything will make sense, I swear. I know what you want. And I want nothing more than to give it to you. Just please let me show you?"

She stares at me, indecision clear in her gaze.

"Mom, trust him. And me. We came up with this plan together and you're gonna be happy, I swear."

I owe that kid big time, because Charlie's words are what finally have Isla relenting.

"Fine."

Charlie goes ahead of us, already knowing exactly where to go. I can feel Isla resisting but she lets me lead her down the hall toward what she thinks is my office. But when we come to a stop outside the mostly closed door, I hear her gasp of surprise.

"This is the part you didn't know about when you saw that paperwork on Gabe's desk. See, you won't be working for me any longer. There's a new man in charge." I knock on the door and push it open to show Dom seated behind my old desk, his damn collection of bobbleheads filling the shelves he had installed earlier in the week. He waves at us with a grin.

"Hey Isla, please forgive the idiot for not telling you about this. I need you. I don't want my first job as general manager to be trying to find a new head of marketing."

Isla is speechless, but I'm hoping the tears brimming in her eyes are tears of happiness. Pulling her into my side, I chance a kiss on the top of her head. "Can we show you one more thing?" I whisper, and I feel her nod, just barely.

"C'mon, Mom. This is the best part." Charlie takes her other hand and tugs her a lot more strongly than I would have, back down the hall to where her old temporary office was. Thanks to Dom and his budget, it was furnished sparsely, his theory being we could reuse the furniture in other places once we found a permanent marketing director who could furnish the space the way they wanted.

This is what I had Gabe working around the clock to achieve.

Charlie points to the empty slot on the door, where her new name plate belongs. "Put it right there, Mom."

Isla looks from the door to me. And the relief that crashes over me at the cautious smile playing at her lips is intense.

Turning to Charlie, she says, "Why don't you do it? My hands are shaky right now."

He takes it eagerly and slides the thin sheet of metal in place.

"Looks good, doesn't it," I say casually, squeezing her into my side even tighter. "Meant to be, if you ask me."

She looks up at me, tears that I hope like hell are happy ones making her eyes shine. "Are you sure about this? I thought the team was your dream."

I shake my head. "No, it was a way to fill the time while I figured out my life. And when I realized the only life worth living was one with you and Charlie in it, I knew it was time to move on. Dom's the right guy to take over. I'll still be a financial investor, and technically the owner, but you don't report to me any longer. I'm not your boss as of 4 pm yesterday when I signed the paperwork." I cup her cheek. "I do listen to you, Isla. Every single word. I'm sorry I was an idiot and didn't explain everything about going to Toronto and making Dom the GM right from the start."

She lets out a small, shaky laugh. "Yeah, no more surprises, please."

"Deal," I promise. "I really missed you this week, wonder woman."

"I missed you, too," she whispers back and when she looks up at me, her gaze is heated, full of excitement and promise.

"Oh my God, stop being weird and just open the

door." Charlie's impatient complaint has both of us grinning.

"Fine, fine," Isla says, stepping away from my side. She places her hand on the door handle and pauses, looking back at me and Charlie. "Should I be worried that Dom is going to grumble about budgets?"

I shake my head. "Nope. This didn't come from the team's accounts."

Her light laugh fills my heart. "Oh boy, somehow, I'm even more worried now." Then, she opens the door and gasps. "Oh wow."

We step inside her newly decorated office as a trio. Isla moves farther in, her gaze sweeping across the space. I recruited Juniper to help with a lot of the design choices, including the deep blue accent chairs and white marble-topped table that are in one corner, and the plants scattered throughout the space.

Isla walks slowly toward the white L-shaped desk, her fingertips trailing over the desk blotter and the rose-gold coloured stationary set on top. She drops down into the cream-coloured office chair and gives it a spin as she giggles.

"This is gorgeous."

Charlie walks quickly to his mother's side and starts pointing out other details in the space, the photos on the open shelving, the plants, the subtle placement of some of Isla's favourite team merchandise. Meanwhile, I sit down in the chair across from her desk and watch the two of them.

Nothing in my life has ever felt so right as this

moment. Every decision I've made over the last year, every step I've taken, has led to this.

The only thing that could top this would be making Isla mine forever.

And if I have it my way, that will happen soon enough.

41

ISLA

"Everything's perfect, you are allowed to relax, you know."

I step away from the banner that hangs above the last row of seats behind home plate, spin on my heel, and glare at Luca. "Listen buddy, just because you no longer work here doesn't mean the rest of us get to goof off. Today has to go well."

The damn man chuckles, placing his hands on my shoulders, his grey eyes glinting with amusement. "It will. You've done the work, now it's time to watch it all come together." He rubs his hands up and down my arms, and I have to admit, I feel my tension slowly dropping. "Breathe for me, wonder woman."

That nickname, said with so much love and pride, is my undoing. I sag into his arms, resting my cheek against his warm, solid chest, and breathe in deeply. Only for my brain to suddenly start spinning. "Wait. Did Gabe go down to meet the fire department?"

Luca holds me tighter, and I feel him chuckle. "Yes. They're ready to go after the third inning."

Today's charity game is a short one, only six innings. With it being late March, the weather is unpredictable at the best of times, and since today is just for fun and to raise money for the Little League, it was an easy decision to fill the time with other fun activities, along with the actual ball game.

Gates open any minute now, and the community will get their first real look at the newly renovated Cedar Creek Stadium, home of the Thunder. And it's all thanks to the man at my side. He's the reason this team is looking forward to its best-attended season in almost a decade, with season ticket sales booming, and the first four games already sold out. The players are invigorated from spring training and ready to go, and I've seen more and more people around town wearing our new merchandise on hats, hoodies, and jerseys lately.

"How does it feel to know none of this would have been possible without you?" Luca asks, turning me to face the field.

"I think you've got that backward. This is all thanks to you," I reply, leaning back in his arms. "It does look incredible, though."

Looks, sounds, and feels incredible is more like it. There's been a palpable energy in the building lately. More than just what would be normal now that the players are back in-house, gearing up for the season. Everyone's excited to see how the team is received by the town and the baseball community at large.

"Take the credit, Isla. There's a reason you're the

head of marketing now." He nuzzles my neck, pressing kisses there that make me wish we weren't in a very public place. Just then, a voice comes over the loudspeaker. "Gates are opening in one minute, everyone. One minute to gates opening."

Luca draws back, a nervous smile blooming across his face. "This is it. Let's go let them in."

We walk hand in hand over to the main gates, where the first faces we see are those of our highest-level sponsors, who get to enjoy priority seating right in the front, near the third base line.

"Welcome everyone, thank you for being here today, and for all of your support. Come on in, grab some complimentary snacks from the concession, and take a look around. The game starts in one hour!" Luca steps back and we let the swarm of people pass, many of them stopping to say hi or shake Luca's hand. By the time the crowd is all inside, he's grinning ear to ear. "Holy shit, there's so many people here."

I laugh. "Well yeah, I told you we had a full house today."

"I know, but I don't think I actually believed it until now." He turns toward me, picks me up, and twirls me around.

The next hour flies by, and before I know it, it's time for the first pitch. Charlie actually teared up when Luca asked if he would throw it. He's been practicing ever since, but I can't deny the fact that I'm nervous waiting for him and Luca to leave the dugout and walk to the mound.

And I'm certainly not prepared for what I see when they do.

Charlie is wearing a Cedar Creek Little League uniform but doesn't have his prosthetic arm attached. And at his side is Luca, wearing a grey Cedar Creek Thunder home jersey and a pair of shorts.

"Is he actually walking out there with his leg uncovered?"

I turn at Dom's shocked voice, to see him holding hands with his wife, standing next to me. Guess I'm not crazy for being surprised by the sight of Luca baring his prosthesis for all to see.

"He doesn't do that often, does he?"

Dom shakes his head. "Rarely. He's never wanted to draw attention to it. So why now?" He sounds baffled, but then Luca starts to speak.

"Hi everyone, thanks again for coming out today for our first annual charity ball game between the Cedar Creek Thunder and the Cedar Creek Little League. We've got a lot of fun planned, and I know all of the players are eager to get started. But before my friend Charlie throws the first pitch on behalf of the Little League, I want to make a quick announcement."

I watch as Luca looks down at Charlie with a soft smile before facing the crowd again. "You might have noticed that Charlie and I have something unique in common." He pauses, then grins. "We both love baseball."

That gets some of the crowd laughing. Luca holds up his hand and continues. "But playing ball doesn't come as easily for us as it does for most kids. And the same can be said for plenty more youth in our area. Which is why I'm proud to announce that the proceeds from today will be split between the Cedar Creek Little League and Let's Play Canada, a charity that supports full inclusion in youth sports for all. And I will personally be matching the donation to both organizations. Because baseball is for everyone. And it is my honour to be able to bring the sport I love to all of you here today, and hopefully to many more community members in the future. With that, Charlie, can you do the honours?"

Luca holds the microphone down in front of my son, who loudly and proudly shouts, "Let's play ball!" Then, as the tears start to build behind my eyes, I watch him throw a near perfect pitch straight into Griff's waiting catcher's mitt.

After that, I don't see much of Luca, but I assume he's busy like I am, making sure everything runs smoothly. Once the game is over, Charlie finds me, throwing his arm around me in a sweaty hug. "Mom, that was amazing. Did you see my hit? I got a double. A double!"

"I saw, kid," I say, ruffling his hair. "I'm so stinking proud of you."

He grins up at me. "Thanks. Hey, can I go to Miles's house for a sleepover?" He jerks his thumb over his shoulder, and I glance up to see his friend and his parents standing there. Miles's mom gives me a wave and I wave back.

"Sure. Do you have your key so you can get what you need at home? I might be here a while longer helping clean up."

"Yup. See ya tomorrow. Love you!"

"Love you, too." I watch him go, my heart so full of pride and happiness, I feel like I could burst. He's come a long way from the kid who hated the idea of moving and was facing relentless teasing at school. I know life won't always be easy or kind to him, but right now, today, he's living every moment happy, and that's all I could ask for.

"Did I just hear something about a sleepover?" Luca's warm voice hits me at the same time as his strong arms loop around my middle.

I turn and wrap mine around his neck before pulling his head down for a kiss. "You did. Which means I can enjoy a hot bath and a glass of wine in private."

Luca hums under his breath. "You could. Or you could come back to my place. Did I mention I've got a hot tub on the rooftop deck?"

I lean back and stare up at him. "You absolutely did not! Luca Calloway, you've been holding out on me."

He chuckles, pulling me back in. "In my defense, we're normally at your house because of Charlie and Gus. The one time you came over, we didn't exactly have time for the hot tub."

I shake my head even as he kisses my forehead. "Excuses, excuses. Let's get everything done quickly, so I can go and grab my swimsuit."

"That won't be necessary. It's a very private hot tub." His eyes darken as a slow smirk covers his face. "No swimsuit required."

42

LUCA

In the time it takes Isla to go to her house and pack a bag, not including her swimsuit, I manage to get home and tidy up, put a bottle of her favourite wine in the fridge, and make sure the hot tub is ready to go. I'm second-guessing my last-minute decision to light some candles, worried it's way too cheesy, when I hear the doorbell ring. I go downstairs from the rooftop as fast as I can.

I open the door to see Isla standing with one hip cocked and a smirk on her gorgeous face. "I was starting to think you fell asleep on me," she teases, brushing past me, letting her fingers trail across my chest.

"Nope. Just preparing the hot tub."

Isla lets her bag fall to the floor, her gaze never leaving my face, as she then kicks off her sandals and brings her hands to toy with the bottom of her dark blue Thunder T-shirt. "Good." Her tongue darts out to moisten her lips. "That's good." In one motion, she peels off her shirt, dropping it to the floor as well.

I don't hold back my groan of appreciation as her

lace-covered breasts come into view. "I hope you remembered, no bathing suit required."

She only nods, then pushes her pants down over her round ass, wiggling a bit as she shimmies them down. "I did." Stepping out of her pants, she closes the distance between us wearing nothing but lace. Placing her hands on the hem of my T-shirt, she peels it off before going up on her toes to whisper in my ear, "Let's get wet, Luca."

Before I can second-guess myself, I bend down and grab her behind the knees, straightening up to toss her easily over my shoulder as she shrieks my name. My grin couldn't be wider, as I take it slow going up the stairs. Every step is a challenge, but one I'm fucking determined to beat. Of course, it could be easier to keep my balance if Isla stopped wriggling.

"Stop moving, woman."

"Luca, you're insane. Put me down!"

I smack her lace-covered ass in response. "Are you questioning my ability to carry you up these stairs? I know I'm older than you, but I'm not *that* old."

She falls silent. "No. Of course not. I would never do that, Luca. I trust you."

I reach the top of the stairs, feeling my quad muscles burn. It's moments like this that I resent my condition. A normal guy with my fitness level would be able to carry his partner up a flight of stairs without thinking twice. Whereas for me, that was a massive achievement.

I slowly lower Isla down, keeping my hands on her bare hips in case she's dizzy from being upside down. "Baby, I'm just teasing you." I drop a kiss to the tip of her nose. "I know you trust me, and I don't take that for granted. Now, do you want to get in the hot tub or not?"

It takes a second for the concern to fully fade from her face. Which, honestly, just makes me love her even more. She's always aware, always considerate of my needs and my feelings. Even when she doesn't have to be.

But her perfect smile comes back, filling me with love and warmth. "Lead me to this magical rooftop patio of yours."

I reach behind her and open the door. She steps outside and wraps her arms around her waist with a shiver. "This is gorgeous, but I was an idiot for getting undressed inside."

"A very sexy idiot." I smirk. "C'mon. The hot tub is over here." I lead her past the seating area, to where the steam is rising from the bubbling tub.

"Oh Luca," Isla sighs, and any doubt I had about the candles being too much is banished.

I push down my shorts and underwear at the same time, tossing them to the side. When Isla turns back, her gaze immediately drops to my cock, which is already hard.

"Someone's eager," she murmurs teasingly before reaching behind her back and unsnapping her bra. The straps fall down over her shoulders, then to the floor.

"You've been teasing me in nothing but lace for far too long, wonder woman. This is what happens."

She shimmies out of her panties next, and then she's naked. And still shivering.

"Get in the water," I command as I move to the chair

I placed next to the tub. She does as I say, sighing as she sinks into the hot water. I remove my prosthesis and the liner underneath as quickly as I can, setting it carefully to the side, far enough from the water. Then, in two hops, I'm at the edge of the hot tub. If I was with anyone other than Isla, I might feel self-conscious about having to do that, and the way I have to swing my legs over the edge to get in instead of stepping in like a normal person. But with Isla, I don't give it a second thought.

As soon as I'm seated in the water, she glides over to me, placing one knee on the bench on either side of me, coming to straddle my hips. I tangle my hands in the hair just above her neck and pull her in for a long, deep kiss.

"So. Rose and thorn for today?" Isla asks when we finally part.

"No thorns. Only roses."

"No." Isla laughs, pushing me away when I try to move back in for a kiss. "I'm serious! Rose *and* thorn for today. I'll go first." She tilts her head to the side, as if she's thinking about her answer. "Okay. I've got it. My rose was watching Charlie throw out the first pitch with you by his side. And my thorn was worrying about the possibility of a rain delay all morning."

"Mother Nature knew better than to mess with all of your plans." I smile and press a kiss to her forehead. "Fine, I'll play. My rose was seeing all of our hard work pay off, with a stadium full of happy, excited fans. And my thorn was not getting to watch the game with you."

She rolls her eyes, but I just shrug. "Hey, it's true. Next game, I want to watch with you on one side and Charlie on the other. That'll be a perfect day."

Isla melts into my arms at my simple words. "How are you so sweet?"

"You make it easy, wonder woman." I lean in and kiss her again.

And again. And again. "Are you warming up?" I eventually ask in between kisses.

I can feel her lips curve upward as she nods and continues to kiss me. On my lap, her hips start to move, rocking back and forth along my cock that's trapped between us. The friction, the warmth of the water, and the feel of her naked body pressed against mine, it's sensual perfection.

I moan, dropping my lips to her bare shoulder and lightly sucking the skin there, letting my teeth graze over it. She gasps, her nails digging into my back.

"Fuck, Isla, you gonna just ride against my cock like that, baby? Is that gonna get you off, or do you need more?" I lift my head and take in her flushed cheeks, lush lips that look well-kissed, and I smirk. "Or do you trust me to know what you need."

"That depends," she says, the words coming out breathy. "Are you going to dirty talk and tease me all night, or are you going to make me come?"

"Who says I can't do both?" I counter, but my hand is already moving down, under the water, sliding in between us and zeroing in on her clit. I pinch it lightly, making her gasp. Her hips still as I play with her, my thumb and fingers dancing around her pussy, toying, teasing, and spinning her even higher. When her head falls back with a sigh, I take advantage and suck her nipple into my mouth, releasing it with a pop, only to do the same on the other side. My cock is throbbing, aching, desperate to get inside of her and find release, but I hold back.

This is about her.

I slide one fingertip inside of her, dragging it out slowly before pushing it back in, deeper this time.

"Oh Luca," she moans, rocking her hips up to try and push me in even farther. I let it happen. Knowing she's as desperate as I am has me wanting to throw my plan to tease her into a frenzy off the fucking roof.

"Give me one right now, baby. Come all over my fingers and then you'll get my cock."

I thrust two fingers in, curling them to find the right spot to apply pressure. I capture her lips with mine and kiss her through her orgasm, feeling the pulse of her inner walls around my fingers as she comes.

She pulls back first with a gasp, her eyes glazed with pleasure. "Fuck me, Luca."

I shake my head. But before she can react, I say, "I'm not going to fuck you. I'm going to make love to you. Dirty, sweet, fast, slow, rough or gentle, I don't care. But you're the love of my goddamn life, Isla Forrester. So I won't fuck you. I'll worship you."

My cock pushes into her swollen pussy, and she cries out my name. It's awkward, only having one leg to push against the floor of the hot tub. But a lifetime of adapting to one leg has me strong enough that I can match Isla's movements well enough. And fuck, it doesn't even matter what I do, the simple sensation of her body against mine, her pussy hugging my dick, the sound of her gasps and cries, it's enough to have me worried I'll lose it too damn fast.

I grab onto her hips and take control of her movements, slowing her into a smooth back and forth that I emphasize with a push of my hips every time she comes in close. I can tell the change in angle is good for her by the way she whimpers against my lips.

"Oh my God."

The steam swirling around has made her cheeks pink, her hair damp and curling around her head, and I swear, she's never looked more beautiful than she does right now, coming undone in my arms.

I let my own head tip back as she writhes on top of me, the squeeze of her around my cock dragging out my own orgasm as I let go inside of her. Eventually, her body relaxes, going limp in my arms, and I hold her tightly against me, savouring the intimacy between us. I could spend forever loving this woman, and I fully plan to.

I have no idea how much time passes before she lifts her head, looking at me from sleepy eyes. "I love you."

The simplicity of those three words is misleading, given the immense depth of emotion they stir within me. My eyes close as I absorb them into my heart. It doesn't matter how many times she says it, I'll never get tired of hearing it.

"And I love you." I stroke my fingers over her face, noticing how the skin that is out of the water is chilled. "Let's go inside and warm up."

She nods and moves off my lap, climbing out of the hot tub and quickly grabbing one of the oversized towels

I hung up before she arrived earlier. "Do you need any help?"

I've already leveraged myself onto the edge of the tub and swung my legs around, but I give her a grateful look. "Thanks, baby. It's fucking cold, so maybe just my towel, and stand nearby in case I slip on the wet floor?"

She doesn't bat an eye, moving to my side, and handing me a towel. I stand on my one leg and hop to the chair next to my prosthesis. Drying my leg takes a minute, and then I roll the liner back on and slide my limb into the prosthesis.

Hand in hand, we make our way back down the stairs and into my apartment. As soon as we hit the bottom of the stairs, I come to a stop. "Shit, I forgot to put the lid on the hot tub." I kiss her head. "Be right back."

"Okay," Isla says with a smile. "I'm going to text Charlie to check-in, anyway."

I'm not gone long. But apparently, I'm gone long enough for Isla to check on her son and put on one of my dress shirts.

Fuck me. The damp towel wrapped around my waist is cold, yet even still, my cock hardens underneath it at the sight of her.

"Stealing my clothes?" I ask in a husky voice. "Not that I mind, it looks better on you than me."

Her fingers toy with the top button on the shirt, grazing over the bare skin revealed there. "My towel was wet, this was the first thing I could find."

"I'm not complaining, baby. Not at all." I step closer to her, reaching one hand out to grasp her behind the neck and pull her in for a kiss.

A different kind of shiver runs through her as she runs her hands up my back. The damn towel is just barely staying on, thanks to my cock trying to push through the fabric. And when she presses her hips into it, I swallow down a groan.

"The question is, what are you wearing underneath it?"

She steps back with a coy smile. "I didn't have time to put on anything else."

"Perfect." I smirk. "The only thing I like better than you wearing my clothes is you wearing no clothes at all. My room. Now."

EPILOGUE
ISLA

THE BIG DAY is finally here. We're hosting the season opener at home, and the energy throughout the stadium and offices is electric.

"Okay, so everyone knows where they're stationed? We want as much content as possible, both for live posting and future posts." I look at the team of interns I put together for today. "Nick, you're monitoring our socials for comments?"

"Yep, I'm on it," he replies, waving his phone in the air.

"Great. Make sure you let me know if anything seems off. And all of the in-game entertainment is fully set up, yes?" I look to the intern in charge of that, who nods. "Make sure you have water on hand for the mascot. That costume gets hot." She gives me a thumbs-up.

I look back down at my checklist and let out a satisfied sigh. "Alright, team. I think we're ready. Go Thunder!" Everyone cheers and then heads off to do their assigned jobs. And I finally let myself sit down. Just for a second.

Of course, that second is when Luca finds me. "Already slacking on the job, wonder woman?" he teases, coming into the now empty conference room.

I glare up at him. "Slacking? Seriously?"

He chuckles, sitting down next to me, and pulling my chair closer to him so he can reach out and tug me into his lap. I go without too much resistance because being held by Luca is the best possible way to unravel the tension I'm carrying today.

"Have I thanked you for not only seeing my vision for this team but bringing it to life even better than I could have imagined," he murmurs, resting his chin on the top of my head. "You should see the crowd out there. I don't think there's more than a handful of Cardinals fans, it's a sea of grey and blue."

I smile. We've got a sold-out stadium for the home opener, and I couldn't be happier. "We'll have to make sure to beat them."

His chest rumbles with his sound of agreement. But then the radio on my hip crackles. "Isla, can you come to the announcer booth, please?"

I sigh at Luca. "Sorry."

He leans forward and kisses me again. "Go. Be amazing."

I pick up the radio. "On my way."

The rest of the day goes by in a blur. I don't get another chance to sit down or talk to Luca and Charlie, who are watching the game from the owner's box, along with Juniper, my mom, and Luca's parents. I'd be jealous of them if I had a moment to think about it. But the next time I see any of them is long after the fans have left and the stadium is quiet. Exhausted, I make my way outside to see Luca chatting with Dom in the staff parking lot.

"Great work tonight, Isla," Dom says. "I don't want to see you in the office before nine tomorrow. Got it?"

I smile tiredly. "Deal. But only if you agree to the same." We've both been starting our days well before eight, and I'm guessing I'm not the only one grateful that today went off without a hitch.

"See you in the morning. I better get home before Coral thinks I fell asleep at my desk."

We wave goodbye, then Luca drapes his arm over my shoulders and steers me to his car. "Come on, wonder woman. I'm going to take you home, run you a bath, and put you to bed."

———

I sleep like the dead for seven hours, then wake up in a panic before I remember what Dom said about starting work later today.

But as soon as I step foot in the office, I'm reminded that the heavy workload involved in managing the marketing department for even a minor league sports team doesn't slow down once the season starts.

My morning flies by, and then it's time for my debrief with Dom. I make my way down the hall to his office, my eyebrows raising when I see Luca in there, chatting with him.

"I thought you were going to the lab today and work on setting up your equipment?" I ask.

He turns to me with a smile. "I did for a couple of hours, but then I decided to surprise you and take you out for lunch to celebrate a successful opening day."

I go to reply, and Dom interrupts me. "That's sweet and romantic and shit, but if you're gonna be here, you need to sit down and shut up so we can get this meeting over with."

I stifle my laugh and take a seat in front of Dom's desk, opening the notes app on my phone where I have everything I thought of yesterday.

It takes us close to an hour to go through it all, but eventually, I set my phone down. "That's it on my end. Overall, everything ran smoothly, but there's those few tweaks we can make quickly enough. We'll be ready for the next game."

"Perfect. Thanks for all your work, Isla. Yesterday was fantastic."

Then, his gaze goes to Luca, who's sitting over on one of the chairs off to the side of Dom's desk. "Nothing to add, Calloway? I'm sure you've got some opinions."

Luca looks up from his laptop with a grin. "Are you kidding? There's not a damn thing I would've changed about yesterday, except maybe for the two of you to not have had to work so hard, so you could actually enjoy it. That game was fucking amazing. Griff's homer in the sixth?" He whistles. "Pure magic." Then Luca stands up and walks over to stand behind me, his hands resting on my shoulders. "But if you're done here, I'd like to steal your head of marketing away for lunch."

Dom rolls his eyes good-naturedly. "I guess so, but you have to bring her back this time. We've still got work to do."

My cheeks heat in response to his obvious dig at last week, just a few days before the home opener, when I was working insane hours every day. Luca came by the offices to take me to lunch, only to actually steal me away to a day spa where he treated me to a couples massage. Needless to say, I didn't go back to work that day.

"We'll be back in an hour," I say firmly, then I turn to leave. Luca follows, his hand finding mine as we go down the hall to my office. Even now, after a couple of weeks spent working in this space, I still mentally swoon when I step inside. It's as if Luca somehow saw into my head and pulled out every idea for the perfect office I've ever had. In reality, I know they had help from Juniper, but still. There's not a single thing I've wanted to change in the space, with the exception of adding some more personal photos to the shelves along the wall.

Luca wanders over there now, as I go to my desk to get my purse. But when I hear him make a quiet sound of surprise, I pause and smile to myself. I know he's just seen the one I added a couple of days ago after finally finding the perfect frame for it.

"I've never seen this one." His voice is raw with emotion, and when I move to his side, I slide my arm around his waist and lean my head on his shoulder, looking at the photo. It's Luca and Charlie, standing on the pitcher's mound the day of the charity game. Charlie's grinning at the crowd, while Luca is smiling down at him. I remember that moment, but it wasn't until I saw the photo, taken by one of our media team with a long-range camera lens, that I actually saw the look on Luca's face. He truly loves my son, and this photo captured it perfectly. And that is something I never want to forget.

"Can I get a copy?"

"Of course."

He turns and kisses the top of my head, and when I look up, his dark eyes are shining. I lift a hand to cup his cheek, and we stay like that for a long moment, no words needed to express the love we have for each other.

But the moment is interrupted by a knock on my door. As one, we turn to see Gabe, once Luca's assistant and now Dom's, standing there. "Sorry to interrupt, but I think Dom might need you in his office, like, now." He's looking at me but then glances to Luca. "Maybe both of you."

He pivots and hurries away, and Luca and I look at each other. "What could that be about?" I ask as we start toward the door.

"No idea," he replies and we quicken our pace back down the hall to Dom's office. When we get there, we find him leaning against the front of his desk, arms folded across his chest. And sitting in the chair in front of him, with his head in his hands, is Brady Dixon.

"What's going on?" I ask as we come in, Luca closing the door behind us.

Dixie lifts his head, his expression one of pure overwhelm.

But Dom speaks first. "Dixie's got something to

share, we were just waiting for everyone to get here so he only has to say it once."

There's a knock on the door, and Rafe walks in, going straight to Dixie's side. "Dix? What's up? You okay?"

We're all looking at the player, whose face has gone white. My heart sinks. This can't be good. Maybe his parents are sick, maybe he's sick, maybe he got an offer from another team. No matter what it is, losing the star player that Luca and Rafe sought out to anchor the team, right as the season is getting started, is the worst thing that could happen.

"I'm okay, but..." He takes a deep breath. "Fuck. I can't believe I'm gonna say this. I didn't...I never..."

"What is it, Dixie? Just say it," Rafe says firmly.

Dixie looks up at him with wide, panicked eyes.

"I'm gonna be a dad."

Thank you for reading The Game Changer! I hope you loved Luca and Isla's story. Please leave a review wherever you purchased your copy.

If you want to see what it was like on moving day for them, you can download their bonus scene by signing up for my newsletter. Just visit this link, or scan the QR code:

https://bit.ly/JuliaJarrett_TGC_bonus

And, you can preorder the second book in The Cedar Creek Thunder, today.

ACKNOWLEDGMENTS

This book nearly didn't happen. In fact, if not for the unwavering support and encouragement of certain people, it would not have existed.

I wrote this book during an extremely difficult time in my life, and struggled to get the story out the way I wanted to. But through it all, my friends and family were there to keep me going.

So, thank you to Carolina, Kelly, Erica, Chris, Alex, Theresa, Chelle, and my badass babes who all encouraged me along the way.

Special thank you to Misty, for inspiring Luca and Charlie's experience with ABS. For lending your knowledge, and helping me capture their stories authentically. And, to BT, for reading through Luca's sections, ensuring everything was accurate for a man living with a prosthetic leg.

I vowed to myself that with this new series, I would challenge myself to include elements in my stories that I've always wanted to. To be inclusive, and diverse, in a way that felt right to me, and that I could confidently do knowing I had done my best to be accurate, sensitive, and above all respectful.

I hope you love the Cedar Creek Thunder as much as I do.

XOXO Julia

ABOUT JULIA JARRETT

Julia Jarrett is a busy mother of two boys, a happy wife to her real-life book boyfriend and the owner of two rescue dogs, one from Guatemala and another one from Taiwan. She lives on the West Coast of Canada and when she isn't writing contemporary romance novels full of relatable heroines and swoon-worthy heroes, she's probably drinking tea (or wine) and reading.

For a complete listing of Julia Jarrett books visit
www.authorjuliajarrett.com/books

ALSO BY JULIA JARRETT

<u>Vancouver Tridents Series</u>

Break The Rules

Fake The Game

Catch Her Heart

Steal A Kiss

Curve Into Forever

<u>Dogwood Cove Series</u>

Always and Forever

Rumours and Romance

Work and Play

Truth and Temptation

Then and Now

Passion and Promises (A novella collection)

<u>Donnelly's of Dogwood Cove Series</u>

Dare To Kiss You

Hate To Want You

Pretend To Love You

Promise To Marry You

Dare To Marry You (A holiday novella)

One Night To Win you